# PRAY FOR MERCY

## BOOKS BY D.K. HOOD

Detectives Kane and Alton prequels

*Lose Your Breath*

*Don't Look Back*

Detectives Kane and Alton Series

*Don't Tell a Soul*

*Bring Me Flowers*

*Follow Me Home*

*The Crying Season*

*Where Angels Fear*

*Whisper in the Night*

*Break the Silence*

*Her Broken Wings*

*Her Shallow Grave*

*Promises in the Dark*

*Be Mine Forever*

*Cross My Heart*

*Fallen Angel*

D.K. HOOD

# PRAY FOR MERCY

bookouture

Published by Bookouture in 2022

An imprint of Storyfire Ltd.
Carmelite House
50 Victoria Embankment
London EC4Y 0DZ

www.bookouture.com



ISBN: 978-1-80019-861-6
eBook ISBN: 978-1-80019-860-9

*To Helen Jenner, for her professionalism, skill, and compassion.*
*You are a legend.*

# PROLOGUE

"I'm frightened! *Please*... I'll be good... Let me out!"

"Make one more sound and you're never coming out." As the key turned, the tumblers fell in the lock, trapping them in darkness.

Terror gripped them and tears stung their eyes as footsteps disappeared down the stairs. There would be no escape from the torment. Teeth chattering as cold seeped from the tiles through worn clothes and into young bones, they pulled their arms inside the thin T-shirt to keep warm. Hugging a bony chest with freezing fingers, as shivers wracked their body and goosebumps spread all over their flesh. It was so dark in the closet and the strange smell threatened to suffocate them, but they clung to the tiny shaft of light peeking through the crack alongside the door and wall.

The tiny beam of light shone directly onto cobwebs. In the lacy woven silk, a fat spider moved up and down, back and forth, its front legs working to repair the damage they'd inflicted. The spider was always there, staring, watching, threatening. They'd tried to squash it under their shoe but had tripped and fallen into the web. Batting at their hair, sure the hairy monster would crawl into their ear and eat their brain, they'd bitten their lip to keep silent. Convinced the spider was bent on revenge, when its black eyes fixed them with a glassy stare and it dropped an inch away from their face, they hammered on the door. "Let me out. *Please*. Let me out."

Footsteps came, through the house and up the stairs, slow and deliberate. Panic gripped them. There would be no supper again tonight. Screaming wasn't allowed. Children didn't scream. Children didn't cry. Children must not be seen or heard.

Shocked awake, they sat straight up in bed, with the lingering smell of mold and rose perfume still clinging to them from the nightmare. It was always the same. Alone in the dark closet with the spider. The old lady would come, a faceless blur to drag them away. They remembered the smell of the leather belt and her insane singing as the belt came down countless times across the bruised flesh of their back and thighs. She would choose only tunes with numerous verses, and each time the beatings continued until the end of the song. Battered and bruised, the old woman returned them to the closet with a warning to behave or there'd be no breakfast either.

Wiping at the sweat coating their face, they stared into the darkness trying in vain to control the rage. The memory wouldn't leave. The nightmares never stopped. With trembling hands, they pushed wet hair from their face, turned on the bedside light, and stared at the photograph they'd cut from the newspaper of the quilting club's last outing. The members all looked the same—old, white-haired, and small. They had no true recollection of the face of the lady who'd cared for them—trauma had erased that unpleasant memory, so their shrink had told them, but the smell of rose perfume and a musky damp odor had remained in a cloud of terror. Not one feature distinguished one woman from the other in the picture or triggered a memory of the person who'd made their life hell—but they'd remembered the quilting circle. They'd had to be extra quiet when they came for their weekly meeting. All the women had one thing in common: They all lived in Black Rock Falls—and they were all going to die.

# ONE

## SUNDAY NIGHT

The sensation of someone being there prickled her skin. Agnes Wagner had lain awake for hours unable to sleep. Alone in the darkness, she watched the light from the full moon shine through the budding tree outside her bedroom window, and with each breath of wind, leopard spots would bound across her wall. At times, she'd imagine being in the jungle and watching the wild cats play with their cubs, but the last few nights it wasn't the creak of the branches brushing the side of her house that had stolen her sleep. Fear gripped her at the unusual shuffling and rattling of doors she couldn't explain. The long winter was coming to an end, and it wasn't the drip of melting snow or the whooshing slide as chunks of ice fell from the roof and landed in a plop on the ground that worried her. Frightened of someone murdering her in her bed, she threw back the blankets and pushed her feet into slippers. Moving wasn't so easy these days and she took her time pulling on her robe. The sounds came again and Agnes stood for a moment listening. The loud thumping of her heart filled her ears, drowning out the strange noises. It wasn't rats or other critters inhabiting her roof. She'd had the pest control man stop by and he'd given the house a clean bill of health.

The idea of sneaking downstairs in the dark to go check the doors and windows again went against her usual sound judgment but remaining in her room, terrified someone might come in and kill her, wasn't an option either. Bad things happened at night and no one in their right mind would go downstairs in the middle of the night, let alone under a full moon. She'd seen the movies and read the books. Her imagination took flight, creating terrifying scenarios, and she paused at the bedroom door. In the movies, it was always teenage girls or college boys who became the victims of a serial killer, and she was in her seventies. *I'd be no fun at all to murder—no fun at all.*

Overriding common sense, she turned the sturdy lock on her bedroom door, pulled it open a crack, and, heart pounding, peered into the dark hallway. The nightly rounds of the house to check doors and windows had become a ritual. Waiting and listening, she flung the door wide. Underfoot the floorboards creaked as she grasped the banister and made her way down the stairs. Halfway down she could see through the hallway to the windows on each side of the front door and stopped mid-stride at the supernatural-sounding laughter. As ghostly shadows glided by, she swallowed hard, wishing she hadn't sat up late watching horror movies. Taking a firm grip of her overactive imagination, she headed down the stairs.

With each step the house grew colder until the air was freezing and goosebumps rose on her flesh. The furnace was new and she'd never had any problem with the heating before. As she took the last step, and turned to check the back door, she froze with one hand pressed against the wall as the door to the cellar moved. It squeaked, opened a little, and then almost closed before opening again to allow an icy cold wind to rush up the cellar steps and cut a path to her. Earlier, the maintenance man had come by to check a faulty lock on the basement trapdoor. Perhaps he'd neglected to shut the door properly or left a window open? The old house was once part of a ranch, and the trapdoor used to drop produce directly into the cellar. Doubt crawled up Agnes' spine. Hadn't she checked the cellar door before going to bed?

Breathless with fear she stared at the door. Horrific stories of people venturing into dark cellars and vanishing forever came to the front of her mind. Nobody in their right mind went into a dark cellar in the middle of the night but, all alone, she had little choice. The strange noises came again with ghostly whines on each flow of air. Trying to ignore the ice-cold tremors sliding down her back, Agnes pulled open the door and stared into the abyss. She searched for the light switch and an instant later the cellar flooded with muted light. She heaved a sigh of relief. No one haunted her cellar, the trapdoor appeared to be secure, but the window at ground level was wide open. She found the hook she used to pull it shut, nodding to herself as it closed with a satisfying click. Behind her the furnace groaned and whined. Still shaken, but proud of resolving the problem, she headed back up the cellar steps, secured the door, and just to be sure, walked through the kitchen and into the mudroom to make sure she'd locked the back door before heading upstairs.

Spooked by the experience, she paused, staring at the moving shadows creating mythical creatures of the night on the wall beside the stairs. Hairs rising on the back of her neck, she hurried up the staircase, and glad to be inside her room, slipped the lock and switched off the light. As she turned toward her bed, a movement across the room caught her attention. She laughed at her stupidity as she stared into the long mirror taking up her entire closet door. In the moonlight, her reflection peered back at her, but then something moved over one shoulder. Terror gripped her as an apparition of a white face with sightless black eyes wearing a thin black smile floated toward her. She gasped, clutching her chest as a disembodied white fist clasping a knife, raised high and its deadly sharp edge sparkled in the moonlight as it struck deep into her neck.

# TWO

## MONDAY

Sheriff Jenna Alton stretched and looked at the time. She gasped and fell out of bed, tripping over her slippers as she hurried to the shower. As work was quiet in Black Rock Falls of late, she'd taken a day for herself. She'd be heading out to Helena with Dave Kane, second in command and the love of her life, and good friend Dr. Shane Wolfe, the medical examiner. Intending to have been up at five to tend the horses, she suspected Kane had tampered with her alarm clock again. Kane had the unique ability to wake up at precisely the time he planned and hated the sound of an alarm. He'd leave her sleeping and head out to do the chores himself, returning most days to work out with her before leaving for the office, but today they'd be meeting Wolfe and taking the chopper to Helena.

Life had changed dramatically since arriving in Black Rock Falls, Montana. She'd once lived as DEA agent Avril Parker and been darn good at her job. After spending a horrific four years undercover, she'd brought down drug cartel kingpin Viktor Carlos. Although he'd ended up in jail and many of his cohorts had died in a gun battle, it was Jenna who'd received the life sentence. No longer able to work due to the threats on her life, she'd taken the offer of plastic surgery and a new name. In witness protection, with a cool ten million in an offshore bank account, she'd joined the backwoods town of Black Rock Falls as a deputy, and after becoming acting sheriff, had decided to run in the local elections. To her delight, the townsfolk had elected her as sheriff in a landslide and she was now on her second term.

She showered and dressed in lightning speed and headed for the kitchen. Inhaling the smell of hotcakes, bacon, and coffee, she went to Kane as he stood at the stove and wrapped her arms around him. "Morning. Why didn't you wake me?"

"Oh, I figured a day off should start without chores." He turned to kiss her cheek. "And our workout can wait. You'll need all your energy for shopping." He chuckled. "Should we hire a truck for the day, to carry everything?"

Jenna met Deputy Dave Kane a couple of years later when the off-the-grid ex-military sniper had applied for the position of deputy sheriff. It had not been until the arrival of Dr. Shane Wolfe that she'd discovered the men came as a package deal. Wolfe was Kane's handler with contacts up to the Oval Office, and after a couple of years, she'd discovered POTUS had concealed Kane's true identity with plastic surgery. She understood Kane would never reveal his birth name and not even Wolfe had the clearance to find out. One thing was for sure, whatever Kane kept locked in his memory was valuable information to the enemies of the free world and they'd placed a bounty on his head. If they ever discovered he was alive, all the nasties would come out of the woodwork to take him down or, worse, capture him for interrogation. For this reason—she'd never understand why—the powers that be had sent Kane and Wolfe to Black Rock Falls, but she was over the moon to have their experience in her team, and in the last few years they'd become like family.

Laughing, Jenna took out plates and silverware. "Maybe.

We both need new boots, jeans... well, everything." She held out the plates as he loaded them with food. "Will Duke be okay at home today?"

"Yeah." Kane tossed his bloodhound a strip of bacon and filled two cups with coffee. "I don't think he'd enjoy being dragged around the stores all day." He headed for the table and sat down, pulling his plate toward him. "He has the doggy door, food, and heating. I'm guessing he'll sleep all day as usual. I notice that Pumpkin"—he offered the black cat a piece of his bacon—"has been sleeping in his basket with him. I think Duke enjoys the company."

"Me too." Jenna looked at him appraisingly. His dark blue pants and cable-knit woolen sweater matched his eyes, and, as always, he'd polished his boots to a mirror finish. He'd wear a long black coat and his Glock in a holster at his back. "I like it when you dress up for the city. Not that I don't like the all-black gunslinger look you have around town, but the bad-boy persona look is good too. You look so slick and handsome."

"You look pretty good too." Kane gave her a lopsided grin. "But then you always look good to me."

After breakfast they headed to the medical examiner's office. The chopper sat on the helipad on the roof and Wolfe was busy making his final preflight checks. It was still bitterly cold and the windchill factor sucked the heat from Jenna, making her cheeks stiff. All around lay the evidence of the ending of a hard winter. Icicles dripped from gutters onto the once pristine snow to leave pockmarks. Gardens resembled great pans of hotcake mixture bubbling on a stove. The blacktop wound through great piles of once white snow, topped with gray ice crystals and littered with twigs, leaves, and bits of garbage.

Pulling her coat tighter around her, she waited as Kane talked to Wolfe and noticed him handing Wolfe something and them both laughing. When Kane walked back to her side, still chuckling, she looked at him. "What's so funny?"

"As Wolfe is heading in the opposite direction to us, I asked him to drop by a store for me." Kane smiled. "He said he had a list a mile long from his girls and figured one more stop wouldn't make much difference."

Jenna nodded. "We could split the girls' list." She frowned. "He'll be in meetings most of the day."

"Yeah, but he has a two-hour break between one of them this morning, so he'll be fine." Kane headed for the chopper. "Let's go."

When they arrived at Helena airport, Jenna discovered Kane had already organized a rental. They all climbed inside and Kane headed for the ME's offices and they dropped Wolfe off. Everything he needed to do was in walking distance, so they headed into town to enjoy a morning of shopping. By the time they staggered into a local diner for lunch, Jenna's feet ached. She sat down at a table and peered at the menu. "Have you eaten here before?"

"Yeah." Kane sat down opposite and waved over the server. "I came here with Jo and Ty over the weekend of the convention. It's not Aunt Betty's but it's okay. The chili is good and the pumpkin soup."

Jenna smiled. "I'll have what you're having and coffee... lots of coffee."

"Sure." Kane ordered and leaned back in his chair staring out the window.

"Dave, is that you?" A statuesque blonde woman in her early twenties stopped at the table and flashed a perfect white smile. "What brings you into town?"

"Ah..." Kane stood and smiled at her. "Poppy, nice to see you again."

*Poppy?* Jenna looked from one to the other. Kane had never mentioned anyone called Poppy. It wasn't a name she'd forget.

"Well, aren't you going to ask me to join you?" Poppy's smile hadn't faltered. "Or introduce me to your friend?"

"Ah..." Kane looked at Jenna. "I guess. Poppy this is my boss, Sheriff Jenna Alton."

*His what?* Jenna gaped as he pulled out the chair beside him for Poppy to join them. She waited for the server to pour coffee and stared at Kane and raised an eyebrow in question as Poppy ordered a meal.

"I feel like I know you, Sheriff." Poppy squeezed Kane's arm. "Dave's told me so much about Black Rock Falls. It sounds like an interesting place to work."

Taking her time to sip her coffee, Jenna shrugged. "I guess that depends on your definition of *interesting*. Personally, I find discovering dismembered corpses and chasing down serial killers frightening. I'm never sure when I step out of my door if I'll get to return home again."

"You've never left a case unsolved, have you?" Poppy leaned forward. "I guess having Dave to profile for you has helped. I'm so interested in serial killers and how you managed stop them. It's a compulsion—no an addiction to kill. Is that why you send them to jail rather than gun them down... to make them suffer?"

"I don't think that's an appropriate question." Kane's brow furrowed. "Every case is different. It's not something we can generalize."

Hackles rising, Jenna wondered if this woman worked for the media. "I don't shoot people unless they're trying to kill me, but do I send serial killers to jail to make them suffer? You bet your ass I do." She caught the flash of amusement in Kane's eyes but kept her attention fixed on Poppy. "Why the interest? What line of work are you in?"

"Me? Oh, I'm a deputy out of Cedar Canyon." Poppy smiled at Dave. "I first met Dave at the behavioral analyst convention a few years back. I went, like he did, to learn more about the workings of the criminal mind. Then I ran into him again at the last one before Halloween. It's a small world, isn't it?" She did the squeezing thing again and laughed. "We had a great time."

Jenna leaned back as the server slid plates of food onto the table. She lifted her gaze to Kane and then moved it to Poppy. "That must have been an enjoyable weekend. I was a little preoccupied when Dave came home to discuss his trip, so I guess meeting you again slipped his mind."

"That was the week a serial killer escaped from jail." Kane's head bent over his chili. "I was kinda busy."

"Well then, never mind." Poppy chuckled and picked at her salad. "I had planned to make contact with you, Sheriff, later in the year." She turned her attention to Jenna. "Dave mentioned you planned to take on more deputies this year. I'd value the opportunity of working with you and Dave."

Meeting her gaze, Jenna kept her expression bland. "We always look forward to experienced candidates for any position." She lifted her fork. "When we do, we'll advertise as usual. It depends on what I'm looking for at the time." She lifted one shoulder in a half shrug. "I already have three qualified deputies on my main team. I was considering a second team to handle the day-to-day running of the office when we're busy. So, it might only be a few days a week to start."

"Hmm." Poppy shrugged. "Maybe we can work something out? A temporary position perhaps? I could take leave and come to Black Rock Falls for on-the-job training in criminal behavior. I'd sure learn more about it there than in my little town."

Noticing Kane's blank stare, Jenna pulled a notepad and pen from her purse. "What's your last name?"

"Anderson, Poppy Anderson out of Cedar Canyon. Sheriff Tom Griffin will give you a reference if needs be. He's a friend of Mayor Petersham."

Folding the notebook and pushing it back into her purse,

Jenna smiled at her. "There you go. Now I'll be sure to look out for your application."

"Thanks. What brings you to Helena?" Poppy became more animated. She poked Kane in the arm. "Why didn't you give me a call to let me know you were coming?"

"I didn't know myself until yesterday." Kane shrugged. "Most times, we don't get enough downtime to leave town."

Feeling like a third wheel, Jenna ate slowly, uninclined to chat, but Poppy's attention had moved to her. "We're here to do some shopping. When we get a break, we like to get away from town for a spell and spend time in the city."

"Are you staying at the same hotel as before, Dave?" Poppy pushed away her plate. "Maybe we can get together later for dinner?"

"Ah... no, we're heading back this afternoon." Kane went back to eating. "We came in the medical examiner's chopper. Maybe some other time?"

"I'll hold you to it." Poppy stood and opened her purse searching for bills.

"My treat." Kane gave her a smile. "It was nice seeing you again."

"Until next time then?" Poppy bent and kissed him on the cheek and giving him a flash of white teeth hurried out the door in a cloud of perfume.

Staring after her, Jenna waved to the server and ordered more coffee. She turned to see Kane eyeing her over the rim of his cup. She looked back at the server. "Apple pie, hot with ice cream."

"I'll have the same." Kane grinned at her. "What? You look fit to draw down on me."

"Why did you introduce me to her as your boss?" Jenna leaned back in her chair and waited.

"Respect." Kane shrugged. "She uses people to get ahead. All that squeezing my arm was just testing your reaction, Jenna.

When I ignored her at the last convention, she came right out and asked Carter and Jo if I had a girlfriend and both gave her a negative answer. She knows I'm your deputy and probably made the connection. She was using us and I don't think it's any of her business to know the reason we're in town, or the status of our relationship, so I kept it professional."

Shaking her head, Jenna dug into her pie. "She seems like a close friend. How come you haven't mentioned her before?"

"I met her when I was staying here in Helena, before I went to Black Rock Falls, and I have no idea why I kept her phone number." Kane met her gaze. "When I arrived in Helena, Wolfe sent me to the convention, mainly, I figure, to keep me focused. She just happened to sit next to me and pestered me until I talked to her. We had lunch together." He opened his hands wide. "After being holed up in a hotel alone for so long, it was nice just talking to someone about normal things for a change. Before I came here, the conditioning was intense. Poppy was like being normal again, I guess." He grinned. "I might be old-school when it comes to relationships but I do enjoy female company. I'm not a monk."

Jenna swallowed a mouthful of pie. "I see."

"I didn't mention meeting up with her again at the convention because it wasn't relevant." Kane shrugged. "The last time we met, she had her sights set on Carter and every time she pulled me into a conversation, I talked about you."

Placing her fork on the plate, she smiled. "So she said. I guess at that time we were keeping our relationship private, so you couldn't tell her you were involved with me?"

"Trust me, keeping it secret makes life difficult." Kane shook his head. "You know, anytime I'm out with Carter, we're surrounded by women. It's like they're sucking me into a whirlpool... and I'm running out of excuses. I'm not too sure what it is about him, animal magnetism or whatever, but they follow him around like a fan club. There were so many, I can't recall all of their names."

Jenna laughed. "You remembered Poppy's name just fine."

"That one I remembered because we had history." He grinned at her.

Jenna took a tissue from her pocket and wiped the lipstick from Kane's cheek and dropped it into Poppy's untouched coffee.

"I'm sorry she spoiled our lunch but she kinda invited herself, didn't she? Like I said, she's pushy." Kane sighed. "I didn't mention her for the deputy position because I didn't consider her suitable."

"If I receive an application from her, we'll discuss her with the team as usual." Jenna sipped her coffee and waited a beat. "She won't be a problem if she's chasing after Carter, will she?"

"Nope." Kane snorted with laughter. "Although that may be over now too. You see, Carter offered her a way to get close to Jo. When Poppy mentioned seeing the posters—TODAY'S SPEAKER: WORLD-RENOWNED BEHAVIORAL ANALYST SPECIAL AGENT JO WELLS—I told her that Carter was her partner, and Poppy suddenly became his best friend." He grinned. "It didn't get her far. Carter could read her like a book."

"Hmm." Jenna leaned back in her chair and smiled. "We have so few new people wanting to work with us. We'll look at her file and maybe we can offer her a temporary position. We do need help, especially when the rodeo circuit hits town, which, added to the festivals all year... If another serial killer decides Black Rock Falls is an ideal hunting ground, we're going to be calling on the other counties for help again this year."

The phone vibrated in Jenna's pocket and she stared at the screen. "It's Rowley." She accepted the call. "Anything wrong?"

*"You need to get back here ASAP. We walked into a bloodbath out of Snowberry Way."*

# THREE

Jenna looked at Kane and mouthed the word *murder*. She pulled her notepad from her purse, and Kane handed her a pen. "Okay, what have you got for me?"

*"An elderly stabbing victim, we believe to be Agnes Wagner out of Snowberry Way. Multiple stab wounds, face and upper torso. There's no sign of a murder weapon. Rio is capturing the scene. Webber and Emily are on their way."*

Mind spinning, Jenna took a calming breath. "Okay, follow procedure. Emily knows what to do with the victim. Make sure she bags the victim's hands. Who found the body?"

*"Rio and me."* Rowley cleared his throat. *"It was really weird. When I arrived this morning to open up, there was an address scrawled on the glass door. I took a picture of it with my phone and when Rio showed we went to check it out. When we found the house, the front door was wide open. It's secluded out here, so no neighbors close by. We cleared the ground floor and headed upstairs. She was in the bedroom—locked in a closet. We figure she was killed and then dragged in there."*

Chewing on her bottom lip, Jenna frowned. "Did you check the CCTV footage to see who wrote the message?"

*"Yeah, and we made out a figure dressed in black. It looked like a kid, but whoever it was covered up and stuck to the shadows. No prints, zip. It's impossible to make an ID."*

Checking her watch, Jenna nodded. "If someone paid a kid to write an address it wouldn't seem like breaking the law. I'll look at the feed when I get back to the office, but it will be hard to track them down." She thought for a beat. "Okay. It sounds like you have it under control. Search around for the keys to the house. You'll need to secure it before you leave. We'll be back this afternoon and go out and take a look."

*"Copy that."* Rowley disconnected.

Jenna explained the situation to Kane. "We better go and find Wolfe. As soon as he's out of his meeting, we'll need to get back to town."

"An elderly woman out at Snowberry Way?" Kane refilled his cup from the pot the server had left on the table. "Hmm, now that's food for thought. Did Rowley mention if there was a robbery or any signs of a struggle?"

Shaking her head, Jenna drummed her fingers on the table. "Nope, he only gave me the basic rundown. It's just as well Rowley had Rio with him. Rowley isn't too good with messy crime scenes." She pulled out her phone. "While we're waiting, I'll get the lowdown from Rio. He probably took in more about the scene without even realizing it. His memory is incredible." She handed Kane one of her wireless earbuds so he could listen in to the conversation and made the call. "We're stuck in Helena for a time. What else can you give me on the scene?"

*"No forced entry on either of the doors but the ground is disturbed outside the cellar window. I checked inside and there're indistinct marks on the cellar floor. The cobwebs around the window are torn and there are some leaves on the floor, but the window is shut. It's a possible entry point because the height of the window would make it difficult to leave without a stepladder or similar, and we know the killer walked out the*

*front door. There is a trail of blood from the bedroom, as in drips. It's as if they killed the old lady, removed their shoes, and walked out the house dripping blood. I found partial prints on the front door handle, but they appear smudged, so I'm assuming the killer was wearing gloves."*

"What about the house?" Kane leaned toward the phone. "Any sign of a robbery? Could the killer have been searching for something specific?"

*"Not that's evident. I figure the entire house needs a forensic sweep. There were hairs on the bedroom carpet. The victim's, I figure. I collected them and bagged them. I didn't see anything in the victim's hands. She didn't fight back. Maybe she knew her attacker?"*

Jenna exchanged a glance with Kane. "Have you interviewed her neighbors?"

*"There are no neighbors. Well, not for a mile or so. It's isolated out here. The driveway is just rocks. Anyone could've driven here and we wouldn't know."*

Rubbing her temples, Jenna sighed. "Okay, I'll need you both out there until we can get home. If you need to dash back to town and grab something to eat, one of you go while Webber and Emily are there. I don't want anyone out there alone."

*"Copy that."* Rio disconnected.

Thinking it through, she looked at Kane. "What do you think?"

"An attack to the face is usually a crime of passion, which seems unusual in an elderly woman... unless the killer is trying to throw us a curve ball by making us believe just that." Kane twirled his cup in his fingers. "We can assume it's not an elderly person because, from what I recall of the windows in the cellars of those old houses out that way, the root cellars had a trap door and a small window mostly for ventilation. It's set high on the wall and most people use a metal rod to open and shut it. It has a drop of at least six, maybe eight, feet, so a slim person or a young person would most likely fit through. The drop would be too great for the average older person." He frowned. "I'll need more details. For instance, did they attack the eyes?"

Amazed by his insight, Jenna shrugged. "I didn't like to ask Rowley about specifics. He's a bit squeamish, as you know." She stirred cream into her coffee. "Why drag the body into the closet? Most people kill and run. Is that significant?"

"Maybe." Kane sipped his beverage. "It would tie into the damage to the eyes, if any. It would tell me the victim knew her attacker, and even in death, the killer was still concerned they'd be recognized."

"So if she lives alone, are we looking for someone who is well known in the community and has a ton of friends who drop by?" Jenna ran her finger through the sugar she'd spilled onto her saucer and licked her finger. "But Snowberry Way isn't an easy place to get to. You'd have thought she'd have been snowed in all winter." She looked at him. "Most of the older women I've met often spend time with their families in town over the holidays, and some stay right through until the melt."

"All these things we'll take into consideration." Kane opened his hands. "It's not much use speculating until we have more information." He glanced at his watch. "We'll head back to the ME's office. Wolfe's meeting will be over by the time we arrive. I'll grab him a to-go coffee. He's probably starving by now and we haven't got time to stop."

Jenna stood. "Okay, I'll order him some sandwiches as well. I'll fix them up for our meals at the counter."

"My treat." Kane frowned at her. "There's no way you're paying for Poppy's meal. This trip was my idea. Don't get all stubborn on me now."

Jenna grinned at him. "Oh, buttering up the boss won't get you any favors." She giggled. "Well... on second thought... maybe it will."

# FOUR

They arrived in Black Rock falls before four, and after stopping to collect a few supplies from Wolfe's office, climbed into the Beast and headed to Snowberry Way. The roads, now clear of snow, had sustained damage and large potholes dug out by the force of the ice, which made the going slow. Kane maneuvered his truck over the holes and road debris, finally turning into the driveway of the victim. He looked at Jenna. "Well, nobody walked here, that's for darn sure."

Two cruisers and Emily's silver Jeep Cherokee sat in the driveway, and tucked inside a garage was a Ford truck. Kane climbed out into the cool mountain chill and turned to Wolfe. "Why didn't Webber bring the van?"

"He's been and gone." Wolfe pulled on booties and gloves and handed the same to Jenna and Kane. "I spoke to Em before we left and told her to get the body on ice. She took the temperature of the victim at the scene. I'm sure my job here is just about done. She's very capable of handling a crime scene."

Kane smiled. "Oh, I have every confidence in her ability. I'll be glad when she graduates from medical school and can be around full-time. It will take the weight off you a bit." He chuckled. "We might get to go fishing one weekend."

"That will be years yet." Wolfe shrugged. "I'm just glad she spends her time in the office when she's not in class. She's like a sponge and learns so fast. Any exposure to cases, I can give her, is an advantage."

The door to the house opened and Rio walked out to greet them. His serious expression and pale face spoke volumes as he approached Jenna.

"What have we got?" Jenna snapped on her gloves. "Have you made any progress since we spoke?"

"I don't have any other information for you regarding the victim." Rio wet his lips. "We're assuming it's the owner of the house. The vehicle and land title are both in the name of Agnes Wagner. She's lived here for over fifty years. Her husband died ten years ago. She takes care of herself, from what I can make out. There's a full pantry and freezer. She doesn't have any kids. It must have been lonely for her out here by herself."

"Did you visit the neighbors?" Jenna followed him inside the house.

"Yeah, there's only one. The house further up is boarded up." Rio turned to look at her. "They didn't see or hear anything and I'd believe them. The cabin is set way off the road." Rio stood to one side and pointed to the door. "Smudged prints here, drips of blood all over, but the scanner didn't pick up anything solid. As you can see, it's even hard to tell the size of the hand." He pointed to the stairs. "Emily and Rowley are upstairs. I've searched the house. Nothing seems disturbed. The cellar is the only point of entry I can find. Although there's no evidence we can use and no footprints. The melting snow has saturated the ground. On the inside, I found a few damp marks under the window, but if there were wet footprints, they dried. The window is shut tight as well. They left by the front door. It was open when we arrived."

"Okay." Jenna headed for the stairs.

As Kane stepped inside, a musty smell surrounded him. He avoided the blood trail inside the front door and scanned the area. The house was ablaze with light and he smiled to himself. Emily had left nothing to chance and had erected Wolfe's portable lighting all over the house. He moved through a small foyer and the metallic scent of blood hit him like a wall. He turned to Wolfe. "From the blood trail, do you figure the killer was injured?"

"Let's take a look at the scene first." Wolfe headed for the stairs. "Whatever, they walked down the middle of the stairs unhurried. Look how even the blood droplets are spaced. If they'd been running, the spatter would have been uneven and splashed over the handrail. This looks like a cold calculated kill. They were in no hurry to leave."

The smell of blood increased as he climbed to the top of the stairs and followed Wolfe into a large bedroom. Murmurs came from inside, and Rowley and Emily turned as they entered. Keeping to the perimeter of the room, he listened to Emily briefing Wolfe.

"Rio filmed the entire scene with the body in situ and took a million shots before we moved anything." Emily pointed to a blood-soaked patch on the carpet. "The victim is small, maybe five-one or -two. From the blood spatter and lack of defense wounds, I think she was attacked from behind."

"Okay." Wolfe crouched down. "This looks like an arterial spray pattern. Was the neck lacerated?"

"Yeah." Emily pointed to the long marks across the carpet. "Stabbed in the neck, then she turned or collapsed, fell onto her back. From the injuries to the face and chest, it was a frenzied attack." She pointed to the blood spatter pattern where the body had lain. "There's this and a classic spray pattern on the closet mirror, consistent with a frenzied attack."

Engrossed by the conversation, Kane glanced at Jenna's

intent expression and then turned to Emily. "And yet after such an adrenaline buzz, the killer removed their shoes and just walked slowly down the stairs and out the front door. Did you get samples of the blood trail?"

"Yeah." Emily looked exhausted. "I've taken samples from all the contact points made by the killer, fibers and anything else I could find."

"That's good." Wolfe turned to Kane. "What do you make of the killer's behavioral switch?"

"I was going to ask you the same question." Jenna moved to his side. "This is bizarre."

Taking in the scene as a whole, Kane turned slowly. "Something else went on here." He looked at Rio. "Do what you do best. Correlate all the information we have here. What's missing?"

"My first instinct tells me no one can do this much damage without being soaked in blood." He stared slowly around the room. "No bloody footprints."

"Look at this." Jenna had bent over to stare at the carpet. "The house is immaculate and yet there's fluff on the carpet over here. Not much but it's evident."

"Which would suggest something was laid on top of the carpet to walk on." Wolfe turned to examine the bed. "The bed's been slept in, but all the blankets appear to be there."

"How many killers set up a scene beforehand? From this bloodbath, there's no possible way of dragging the victim into the closet without leaving bloody footprints." Jenna peered at the carpet. "Show me the image of the body in situ."

"Here you go." Rio handed her his camera. "The zoom is here." He indicated to a button on the device.

"Were the doors open or shut?" Jenna frowned. "What about the clothes hanging inside? Did you check them for blood spatter?"

"Yeah, we did and the doors were shut. When we arrived,

we followed the blood trail." Rowley stepped around the smeared red line leading from the crimson pool on the carpet to the closet. "I stood here and slid open the door. Someone has pushed the clothes back along the rail to the other end. There's not any blood we could see and no other contact points on the walls or carpet apart from where the victim was lying."

"Doesn't this strike you as unusual, Wolfe?" Jenna stared at him. "The killer must have been soaked in blood. So how did they drag the body into the closet without leaving any trace evidence?"

"From what I can see, the victim fell onto her back with her feet toward the closet." Wolfe pointed to the drag marks. "See here? Those marks would be consistent with her being dragged feet-first. From the image and her position in the closet, she was dragged to the opening and then rolled inside."

"I didn't find any fibers in or around the closet." Emily frowned. "I've missed some vital evidence. None of this adds up, does it?"

"You did a great job." Wolfe smiled at her. "I'll look over your findings and then we'll head back to the office. Once we've put everything together, we'll have a clearer picture of what happened. I'll know more when I've seen the body."

"So, you figure she was disturbed in her sleep, got out of bed, and was attacked?" Jenna frowned. "I would have thought we'd see defense marks if that were the case."

"My thoughts exactly." Wolfe frowned. "More like surprised from behind."

A thought struck Kane and he headed across the room and into the bathroom. "The towels are missing." He rubbed his chin. "Hmm, did they use the towels to avoid leaving footprints?"

"If so, they must have been inside the room prior to the murder. Perhaps they broke in and crept upstairs, placed the towels on that chair close to the blood spot on the carpet. When the old lady headed for the bathroom, they killed her." Jenna opened a linen closet. "White towels. I'll bag one and see if they match the fibers on the carpet."

Kane shrugged. "From what I can see here, this murder was well planned, but why have the towels heading toward the bathroom and not the stairs? Unless..." He headed to the shower and peered at the still damp surface. "Bingo."

"Ah, so they took a shower and carried their bloody clothes in a towel. They dripped blood on the stairs on the way down." Wolfe was at Kane's shoulder. "I'll swab the shower for trace evidence, but I smell bleach. I doubt I'll find anything we can use." He went to work.

"Rio." Jenna glanced at him. "Go check the incinerator and see if they burned up the clothes. I did smell smoke when we arrived, but that's nothing unusual for this time of year."

"Okay." Rio grabbed a few evidence bags, snatched up his camera, and headed out the door.

"So, we have a naked killer in Black Rock Falls?" Emily looked skeptical.

Taking in the room, Kane shrugged. "There're plenty of clothes in this room, male and female. She has a closet full of them, and obviously didn't give her husband's things to Goodwill. Or if this murder was as well planned as it seems, the killer could've had a spare set in their vehicle. It's not as if anyone would see them out here."

"Not that we found any sign of a vehicle and we've searched all over." Rowley pushed up his Stetson.

Kane walked to Rowley's side. "How are you holding up?"

"I'm good." Rowley raised both eyebrows. "Seems watching my twins being born and changing diapers has hardened me. I didn't even spew this time."

Slapping him on the back, Kane smiled. "That's good to know."

"Hey." Rio's voice came from downstairs. "There's been a fire out back. You might want to take a look, Sheriff."

"On my way." Jenna looked at Kane. "Finish up here, I'll wait for you downstairs. I don't want to risk contaminating the scene with ash from the fire."

Kane took the evidence bags from her and nodded. "Sure." He looked at Rowley. "Did you find the house keys?"

"Nope but her phone was beside the bed." Rowley scratched his head and peered around. "Do you want me to search downstairs?"

Scanning the room, Kane shook his head. "Nah, she'd likely keep her purse close by, so look up here." He turned to Wolfe. "I'm guessing you'll be wanting to preserve the scene pending the autopsy results?"

"Yeah, and I'll leave the lights here for now, but we should check the cellar before we go." Wolfe walked around the bed and pulled open drawers. "Ah, here's her purse." He opened the substantial bag. "ID, house keys, and five hundred in bills. So robbery isn't a motive." He tossed the purse to Kane. "We'll need to make sure the place is secured. I'd like to see the point of entry. If someone got through the cellar window, they could again and return after we leave."

"Sure." Kane handed Rowley Jenna's evidence bags and led the way out of the bedroom.

"Okay, Em, that's all we need for now." Wolfe looked at her over one shoulder. "Take all the evidence back to your truck. Rowley will help you. I'll meet y'all downstairs."

They found the cellar and Kane peered into the blackness, glad to find a working light. How many times had he walked into a dark cellar and found a corpse? With all he'd faced in his lifetime, a dark cellar still gave him the jitters. With Wolfe close beside him, they searched every inch. One wall had been used to display tools and had a well-used workbench below. Tools and half-finished projects littered the bench. A wave of sorrow hit him in the pit of his stomach. Agnes probably hadn't disturbed it since her husband died. She must have wanted the remembrances of him around her. He checked the window. "This could be opened from the outside. A knife would lift the catch with ease, and we know they had a knife." He searched the workbench and returned to the window with a hammer and nails. Standing on an upturned milk crate, he secured the window. "No one is getting inside now."

"Good." Wolfe headed for the stairs. "Let's get out of here. It's been a long day. The autopsy will be at ten as usual." He turned to smile at Kane. "Ah, by the way. The mission you sent me on went real well. They'll be contacting you in about a week."

"Great." Kane followed him up the stairs. "At least something in this crazy world is working out right for a change."

# FIVE

## TUESDAY

Exhausted from a disturbed night's sleep and too scared of bears to go to the woodpile for fresh logs for the fire, Jolene Darvish pulled on the thick coat that once belonged to her husband and rubbed the frost on the window to make a patch to see through. It might be spring but it was still freezing high in the mountains. It had seemed a good idea all those years ago to build a cabin at Bear Peak and live off the grid. Injured during his tour of duty, her husband had returned home a different man. He needed solitude and didn't want to mix with the townsfolk. Being young and strong, they'd camped out until they'd built the cabin. She'd worked in town as a dental hygienist to earn enough to pay for the essentials, but Johnny never left the mountain until the day he died. Now all alone, with no kids, her family long gone, she had no choice but to remain through long cold winters and summers with the risk of losing everything in a wildfire.

She peered outside and gasped at the door to her food locker hanging open. With no cellar in the house, they'd built the sturdy building with granite rocks and a thick wooden door. Bears had never ransacked it in the fifty years she'd lived on the mountain. Had she forgotten to lock it? She moved slowly to the front door and found the key, hanging on the bent nail right where she'd left it. If she hadn't locked the door, the key would be in the lock. Taking a deep breath to steady her nerves, she pulled open the front door and peered all around. The cabin backed up to the mountain, giving a clear view all around the dense forest. Moving with caution, she stepped outside and sniffed the air. Bears had a foul smell and the air was fresh and clean.

Making her way to the food locker, her boots crunching on the ice patches on the grass, she peered in dismay at the broken lock. Light filtered inside and lit up the empty shelves. Everything was gone. "Oh no, my chickens."

Heart pounding, she shuffled to the other side of the house, expecting to see blood and feathers. She pressed a hand to her chest in relief. The chicken coop was untouched. Her fat brown hens were still safe and warm inside the shed. She opened the coop and poured food from a metal bin onto the floor, checked their water, and then went back to the house. The firewood could wait. Right now, she needed to head into town to speak to Father Derry at the shelter and explain what had happened. With luck, he'd put her name down for another portion of the donated meat from the local hunters. She'd help out by serving food for a couple of hours, and maybe be able to grab a meal before heading off to the meeting of the quilting circle. It had been a long winter without company apart from the odd phone call. The snow had isolated her for months and, not being able to clear the driveway, she had no choice but to wait for the melt. After checking her purse, she found enough bills to buy groceries to see her through, but not enough to fix the door.

Grimacing, she headed for her truck. Years ago, she could have fixed the darn thing herself, but now in her eighties, everything seemed more difficult. She sighed. Even climbing into her truck was becoming a problem, but it wasn't the end of the world. Living rough had made her resilient. She rarely got sick and often believed her husband was watching over her. Through all the bad times since he'd died, something had always happened to eventually make things right. She glanced at the rings on her fingers. Maybe she could trade one for a new lock? There, problem solved, and it wasn't even eight yet.

The old truck shook and rattled, but she ignored it and turned up the tunes on the radio and sang along. One thing, she still had her singing voice, and somehow no matter how lonely she became, she could turn on the radio and it was like the sun coming out. So many memories came flooding back with those old tunes. It was like reliving a beautiful time in her life.

As she left her driveway and turned onto the dirt road, the truck bounced and scraped over fallen rocks. Living on the side of a mountain had its downfalls and fallen rocks or sometimes boulders were always a possibility after the melt. The old road went from Stanton right up to the top of Bear Peak, the part of the Black Rock Mountain range that resembled the head of a grizzly. Many people had once lived scattered through this part of the forest but not so many now, although the cabins remained. No one wanted to live here since it had become notorious as a murderer's playground. Hikers had found many graves over the years and people intent on murder had continued to stain this beautiful part of the forest with blood.

Driving slowly around fallen boulders, Jolene kept one foot hovering over the brake. The descent was a steep incline, made dangerous by the scattering of soil and pebbles. In parts the narrow winding road fell away to a sheer drop into a gulley that took the runoff from the great Black Rock Falls. As the road snaked around, she could make out the glimmer of water at the bottom of the ravine, like a pale blue ribbon against the black granite rock.

With the radio blaring she didn't hear the motor of another vehicle coming up behind her until it tapped the back of her truck. The sudden impact and increase in speed startled her as her vehicle careered down the mountain at an impossible rate. Panic gripped her as she wrestled with the wheel, trying to make the next bend. The raw edge of the road was coming up fast and glimpses of the trees in the gully rushed by. The menacing truck took up all her rearview mirror and, in a grind of metal, shunted her forward again. Terrified, she pressed down on the brake and, using all her strength, pulled hard on the wheel. Suddenly, the big truck dropped back, and trembling with shock, she wrestled her vehicle tight onto the side of the road to allow it to pass. Fingers shaking, she turned off the radio and waited. What kind of fool does that to an old lady in these parts? She peered into her rearview mirror, but instead of passing, the truck just sat there as if daring her to move. She opened her window and waved it past, trying to make out who was driving, but all she could see was the silver grill glistening in the sunlight.

The engine revved and the big truck edged closer and then stopped. What did it want her to do? All Jolene could see was thick bull bars moving closer. The roar of a powerful engine filled the cab and she wound up the window and locked the doors. The jolt came again lurching her vehicle forward. Terrified, she rolled her vehicle down the mountain, moving a little faster than comfortable to get away from the menace behind her. In seconds the truck was on her. The impact as it struck the back of her vehicle, flung her forward, locking the seat belt painfully across her chest. The truck behind her roared and propelled her forward toward the edge of the mountain. She screamed and, pressing both feet on the brake pedal, used all her strength to slow down. The smell of burning rubber filled the cab as the brakes locked and the tires skidded along the dirt road. Desperately turning the wheel to make the corner, her old pickup slid sideways. Behind her, the roaring truck's wheels spun, sending clouds of dust and gravel into the air, and pushing her toward an open expanse of sky. "Stop it!"

Out of control, Jolene screamed in terror as her front wheels reached the edge of the road, but all at once the truck eased off and she bounced around the turn. Heart in her mouth, she couldn't suck in a breath, but somehow spun the wheel to gain control. Ahead on the left, a neighbor's driveway loomed like a beacon of hope. Accelerating, the truck's back wheels slid over the gravel as she aimed for the open gate. Behind her the truck roared past in a blast of airhorns and Jolene sat for a long time taking deep breaths. She'd met many fools in her lifetime but not one of them had tried to kill her—until now.

# SIX

Pulling on her gloves, Jenna stopped on the front porch to inhale the crisp pine-scented breeze, and after taking one last look at the snow-capped mountains, she climbed into the Beast. With Duke safely in his harness on the back seat, she turned to Kane as they headed for the office. "That poor murdered woman. She has no one left in the world to claim her body. I called both lawyers in town and one of them has a copy of her will. I asked him if anyone would benefit from her death, but he informed me that there were multiple beneficiaries. Agnes Wagner was a devoted church goer and left her entire estate to charity. She mentioned me in her will as the founder of the Broken Wings Foundation, he was able to speak to me without a court order. The foundation for battered woman will get the bulk of her estate."

"So, you could be a prime suspect?" Kane flicked an amused look in her direction. "That being your pet charity and all." He chuckled. "Don't worry I'll give you an alibi. I owe you that much after allowing you to be waylaid by Poppy."

Jenna laughed but she had been a little jealous. "You're making too much out of it, Dave. I'm not threatened by her. I trust you. It's taken me years to get you to commit to a relationship. I know you're not the kind of guy to jump in boots and all after meeting a woman."

"So, if she sends in an application to work with us, you'll accept it?" Kane looked at her skeptically. "I said she was a rookie, but now I come to think of it, she'd be in her third year of service by now. She might be an asset."

Staring at the melting patches of snow, forming blue reflective patches across the lowlands, she shrugged. "She's inexperienced by her own admission. The last rookie we had working with us was murdered. You do remember that don't you?"

"Yeah, it was nasty." Kane turned into Main and slowed to allow a woman to cross the road with two kids in tow. "I'm thinking, if she wants experience with how we handle serial killers, she can go through our files and I'll explain the profile I came up with in each case."

Turning her head slowly to look at him, Jenna couldn't contain the chuckle. "Really? She could do that by reading our casefiles. From what she was saying, I assume she wants hands-on experience." She allowed the grin she'd been trying to contain burst forth. "Oh, I can give her that—but she'd not be working with you. You're my partner. First up, she'd be pulling duty at the Triple Z Roadhouse to see just how rowdy those rodeo boys can get. Then I figure a few days patrolling the showgrounds with Rio or Rowley and seeing how things are done in a backwoods town would add to her experience."

"Poppy hasn't had the training you've had, Jenna." Kane gave her a sideways glance. "I doubt she's had much experience at all in that tiny town. I can't see the sheriff there working out with her every morning like we do."

"Exactly." Jenna scrolled through her files on Agnes Wagner's murder. "She'd be a liability in a crisis, and if she's as soft as you say, I wouldn't allow her to work with us on a homicide anyway. I know nothing about her and, if you haven't been in contact with her between the first conference and the last, neither do you. I'm sure as hell not risking my life taking down a serial killer with someone I don't trust watching my back. That's if we happen to have a case at the time." She glanced at him. "You can't help every damsel in distress, Dave. If she wants to work here for a short time to get experience, it will be on my terms... as you told her. I'm the boss."

"I didn't intend on training her for combat, Jenna." Dave pulled into his space outside the sheriff's department and turned to look at her. "She asked for my help at the conference and I blew her off. I figured she was coming on to me but now she seems genuinely interested in profiling." He slid her a look and held it for a long time. "As you hadn't planned to advertise the job for few months yet, you have time to think about it and she might not apply. I'll keep out of it, if that's what you want, but we'll sure need some help around here soon."

They spent the time before the autopsy correlating and updating the files on the homicide. They moved on to checking out the CCTV footage, but the fuzzy image gave them nothing to work with at all. Bobby Kalo had no luck after using all the FBI's software to come up with a viable image. Jenna suggested floodlights for the front of the office, but no doubt she'd get complaints from the people living opposite on Main. When Kane's stomach started growling, she took a brisk walk to Aunt Betty's to give Duke a run and collect takeout before settling back to work. Nothing much had happened in town since the melt. It was as if the townsfolk were all emerging from hibernation and too busy to get into trouble. The time for the autopsy came around fast and she looked at Kane across her desk. "Ready to leave? It's coming up to ten."

"Yeah. I'll leave Duke with Maggie." Kane led the way down the stairs down to the main floor.

"Anyone want to observe the autopsy?" Jenna turned to Rio and Rowley.

"I would." Rio stood and grabbed his coat. "This case is a real mystery. From what I've discovered about the victim, she didn't have any enemies. She was a liked member of the community, although she's stayed in her house most of the time since her husband died."

"I'll pass." Rowley looked up from his computer screen. "I'm checking out people who the victim used to see regular. I have a pile of invoices from local contractors we found at her house and I have her phone to hunt down who she contacted before she died. I might get a clue as to why someone killed her."

"Okay." Jenna led the way out to Kane's truck and stared into the sunshine. "Nothing better than an autopsy to ruin a perfectly good day."

They all piled into the Beast for the short drive to the ME's office. Jenna ran the evidence through her mind. The ashes she'd bagged from a fire pit out back of Agnes Wagner's house were just that—ashes. Not one fragment of material remained, if indeed the killer had burned the bloody clothes at all. She had no idea if Agnes usually incinerated her garbage. Jenna pushed her thoughts to one side as she swiped her card on the entrance scanner. There was something quite disturbing about the ME's building. Although Wolfe had gone to great pains to make the foyer and the visitors' area warm and comfortable, with air fresheners strong enough to prevent the usual odors from the mortuary escaping and causing concern, the move through the two sets of electric glass doors, from a warm vanilla-scented area and into a cold chemical environment, always brought the seriousness of the examination rooms into sharp focus. Out there was comfort and consolation, but once through the doors, the stark reality of the brutality one person could inflict on another was frighteningly real.

The morgue was a reality check too. As sheriff, it was her responsibility to apprehend the often twisted and maniacal offenders who preyed on her townsfolk. Jenna had come to realize, especially since working with Kane, that although the brain chemistry that created a psychopathic serial killer might be in the genes of a person from birth, a great majority of the afflicted never murdered. It seemed that traumatic experiences as a child —sometimes by bullying or humiliation—triggered violent episodes. So it seemed that a vicious circle of circumstances created most of these killers, and once they released the beast, like a genie in a bottle, they could sometimes control it for a time but never put it back. Many had tried to help these people and many had died believing they could reason with a mind often conflicted by multiple mental disorders, but in her experience, there was no cure.

She shucked her coat and pulled scrubs over her clothes, adding a mask and gloves before following Kane and Rio into the examination room with a red light burning outside. Emily was missing but Wolfe was staring at X-rays and Colt Webber was busy arranging instruments on the silver tray on a cart. She glanced around at the stainless-steel benches, sinks, and wall of drawers to store corpses. The room was much like any other operating room, with the lights above the gurney, but where the body of Agnes Wagner lay, the cold metallic bench had a drain at one end. She swallowed hard at the sight of the two bluish white feet poking out from under the sheet, one with a dangling toe tag. Who would attack and kill a kind elderly woman? What was their motive? Nothing was missing from the house, as far as she could figure. The killer hadn't broken in to steal anything. They'd found cash in the victim's purse. Had the killer targeted her for a reason? If so, what would possibly induce someone to hurt her in such a violent way? So many reasons spun around in her mind in a carousel of question marks. As Wolfe went to the gurney and pulled back the sheet. Jenna summoned her professional side. She'd need it. This senseless murder had shaken her to the core.

# SEVEN

Shane Wolfe moved his attention to his silent audience. He wondered how Kane and Jenna managed to portray a visual of complete calm, as if they were devoid of emotion, especially when both of his friends just happened to be the most caring people he knew. The solemnity of the occasion shimmered through the room, giving his workplace the feel of a funeral home, where the need to keep their voices to a whisper as a mark of respect was paramount. The problem with that attitude was it would get them nowhere. Silence in a funeral home was one thing, but not in his examination rooms. Active discussion was essential to solve the puzzle of a case, and if he needed a cattle prod to get them springing into action, he might well consider it. He leaned against the counter and moved his gaze from one to another. "I'm aware, seeing a kindly old lady brutally murdered has been a shock. Agnes Wagner is a stereotype of the grandmas we loved and we all feel a connection, which makes watching the autopsy more difficult. I'd like y'all to consider a very important aspect of why we perform autopsies." He waved a hand toward the body on the gurney. "Agnes here can't tell us what happened or who did this to her. By using forensics and investigation techniques, we'll be able to hunt down who killed her and why. We're all highly skilled and together we'll catch the person who did this, b*ut* we must start with the autopsy. Allow me to speak for Agnes by telling y'all what happened." He pulled back the sheet.

"What made the sharp force trauma injuries?" Kane moved forward as if breaking the spell on the room. "A screwdriver?" He peered down at the mangled body and then up to the X-rays displayed on the screen. "No, not a screwdriver, not from the bone damage."

Moving to the screen array, Wolfe nodded in agreement. "I'll need to examine the damage to the bone but I'm not seeing a typical saw injury, say from a hunting knife. The width of each incision would preclude a kitchen knife or similar as well. We're seeing puncture wounds here. I would suggest a thin blade of about six inches long caused the injuries. I'll take measurements as we go."

"Do you mean something like a meat skewer?" Jenna's eyes peered at him over the top of her mask. "But what about the neck injury?"

"That would be easy to inflict." Kane shrugged. "The victim wouldn't be standing still after the initial attack, and with the blade buried in her neck, a twist or turn to get away would've caused the tear."

Wolfe smiled behind the mask. The discussion had begun and the team was looking at the victim objectively. "You've gotten it in one." He nodded to Kane. "I'll open her up and we'll measure the depth and angle of the wounds. This will give us an insight to the killer."

He went through the careful dissection. Stopping each time to answer a question or two from the team. "Okay, we have a hematoma on the back of the skull consistent with someone grasping her hair. For the bleeding to be evident under the skin, it happened before she expired. So, we can say, the killer grabbed her by the hair with their left hand and stabbed her throat with the right. The throat puncture is consistent with a downward thrust from a right hand. This injury would have caused the arterial spray on the carpet. The hematoma at the back of the skull also indicates the killer waited until she collapsed before stabbing her face and chest, or the collection of blood under the skin would have been minimal if any."

"You sayin' the killer attacked from behind, struck, and then stepped away?" Rio leaned against the counter in a relaxed pose. "If so, it wouldn't have been difficult to have avoided the blood spatter if they used the victim as a shield. That's possible, isn't it?"

"Yeah, but the arterial spray is immediate, so it would be near impossible not to be splashed, especially if the victim is trying to get away." Kane looked at Wolfe. "So, we can assume the killer struck from behind and the victim staggered forward before falling. How come she fell on her back?"

"If someone stabbed me in the neck in a confined space, I'd grab my throat and turn to defend myself." Jenna frowned. "I assume the loss of blood was so great she collapsed and fell."

"Some people freeze in an attack situation, but I figure they frightened her and she tried to get away." Kane shrugged. "It's the classic flee-or-fight response. Your reaction is to fight, Jenna, because it's part of your training, or more likely your mind is gene-programed to fight back. Look at the evidence—Agnes fled."

"Gene programmed?" Jenna's gaze sharpened. "What do you mean by that?"

"The more research they do into gene sequencing, the more we know about why we act the way we do." Kane met her gaze. "They have known about the fear gene for a while. People without it, like me, go into dangerous situations without fearing they might die. Then there's the warrior gene. Those of us who run into danger to protect everyone, and now the star gene."

"Aliens from outer space?" Jenna snorted. "I've heard about that one."

"Haven't you noticed how technologically advanced kids are who can't walk yet?" Rio tapped his head. "It's all in there just waiting to be activated."

"Yeah, I agree but getting back to the autopsy." Kane looked at Wolfe. "If she passed out, would she fall straight back?"

Wolfe looked from one to the other. "Yeah, that's possible. Y'all have some good theories. I've another to throw into the mix. What if she'd had a coronary? Her heart is in shreds but I'll do blood tests to confirm." He lifted his eyebrows. "I have all the latest research into DNA, if you want to read it."

"I sure do." Kane nodded.

"Wow!" Rio chuckled. "If you and Jenna get together and have kids, do you have any idea what a guy your size with a double dose of fear genes or a woman like Jenna would be capable of?" He narrowed his gaze. "Forget about combat robots, the military could enlist your kids."

"Ha, ha, ha. Very funny." Jenna shot him a glance to freeze Black Rock Falls Lake.

"The attack on the face and eyes is significant." Kane ignored them and bent closer to the body. "The killer didn't want her to see them and then there's the reason they dragged her into the closet." He shrugged. "That reason is complicated and could be a contradiction of some kind. I figure the killer might know her and wanted to hide what they'd done to her from anyone coming here."

"Yet they left the front door wide open." Rio let out a long sigh. "That moves us away from the hiding-the-crime theory. More like, the 'come see what I did' theory."

Wolfe took measurements of the incisions and frowned. "I thought at first maybe a screwdriver, but from the damage to the bones, the scoring is indicative of a sharp pointed instrument." He pointed to indents on the flesh of the chest. "This is what I see usually in fights, they're very similar to injuries inflicted by knuckles. I figure someone had their fist wrapped around the handle of an icepick and used it in a downward thrust, as if punching it into the flesh." He looked at Jenna. "The measurements fit the width and length of a domestic icepick with a wooden handle."

"There doesn't appear to be any head injuries apart from the hair-pulling hematoma and the sharp force trauma." Jenna peered at the X-rays. She turned and looked back at Wolfe. "We'll need to take a team back to the victim's house and do a sweep of the yard to see if the killer tossed the murder weapon in the grass." She looked at Rio. "Get on the phone and find me some metal detectors."

Wolfe nodded. "Leave this with me and head out now. I'll finish up and send you a report. I'm still waiting on the trace evidence samples from the shower. I did find traces of blood but nothing else. The sample isn't good but I'm running it against Agnes' DNA. If it's her blood, we know the killer washed before leaving the house." He met Jenna's eyes. "Unless she died from a coronary, I'd say cause of death is blood loss from sharp force trauma. From the evidence we have at hand, I can give you an approximate time of death. The fact she was in bed and obviously disturbed, and considering the temperature of the body, I can put the time frame between six at the earliest last night to when the body was discovered this morning, but factoring in the room temperature, I'd say she probably died between midnight and two this morning."

"Okay." Jenna turned to look at her deputies. "Let's go, we have a murder to solve."

# EIGHT

In the truck on the way back to town, Jenna stared at the melting landscape, glad to see the green awakening of spring at last. Winter had seemed to last forever and she yearned to stand in the sunshine and not be constantly chilled to the bone. As Rio chatted in the back seat on his phone, trying to locate metal detectors, she allowed the case to percolate through her mind, mentally listing the correct procedure for apprehending a killer. She had Rowley working through the contacts on Agnes' phone to get information from her friends. When she got back to the office, she'd work through the information and send Rowley and Rio out to search for the murder weapon. Kane she'd set to work finding a possible motive for killing the poor woman and profiling the suspect.

"There are so many aspects to this case that don't make a whole lot of sense." Kane turned onto Stanton and headed down a shadow-striped highway. "The frenzied attack is more what I've seen from a jealous lover. Often killing isn't on their minds at all. In a jealousy kill, they usually want to inflict pain and suffering by attacking what's most important to the victim. The woman is no longer the person they loved. They see a twisted ugly person, someone who has betrayed them. They want people to remember them as they see them and not as they were before the attack. Disfigurement is usually because they have the 'if I can't have her, nobody else will' mentality, but they don't attack the eyes."

Interested, Jenna turned to him. "The last case we had where the face was attacked post-mortem, the victim was a schoolkid murdered by a jealous teenager. This is an old woman. How does it compare?"

"From what I recall, in that case the killer believed the girl was watching her even in death." Kane shrugged. "There's a deal of hate in this murder as well, but seems to me it was well planned. I don't believe the killer struck from behind because they wanted to prevent blood spatter. I'm thinking it was because they were frightened of Agnes seeing them."

"So, you figure this suspect is young?" Rio's eyebrows rose almost to his hairline. "I can't see a kid having a knowledge of forensics to cover their tracks. They went to great pains not to leave evidence behind. Trust me, living with my impulsive twin siblings, if they decided to murder someone, they'd make one hell of a mess of it." He shrugged. "This wasn't a thrill kill. It was messy, yeah, but look at the scene. It was almost clinical, wasn't it? They covered their tracks too well. Looking at the almost precise placing of the stab wounds, I figure they took their time."

Glancing from one to the other, Jenna considered both arguments. "I don't think Kane is suggesting a thrill kill. I'm thinking it's more like a violent home invasion, as if they hunted down Agnes and murdered her for a reason." She rested her gaze on Rio. "What you say makes sense too. They planned the kill and took their time." A shiver went down her spine. "If they used the shower, collected the evidence, and burned it before they left, they have no fear of being caught—this makes them very dangerous." She glanced at Kane. "It's not only the good guys who lack the fear gene."

As Kane parked the Beast outside the sheriff's department, Jenna could see people crowded around the front counter. Blasted by a cold gust of wind that seeped through her clothes, she gathered her things and headed for the wide glass doors. The remnants of the address someone had scrawled over it were no longer visible. She pushed open the door to find a crowd of elderly women talking nonstop to a bewildered Rowley and a flustered Maggie. She waited for Kane and Rio to follow her into the foyer and cleared her throat. "Ladies. If there's a problem, we'll speak to each of you, but one at a time, please."

Faces, red from shouting all turned toward her and spoke at once. She held up both hands, and rather than raising her voice, lowered it. Using this method often made people stop shouting and strain to listen to what she had to say. Thankfully it had the desired effect. The women fell silent and stared at her. "Settle down, take a seat, and I'll get to everyone. Please give your names to Maggie." She glanced up the stairs to her office and back at the elderly women. "Send them along to Deputy Kane's desk. We'll speak to them down here." She looked at Rowley. "You'd better come and explain what's happened."

She walked to Kane's desk, pulled out a chair sitting beside him, and looked at Rowley. "Who are all these women?"

"That was my fault." Rowley glanced back at the crowd. "I went down Agnes Wagner's contacts list and made a few calls." He pushed his hands into the front pockets of his jeans and shrugged. "I mentioned Mrs. Wagner had died and we needed to know who'd seen her last. All but one of them had seen her recently and none of them would give out any more information over the phone. They all wanted to speak to you because they don't trust strangers calling out of the blue. Well, all but Mrs. Mills, Wolfe's housekeeper. She was having lunch with Mrs.

Jacobs—ah, that's Rio's housekeeper—and they both said they'd drop by. Well, seems they all showed at once."

Not surprised by the women's reaction, Jenna nodded. "Okay, Maggie will sort them out." She leaned back in her chair. "I need you to go with Rio and drop by Mrs. Wagner's property to hunt down the murder weapon. It's probably an icepick or similar. Rio has the details and has metal detectors for you to use." Beside her, Kane's stomach rumbled, reminding her it had been six hours since breakfast and Rowley had been stuck in the office all morning. "Grab a quick bite to eat and then head out with him to the victim's property." She waved him away. "Get at it."

"Yes, ma'am."

As Rowley walked away, she turned to Kane. "Thoughts? Apart from what's on today's specials at Aunt Betty's?"

"Oh, I already know them. Susie sends me a text every morning." Kane rubbed his belly. "I'm sure, I'll survive another hour or so." He indicated with his chin to the women seated in the foyer. "The women have settled down now and before we take individual statements, maybe we should speak to them as a group." He collected pens from the top of his desk and dropped them into the bottom of a candy jar. "I figure they're involved in a group activity or maybe they help out at the shelter. They must all have something in common."

Jenna pushed to her feet. "That works for me. Grab a notebook and take down anything we need to follow up on." She made her way through the office and stood in front of the women. She caught sight of Wolfe's housekeeper and smiled at her. "Mrs. Mills, I need a spokesperson. I assume you all know each other?"

"We do." Mrs. Mills stood and her lips quivered. She seemed almost on the edge of tears. "What happened to Agnes?" She shook a finger at Jenna. "Don't tell us she died in her sleep or some other fanciful nonsense. I've been working for the ME long enough to know the deputies don't go around calling everyone unless something's wrong."

Scanning the concerned faces, Jenna straightened. "You'd know that I'm not able to give you details of the case, but her death is suspicious. So we need you, her friends, to give us as much information about her as possible. For instance, when you last spoke to her, did she mention having anyone drop by? Was she getting quotes for work around the house? Has she mentioned if she was concerned about anything?"

"I last spoke to her on the phone not three days ago." Mrs. Mills' brows knitted into a frown. "She mentioned having a new furnace fitted and having to leave the window open in the cellar. A critter had crawled inside the cellar and died. She complained about the smell, but she would have closed it by now. We all met this morning, for the first time since the melt, for our quilting circle but she didn't show and she's never missed a meeting. We used to hold our meetings at one of our members' homes, but now we have a nice cozy room at the town hall we can use from ten until two."

Jenna frowned. "No one thought to call her?"

"Of course, we called her." Mrs. Mills' eyes filled with unshed tears. "Now we know why she didn't pick up. I had planned to drive by her place as soon as the meeting ended."

Jenna didn't have to glance at Kane to know he'd be taking notes. His solid presence beside her had calmed everyone down. She wasn't sure how he did it, but she'd seen the Kane effect many times. The townsfolk felt safe when he was around. Turning her attention back to Mrs. Mills, she sighed. "I know this is difficult, but we desperately need information. Anything you can remember will help. Do you recall if Agnes mentioned the name of the contractor?"

"That would be Trey Duffy." A small woman, with a round face peeking out from under a knitted hat embellished with roses, stepped forward. "I recommended him. He replaced the furnace in my cellar as well. He did a fine job, took away my old furnace, and cleaned up all the mess afterward." She cleared her throat. "Many of us use the same contractors. People we think we can trust—this being Black Rock Falls and all."

"May I have your name?" Kane moved closer to the woman. "What other contractors do you share? Do you have their contact details?"

"Mrs. Harriette Jefferson out of Stanton Road and, yes, I do, right here on my phone." Mrs. Jefferson's cheeks blushed bright red. "I'm a widow and need help with a few things from time to time—we all do."

"Can you give them to me, please." Kane moved closer and took the details. "Anyone else?"

"Many of us call Colby Hahn if we need a handyman, or Archie Bueller if we need a gardener." Mrs. Jefferson gripped her purse in front of her like a shield. "I do recall Agnes mentioning Colby did some fixing up at her place before the snow."

Jenna held up a hand to get everyone's attention. "Okay, did anyone here see Agnes at any time before Sunday?"

"I did. I'm Mrs. Jacobs, Deputy Zac Rio's housekeeper." She nodded to Jenna. "Nice to see you again, Sheriff."

"And you too."

Not wanting to chat, Jenna slid a meaningful glance at Kane, to block the unnecessary chatter.

"Can you elaborate?" Kane stared at her, pen raised. "When, where, and approximate time."

"Aunt Betty's Café last Friday. We met at one and stayed until about two." Mrs. Jacobs smiled. "I have to be home for when Cade and Piper come home." She rolled her eyes. "Well, let's say I have to be there to make sure they get home and aren't sneaking off to the computer shop or hanging out in town. Zac likes to make sure they're at home in case he's held up here."

"Okay." Kane made copious notes on his screen.

Thinking for a beat, Jenna cleared her throat. "Was there anything in her conversation with you about any problems she was having, or any worries, prowlers or the like?"

"Well, she'd changed the furnace because it was making a noise and keeping her awake at night." Mrs. Jacobs stared into space for long seconds like an automaton that needed winding or a server drop out freezing an image on a screen, and then all at once, she came back on line and blinked. "Not that I recall, but you really need to know about Jolene Darvish's near-death experience this morning. She lives out on Rocky Road. The poor woman is all alone out there and the melt has caused rock-slides. The mountain road to her home is covered with debris." She heaved a long breath. "Now Jolene isn't the skittish type, but she told me a truck was tailgating her this morning and came close to running her off the road. You know that road up to Bear Peak is twisty and can be darn right dangerous. What fool drives like a maniac in that neck of the woods?"

Concerned, for the woman's safety, Jenna glanced at the group of people. "Is she here today?"

"No, she is not." Mrs. Jacobs lifted her chin. "She left to drop by the general store before Deputy Rowley called us. We couldn't let her know about the calls. Jolene turns off her phone when she's not using it to save the battery."

"Jolene told me she figured someone was following her on the way to town this morning." Mrs. Mills pushed her glasses up from the end of her nose and leaned closer to Jenna. "She said the truck tapped the back of her vehicle coming down the mountain. It gave her a shock when they followed her right to the town hall, but when she turned in to the parking lot they drove on by."

"We'll need to speak to her." Kane looked at Jenna. "I'll head down to the general store and see if she's still there." He stared down at Mrs. Mills. "Can you give me a description?"

"She's wearing a pink knitted hat, a green coat, and sturdy

brown boots." She waved him to the door. "She walked from the town hall, so she might be walking back to pick up her vehicle, or she'll stop by Aunt Betty's Café. Some of us go there after our meeting."

Jenna looked at Kane. "Go, I'll take care of things here."

# NINE

Zipping up his jacket against a freezing gale blowing from mountains still tipped with snow, Kane headed for the Beast, and almost tripped over Atohi Blackhawk, a Native American tracker and close friend. "Hey, sorry, I didn't see you." He pulled down his woolen hat over his ears.

"Has something clouded your eagle eye?" Blackhawk stepped back and looked at him with curiosity. "Or do you have something of great importance on your mind?"

Kane opened the door to the Beast and turned to his friend. "I'm hunting down an elderly woman. Do you need to speak with me?"

"Yeah. I'll come with you. We can talk on the way." Blackhawk walked around the hood and slid in beside him. "No Duke today?"

Kane shook his head. "Nope, he's with Maggie at the office. We had to attend an autopsy today and Duke would rather be where it's warm and Maggie supplies him with a constant supply of food." He flicked him a glance and started the engine. "What's the problem?"

"The harsh winter has caused a few rockfalls high up in the

forest." Blackhawk waved a hand toward the distant endless expanse of spring fresh green pine trees. "The ice has uprooted many of the pines and it's widespread. There's been subsidence and landslides are plenty. A mudslide caused by the removal of trees for the ski resort is possible. Rubble is rolling down the mountain and it's only a matter of time. One day of rain and people are going to be killed." He shrugged. "Mayor Petersham needs to get crews out to stabilize the areas north of Bear Peak before there's another slide and the road is blocked completely. The service road to Glacial Heights Ski Resort has subsided and fallen down the mountain in a few areas too." He blew out a long breath, filling the cab with steam. "I called the road alert hotline twice last week and not one crew has showed." He shrugged. "I tried calling the town council offices and they informed me the crews were out on the highways. If there's a mudslide, the houses along the north end of Stanton and anything in between will be buried. Unfortunately, Mayor Petersham doesn't take calls from me. It will have to come from Jenna."

Kane pulled in front of the general store. "Okay, I'll speak to her."

"Thanks." Blackhawk smiled. "Now, how can I help you?"

"I'm looking for an elderly woman, pink hat, green coat. Someone tried to run her off the road." He turned to Blackhawk. "You go right and I'll go left." He slid out of the Beast and headed into the store.

General stores always have their own distinct smells that change with each step through different aisles of products. Going right might have been in his best interest as going left took him through the bakery section. With his stomach growling like a grizzly, loud enough to turn heads, he scanned the store and then spotted a pink hat. Edging his way around customers, he sidestepped a screaming child demanding a candy bar, his cheeks wet with tears. When the child's mother looked at him, she snatched up her son.

"See, you made so much noise, someone called the deputy." The woman dabbed at the child's face with a tissue.

Kane's attention fixed on the pink hat moving away down another aisle but stopped to look at the little boy. "What's up?"

The little boy's eyes widened and he turned his face into his mother's shoulder. Kane met the woman's gaze. "Is everything okay here?"

"Yeah, it's a battle to buy anything. Danny insists I buy candy at every store." She hoisted the little boy onto her hip. "He's already had candy once today."

Glancing over the woman's head to the bobbing pink hat, Kane dropped his attention to the little boy, who was now peering at him from between his fingers. "You be good for your mommy. Okay?"

When the little boy nodded and pushed a thumb into his mouth, Kane hurried away. He caught up with the pink hat just as Blackhawk turned into the aisle from the other end. They grinned at each other and the woman spun around and looked from one to the other. Holding up one hand, Kane smiled. "Jolene Darvish?"

"That would be me, yes, officer. I'm glad to see you." Jolene Darvish glanced nervously at Blackhawk. "You see, I'm convinced someone is following me."

The lavender perfume she was wearing shot him back to his own grandmother with such clarity it stopped all other thoughts in their tracks. Biting back a shudder of memory, he gave himself a mental shake. "Yeah, I know. Mrs. Mills told me, but it's not Atohi. He's a good friend of mine." He walked beside her noticing the list of prices she'd been calculating as she selected groceries. "When you're finished here. I'll give you a ride to the sheriff's office, all the quilting circle is there. I'd like to know more about the person who tried to run you off the mountain road."

"That's very kind of you." She glanced at the list in her hand. "I only need a can of pumpkin soup, but if I forgo my coffee at Aunt Betty's, I can buy two."

Concerned about the frail old woman, Kane looked at the meager contents of her cart. "Are you all out of food?"

"Unfortunately, I am." She gripped the shopping cart. "I'd put up preserves and sausages for winter and had enough to see me through May, but last night a bear got into my food locker and took everything. I'm lucky they didn't kill a single chicken. I'd gotten a share of the meat donated to the shelter by hunters as many of us older folk do, and it was in the freezer but it took that as well. I put up preserves for people who have a glut of fruit or vegetables for a portion instead of payment. The bear has ruined everything." She cut him a glance. "I'm not going to the shelter. I can manage well enough on my own. I have a small pension but nothing put away for a rainy day."

The idea of a bear not raiding a chicken coop didn't make sense. Something else was going on and he intended to get to the bottom of it. Kane smiled at her. "You remind me so much of my grandma. I miss her very much." He sighed and shook his head. "In her memory, will you allow me to replenish your food locker. I'll come by and check out the place and do any repairs you might need to keep it safe."

"You are a very kind soul, Deputy Kane." She smiled at him. "Yes, I know you. Mrs. Mills never stops talking about what you, and the sheriff, do to help people in our town. I can see in your eyes that I would hurt your feelings if I refused."

Kane smiled at her. "I'll fix up everything and have it delivered. Keep it in the house and I'll make a time to come by and fix up the food locker as soon as I'm able." He grabbed the cart. "Go with Atohi to my truck, I'll be along shortly." He tossed Atohi his keys.

He moved through the checkout and got the cashier to take his order, using the cartload of groceries for the kind of food she liked. He estimated what Jolene Darvish would need for a couple of months, added a few luxury items, gave them the address, and arranged the delivery. He hurried back to his truck and found Jolene Darvish standing on the sidewalk eyeing the Beast with skepticism. He smiled at her. "The delivery will arrive before noon tomorrow."

"Thank you. This your truck?" Jolene Darvish peered up at him from her diminutive five feet. "You don't have a cruiser?"

Kane smiled and opened the door. "No ma'am." He helped her into the back seat.

"Now don't you go driving like a maniac." She touched him on the shoulder as he slid behind the wheel. "I know how you young whippersnappers like speed and my nerves are on edge from this morning."

Turning to Atohi with a grin, he scratched his cheek. "I'll drive real slow, ma'am." He took off very slowly. "Tell me about the vehicle that tried to run you off the road. Did you see the driver?"

"No, it was right on my tail." She met his gaze in the rearview mirror. "All I could see was the grille and the bull bar." She paused a beat as if recalling a memory. "It had GMC on the front."

Kane nodded. "That's good. Now the person following you. Can you describe them?"

"No, I'm afraid I can't." She gripped the back of the seat. "Have you ever had that feeling, deep in the pit of your stomach that someone is watching you?"

Being very familiar with his own gut instinct, Kane glanced at her in the rearview mirror. "Yeah, I know what you mean. It's saved my life many a time."

"That's the feeling." She leaned back in the seat. "Although it might be a bear, waiting in the forest to raid my food locker again." She chuckled. "It can't be after me. The meat on my bones is long gone."

Pulling into his parking space outside the sheriff's department, Kane glanced at Atohi's concerned expression. It was obvious, his friend was thinking the same thing. To a hungry bear just out of hibernation, a vulnerable old lady alone in a cabin in Bear Peak would make a very nice snack.

# TEN

After speaking to the quilting circle members and getting much the same information, Jenna sent them on their way. Kane had taken off again, saying he was dropping Atohi back to his truck. She updated her files and leaned back in her chair. Famished didn't come close to the gnawing in her belly. When she looked up to see Kane walking through the door, she smiled with relief, now they could go and eat—and then her phone rang. It was Rio. "Did you find the murder weapon?"

*"Nope."* Rio let out a long breath. *"We've searched all over, but the killer could have thrown it anywhere, including alongside the roads and there's miles of highway. That's not why I called. I had a call from the principal of the high school to ask why Cade and Piper didn't show for school again today."*

Jenna tidied Kane's desk and turned off his computer. "Mrs. Jacobs was in this morning asking after our victim and mentioned having to be home for them this afternoon, so she must have sent them to school this morning."

*"They're not answering their phones and they're not at home, unless they decided not to pick up the landline either."* Rio

cleared his throat. *"Maybe it was a mistake buying them that truck. It was a mistake to allow Dave to work on the engine, and you know Dave with engines. It goes way too fast now."*

Waving Kane over, she put the phone on speaker. "Are you concerned they might have wrecked the truck?" She raised her eyebrows at Kane. "Dave mentioned Cade was a very responsible driver and I'm sure Piper is as well."

*"Cade is a seventeen-year-old kid, and driving a powerful truck is like pointing a loaded gun—I know it's the norm out here in the West, but back home it was different. I'm heading home to see if they're there. I'll need some personal time to hunt them down."* Rio's boots crunched on the dirt and Jenna could hear his cruiser door opening.

"Dave is right here." Jenna frowned. "Do you want us to help you?"

*"Not yet anyway."*

"What's happening with the twins?" Kane moved beside her. "Are you sayin' that the truck is too much for Cade to handle?"

*"Well, it wasn't until you rebuilt the engine, now it can tow an eighteen-wheeler."* Rio snorted. *"Like I said, it's a loaded gun."*

"I made it safe." Kane looked unimpressed and his shoulders drooped. "It's dangerous out here, and if they'd broken down, anything could have happened. Don't you think I considered the implications of the upgrades before I made them? I took Cade and Piper out a few times in the Beast before I did anything, and Cade especially handled the power just fine and my truck is way more powerful than that old GMC."

*"Oh, don't get me wrong."* Rio started his engine and the sound of tires on gravel came through the speaker. *"I appreciate the work you put into that truck. It's the twins. They seemed to be settling down and now they vanish at all hours of the night."*

He sucked in a breath. *"Well, Piper was home this morning, but Cade didn't roll in until just before I left for work. It's not drugs. I have them tested regular after they ran away from their grandma's and came back as high as kites."*

"It sounds like he has a girlfriend." Kane rubbed the back of his neck. "That would be why he's not picking up his calls. Maybe ground them for a time?"

*"I'm their brother not their dad. It makes it difficult, especially now they're getting older."* Rio sounded defeated. *"Maybe I should talk to Wolfe. He might have some fatherly advice."*

Jenna looked at Kane and shrugged. "Is Rowley on his way back to the office?"

*"Yeah. I'll go and hunt down the twins. I should be back this afternoon."* Rio disconnected.

"Hmm." Jenna tapped her bottom lip thinking. "Do you figure Wolfe will be able to help him?"

"Maybe." Kane shrugged and grabbed Jenna's coat from the line of pegs along the wall. "I need to eat." He whistled Duke and the dog bounded out from behind the counter, his backside wagging and his eyes bright with excitement. "Are you okay to walk? I'll bring you up to speed with what Jolene Darvish told me on the way."

They headed out into the cool spring afternoon and Jenna listened in awe at the poor woman's encounter with the truck. "How on earth did she manage to get away? What do you figure, road rage or something more sinister?"

"It could be a problem." Kane nodded at a woman pushing a stroller who'd given him a wave. "More so the raid on her food locker. I've seen bear raids and they rarely walk away from a chicken coop. From what she said, the bear broke the lock on her door. Now that would be a first. A bear would smash through a door, but they don't have the skill to break a lock, and her preserves were missing as well and she didn't mention any broken jars. If a bear had torn up the place, it would be a mess. It's all too neat."

Jenna pulled her hat down over her ears, the wind was picking up again and blowing tendrils of hair into her eyes. "Like the murder the other night?"

"It sure makes me suspicious, but I doubt the robbery, if it is one, and the road rage are connected. As they took everything, the chances of them returning would be minimal. No one is that stupid." Kane raised one shoulder. "Old folks sometimes drive slowly and if the truck driver was the impatient kind, he might have lost his temper. I'm not sayin' that's an excuse, but if they'd wanted to kill her, they'd have pushed her into the ravine." He glanced at Jenna. "I'll drop by Mrs. Darvish's place in the morning and fix the food locker door unless you have suspects to hunt down?"

Jenna shrugged. "I have names of people who worked for Agnes. We'll need to speak to them, but by all accounts, most of the quilting club has used them for some time and no one has been murdered before now." She pushed open the door to Aunt Betty's Café and the delicious aromas of a myriad of dishes wafted over her. Her attention went to the specials board and she moved to the counter and waited for the manager to finish serving a customer. "Hi, Susie, I'll have the BBQ pork belly burger with onion rings, sweet potato fries, and coffee." She rubbed her belly and sniffed. "Oh, is that peach pie I smell?"

"It sure is and just out the oven." Susie grinned. "À la mode?"

"Is there any other way?" Kane chuckled. "I'll have the same but add a loaded baked potato to my order. I'm kinda hungry." Beside him Duke whined. "Oh, and if you have any leftovers for Duke, I'd appreciate it or he'll take a hotdog hold the bun."

"I always have something for Duke out back." Susie beamed at him. "Take a seat. I'll be right along with the coffee."

The diner hummed with low conversation, even at close to three the place was still busy with a line at the counter and people hanging around waiting for takeout. Jenna had never found the diner empty. Aunt Betty's Café was a goldmine. She led the way to the table reserved for the sheriff's department, next to the window at the back of the diner. As Kane liked to keep his back to the wall, he took the seat opposite her. Susie arrived, placed a plate of leftovers on the floor for Duke and then straightened to pour the coffee leaving the pot on the table as usual before leaving. Jenna leaned toward Kane. "One thing of interest. The women mentioned a new plumber, a young man, they said, in his thirties." She smiled. "They mentioned that he asked a lot of questions, like did they live alone and things like that. He seemed very nice."

"Well, that's a double-edged sword." Kane leaned back in his chair and pulled off his gloves. "He might well be a kind-hearted guy or he might be a murdering psychopath. It's hard to tell the difference until they kill someone." He shrugged. "I figure we add him to our list of maybe suspects. If they all have alibis for the time of Agnes' death, perhaps one of them at least might have seen someone hanging around."

Considering his words, Jenna nodded. "We have to start somewhere. I'll hunt down their details once we get back to the office, and I'll send Rio and Rowley to interview them in the morning." She smiled at him. "I'll have another chat with Jolene while you're busy mending her door. I might be able to get some more information from her after she's had time to sleep on it."

"Good idea." Kane's attention moved from her to Susie as she walked toward them with a laden tray. "Ah..." He helped unload the tray and grinned at Jenna. "Good choice. I could eat a horse." He bit into the burger, licked sauce from the corner of his mouth, and sighed. "Maybe I should have ordered two of these."

Jenna giggled at the look of rapture on his face. "I'm wondering when you're going to ask Susie if you can live here."

"Uh-huh." The corner of Kane's mouth twitched into a smile as he looked at her. "They do say a way to a man's heart is through his stomach, but you know darn well my heart is already taken."

# ELEVEN

After a very pleasant time catching up with her friends, Jolene Darvish walked back to her battered old pickup with Mrs. Mills. "I like Deputy Kane. He told me I reminded him of his grandma and ordered me a ton of supplies. He really didn't give me the choice to refuse." She smiled. "He insisted on dropping by in the morning to fix my door and gave me his card. He said I could call him day or night if I heard anyone around my cabin and he'd have someone drop by and check on me."

"He's a nice man. He was injured—shot in the head, you know." Mrs. Mills leaned closer and lowered her voice conspiratorially. "He has a metal plate in his head, but it doesn't slow him down. Dr. Wolfe thinks the world of him and so do the girls. Both the sheriff and Deputy Kane are like family."

Jolene nodded. "I had the feeling he was all alone in the world. I saw sadness in his eyes when he spoke of his grandma, that's why I agreed to allow him to pay for my groceries. I think if I'd refused, I would have hurt his feelings."

"He'd be a hard person to refuse." Mrs. Mills chuckled. "He has that look in his eyes that stops any argument." She squeezed

Jolene's arm affectionately. "I'll see you next week. Call me for a chat."

With a wave, Jolene climbed slowly into her pickup, placed her basket on the seat beside her, and started the engine. It had been a really nice afternoon and seeing all her friends had made up for the fright earlier. She headed through town and out onto Stanton, enjoying the views. The forest in all its spring glory had changed dramatically each day, and although small patches of gray snow still sat in piles alongside the highway, beyond, the new buds on bushes and trees had exploded into every shade of green and wildflowers had popped up their heads, dotting the woodlands with color.

She turned onto Rocky Road, the old pickup crunching over the gravel smeared across the blacktop from the constant flow of melting snow. The road went from blacktop to packed dirt mixed with rocks, and the numerous potholes made for a bumpy ride. Moving slowly up the twisty mountain road, she caught a flash of light from behind her, the reflected sunlight blinding her for a second and then it was gone. She turned off her radio and wound down her window. Her heart picked up a beat at the sound of a powerful engine and she pressed the gas, willing her old vehicle to move faster. Rounding the next bend, she hit the straightaway and pushed the accelerator to the floor.

In an instant her rearview mirror suddenly filled with the massive grille and grinning bull bar. The truck was gaining fast, eating away the distance between them rapidly. Panic had her by the throat and she looked wildly ahead for an open gate but most folks had abandoned their cabins or secured them. She had no escape from the roaring monster gaining on her. The road was too narrow to pull over and hope it would pass by. Fumbling for her phone, she pressed the side to turn it on, but before the screen lit up, the truck was on her. The jolt from behind knocked the phone from her hand and it fell under her feet.

Crying out in terror, she gripped the wheel as the truck propelled her faster and faster up the mountain. The front wheels of her pickup dropped into potholes throwing her about in all directions. Behind her the roaring engine dropped down a gear and shunted her forward at a greater speed. The long grass at the side of the road flashed by. She wrestled with the wheel trying to keep on the road, but ahead a tight bend was coming up fast—too fast. Hitting the brakes, she swung the wheel hard to the right, but instead of making the corner, her pickup slid sideways and shuddered to a halt in a cloud of dust and burning rubber. Trembling all over, she gaped through the passenger window at the big GMC truck just sitting there as if contemplating its next move. The tinted windows stared back at her like a giant insect, reflecting her old truck. Hand shaking, she turned the key, willing the engine to turn over. The starter whined but the motor refused to engage and then nothing. Her pickup rolled backward toward the gaping maw above the ravine. Standing on the brakes she tried to turn the wheel, but without the engine running, the steering had locked.

She had to get out and unfastened her seat belt and was reaching for the door handle when a huge roar came from the truck. Frozen in terror, she stared as it came for her, moving slowly as if daring her to jump clear. Tormenting her by slowing and then dashing so close she could smell the heat of its engine. Sobbing with terror, she held up both hands. "What do you want? Why are you doing this to me?"

The big truck edged closer, the bull bars touching her door in a kiss of metal. A loud grinding filled the cab as the passenger door crumpled. The window shattered into a thousand pieces, scattering diamonds of glass all over her. As if her pickup weighed nothing, the truck pushed her sideways. The tires screamed as her vehicle inched closer and closer to the ravine. Scrambling to get out, Jolene pushed at the door, it opened a crack, but the wind rushing down the mountain slammed it shut again. The next second the pickup rolled over the edge and the noise stopped. The pickup spun slowly in the air and then made a nosedive for the sparkling blue river. Thrown onto the roof, Jolene's thoughts went to her husband and then the sun blinked out.

# TWELVE

## WEDNESDAY

Deputy Jake Rowley paced the kitchen with his baby girl, Vannah, over one shoulder. He patted her back and talked to her. His wife, Sandy, was feeding Cooper, the other twin, and his daughter refused to settle. He glanced at his watch. He needed to leave for work soon and walked into the family room and smiled at his wife. "I wish I didn't have to go into the office but I have suspects to interview this morning, or I'd grab an hour of personal time."

"I'll be fine. Cooper is just about done and he'll go straight to sleep." Sandy looked up at him. "I figure she just likes being with her daddy."

Grinning, Rowley dropped the little girl into his arms and traced a finger over her pink cheek. The smile she gave him melted his heart. He'd found the twins overwhelming when they'd arrived. Having Sandy's parents living with them, he had the feeling he wasn't needed, but since they'd returned home, he'd formed a special bond with the twins. They recognized him, became excited when he arrived home, and loved cuddles. Best of all, the twins had dropped into a routine, and apart from a few sleepless nights, things had gone really well. "I think you're right. Vannah is a daddy's girl." He looked into the big brown eyes and smiled. "Daddy has to go to work and you need to go to sleep so Mommy can get some rest."

"I'll put Cooper down and grab her, or you'll be late for work." Sandy stood slowly, placed Cooper on her shoulder, patted his back until he burped, and then headed for the nursery. "Are you working with Jenna today?"

Following her, Rowley shook his head. "Nope, with Zac. It's routine, nothing to worry about. I'll meet him at the office and we'll head out." He handed Vannah to her and then kissed her rosy cheek. "You be good for Mommy now." He stopped to look down at his sleeping son and slipped one arm around his wife. "Can life ever get better than this?"

"It does every day." Sandy kissed him. "Now go. I'll see you tonight. Love you." She waved him toward the door.

Sighing with contentment, Rowley climbed into his truck and headed into town. He made it to the office with five minutes to spare, greeted Maggie on the front desk, and looked around for Rio. He strolled back to the counter. "Rio not in yet?"

"Not unless he slipped in and hid somewhere when my back was turned." Maggie raised both eyebrows. "Come here." She pulled out a tissue and dabbed at his shoulder. "You been cuddling those gorgeous twins of yours before work again?"

Rowley laughed. "All the time." He stared out of the glass doors for any sight of Rio's vehicle and sighed. "I guess I'll wait for him at my desk. Anything need doing before I head out today?"

"Nope." Maggie rolled her eyes toward the ceiling. "Ain't one murder enough trouble for you?"

"One too many." Rowley headed back to his desk and checked through the files, reading through Jenna's updates, and called Colby Hahn asking where he could find him. The man had been cooperative and given him a local address. He'd done the same for Archie Bueller.

He glanced at the clock. It was unusual for Rio to be late for work. He'd been very quiet of late and he wondered how his romance with Wolfe's daughter Emily was progressing. They'd had a few dates since the ball at the ski lodge, but Rio hadn't discussed the outcome. Rio played his cards close to the vest and it was always difficult to know what he was thinking. He pulled out his phone and called him. When the phone went to voicemail, he left a message. Maybe he'd decided to take Cade and Piper to school and grounded him from using the truck. Rather than speculate, he collected his things and a statement pad, and went back to the counter. "I'm heading out to speak with Colby Hahn. He's working out of 3 Maple Crescent today. If Rio decides to show for work this morning, ask him to call me."

"I'll be sure to tell him." Maggie made a note and then gave him a wave.

Rowley checked the information on his iPad and headed for his truck. The drive to Maple was only a few minutes and he noticed the handyman's GMC pickup in the driveway. He parked some distance away from number three rather than call attention to his visit and walked to the house. A man, he assumed was Colby Hahn, was around the age of thirty, wearing jeans, a pale blue T-shirt and a ballcap, was replacing the steps to the front porch. He waited for the man to finish using an electric saw to cut a length of wood and walked closer. "Colby Hahn?"

"Yeah." Hahn's eyebrows rose in question as he turned from the saw to look at him. "You didn't mention why you wanted to speak to me. Is there a problem, Deputy?"

The man appeared relaxed but with the number of tools within reach, Rowley pushed his statement book under one arm and rested his palm on his weapon. "I'm Deputy Jake Rowley.

I'm investigating the death of Agnes Wagner out of Snowberry Way. I believe you did some work for her recently?"

"Yeah, I've worked for Mrs. Wagner a few times. This time, she had problems with a few of her doors sticking since the melt." Hahn shrugged. "It wasn't a big job but she's getting older now and doesn't have the strength to pull open the doors when they jam shut."

Hahn's mention of Mrs. Wagner in the present tense surprised him. He'd already told him the woman had died, so was he consciously speaking about her in that way to throw him off or had he misunderstood him? Most people would make a comment about the death of somebody they knew, but he went on as if it didn't matter. He'd make sure Hahn hadn't misheard him. "I see. We found her dead on Monday morning. When did you last work for her?"

"Wednesday and Friday." Hahn brushed sawdust from his shirt. "I had to go back on Friday and give the doors a second coat of paint. I had to run a plane down the sides and the doors were kinda scruffy, so Mrs. Wagner wanted them all painted. They were the doors along the passageway... including the cellar door."

Rowley made notes, adding the man's manner and cooperation and other things he'd observed as he went along. "Would that be the last time you saw her?"

"Yeah, Friday. She paid me in cash and preserves." Hahn smiled. "I have the same deal with most of the older ladies in town. I'm happy to trade in supplies. I don't get time to put up preserves myself and I don't have a wife to help out, so it makes good sense."

Hahn's complete lack of empathy for the death of a woman he'd worked for more than one time set off alarm bells. Rowley's neck prickled in a warning to be careful. He had no backup but had the advantage of being out in the open with the man, and if anything happened, the curious woman peeking out from behind the curtain at him would call it in for sure. He glanced at his information on Hahn and chewed on his cheek, thinking. There wasn't an actual address listed, other than Bear Peak, and that part of the mountain was vast. "Where exactly do you live on Bear Peak? Do you have a property name or a road?"

"Not really." Hahn smiled. "I'm living in one of the old cabins. It's via the fire road accessed by Rocky Road but has no precise address, no. I don't get mail delivered. I have a box at the post office and I use my cellphone and satellite sleeve if necessary. There are many abandoned cabins up there and when I arrived, I needed a cheap place to stay. I hunted one down and moved in." He chuckled. "I found newspapers from the 1960s tied in bundles. The place was sturdily built and it didn't take too much time to fix up." His eyes wrinkled as he stared into the sun. "I've been living up there about a year now. Has the owner suddenly returned? I tried to hunt them down and found no trace of them."

"No, I haven't come about the cabin and people at Bear Peak have been going missing since before I was born. It's not the most popular place to live—darn right dangerous if you ask me. There are countless numbers of old cabins all over Stanton Forest. Most built illegally but they're not hurting anyone and people often use them in the hunting season. Those that do keep them clean and some even fix them up." Rowley looked him straight in the eye. "Can you account for your whereabouts on Sunday night through Monday morning?"

"I'd have been home." Hahn shrugged. "I start early and work through until dark most days, but on the weekends I catch up with my chores and sleep." He gave him a lazy smile. "It's just me, a few chickens, and my guns, so I don't have anyone to vouch for me unless you speak chicken."

"I don't, no." Rowley's mind went to Jenna's notes about Jolene Darvish's run in with a GMC truck earlier in the day.

"What time did you come down the mountain yesterday morning?"

"Going on eight." Hahn indicated with his chin toward the house. "They didn't want me here before the kids left for school, so it was a later start than usual."

Rowley scratched his head with his pen and acted nonchalantly. "Did you see anyone on Rocky Road?"

"Can't say that I did." Hahn frowned.

"Have you ever worked for Jolene Darvish? She lives on Rocky too."

"Yeah, a few times." Hahn looked annoyed. "Is that all? I need to get back to it. I'm almost done and want to head home."

Closing his notepad, Rowley frowned. He wouldn't get any more information from Hahn and thanked him and headed for his cruiser. He pulled out his phone and called Rio. The phone went to voicemail again. "Where the heck are you?"

# THIRTEEN

As the Beast roared along Stanton and the fresh mountain air rushed through the cab, Jenna shivered but didn't have the heart to pull Duke back inside. The bloodhound's head stuck out the window, his long silky ears blowing in the wind as his lips filled with air, moving them away from his teeth in waves to give the impression he was singing along to the tunes blaring from the substantial speakers. She laughed. "Would you look at Duke. He's singing along with you."

"He has great taste in music." Kane grinned and continued to sing in his deep baritone. He shot her a serious glance. "It's only fair he joins in. I do howl at the moon with him when the fancy takes him."

Jenna rolled her eyes. "Yeah, I know. I figured a pack of wolves had invaded us. Is it a full-moon thing and should I be worried? I mean, you're not going to change into a werewolf are you?"

"Not anytime soon." Kane grinned at her and wiggled his eyebrows. "Are you frightened I might bite you?"

"Ha-ha." Jenna laughed. "No, but if you do plan to go feral and run with the pack, I'll be running right alongside you."

"That's good to know." Kane chuckled. "Maybe next full moon you should come out and howl at the moon with us?"

"That's a date." Jenna sighed, looking at the forest flashing by. "I wish we could have ridden up here. It would have been a nice ride in the sunshine. I really need to get out into the fresh air. It was a long winter. I'd kill for a run on a beach somewhere and feel the sand between my toes."

"Shane was telling me the other day his mom has a place in Florida. A condo right opposite the beach." He cleared his throat. "He said if we ever wanted a holiday, we could use it. He plans to take a week down there with Julie and Anna next summer and take them to the parks. Most times it sits empty."

Jenna frowned. "Why not book a place like normal people and head out to Hawaii or somewhere?" She chewed on her bottom lip. "Ah, I see. No bookings, no one knows we're there, apart from the airline."

"We're not 'normal people' anymore, Jenna." Kane's expression became serious. "There are killers out there who have it in their heads to challenge us to catch them. You do understand some psychopaths want someone to stop them killing? This is a few of the type we attract, then there's the ones who believe they can beat us and get away with murdering people in our town. It would be nice to go somewhere, where nobody gives a darn who we are or what we're doing in their town."

Leaning back in her seat and closing her eyes, thinking of Florida beaches, she smiled. "Wouldn't that be nice? Can we ever get away for a few days... like ever?"

"When you employ two more deputies, we can leave the crime solving to Rio and Rowley. With two others to assist them, they'll do just fine and let's face facts here, Jenna, we're only a flight away if they need us."

Jenna opened her eyes as they turned off Stanton and started to make the climb up Rocky Road, heading for Jolene

Darvish's house. "You sure have a point. Okay, the first chance we get, we're out of here."

"That's Rio's truck. What the heck is he doing here?" Kane pulled into the narrow driveway behind him and climbed out.

Jenna scrambled out and stepped carefully around the potholes in the road. She stared into the cab. Rio was just sitting there staring at the road, his face pale, and eyes fixed. "Is he okay?"

"Yeah." Kane pulled open the door. "Are you sick?"

"Nope." Rio dragged his attention away from the road. "I'm waiting for Cade. Seems you're right, Dave. He's been coming up here to visit a girl and he didn't plan on coming home again last night." He turned a weary gaze toward them and shrugged. "I figured I'd wait here for him to drive by. I tried to find him last night, but unless you know where the cabins are up this way, it's like looking for a needle in a haystack and you risk the chance of someone taking pot shots at you. Mountain folk can be darn right unsociable."

"Just how long have you been sitting here?" Kane leaned against the open door.

"Since Piper broke down and told me where he'd headed." Rio shrugged. "Around four yesterday afternoon."

Jenna peered in through the passenger window. "Why aren't you answering your phone?"

"Battery's dead and I didn't think to bring a car charger with me." Rio shrugged. "I'd been calling Cade nonstop all last night. He's not answering either."

"Just a minute." Kane slapped the door shut and headed back to his truck, returning with a Thermos of coffee and a bag of cookies. "Here, these will keep you going. We need to go check on someone." He thrust them at him through the window.

"Thanks." Rio gave them a bleak look. "What do you want me to do?"

Jenna exchanged a meaningful glance with Kane and nodded. "Best you stay here in case Cade slips by. We'll be at Mrs. Darvish's cabin. It's four driveways up. Once we've been there, we'll help you locate Cade." She turned back to the Beast.

"I don't figure that's the way to handle Cade." Kane climbed behind the wheel. "If he wants to keep him home, maybe take his car keys away from him. Walking or taking the bus after having your own ride brings a kid down to earth real fast... Trust me, I know."

It wasn't Cade's behavioral problems that was bothering Jenna. She frowned at Kane. "Rio is a trained officer, very well trained, and his kid brother goes missing. Why didn't he call it in or at least call one of us to help him?"

"Not only that." Kane flicked her a glance and backed out of the driveway, turned onto the road, and headed up the mountain. "Why is he driving around without a phone charger in his vehicle? They're supplied and it's not as if he forgot to bring it with him. He never forgets anything. It's as if he's a different person this morning."

Thinking the same, Jenna nodded. "I agree. This goes way past being angry at his brother. I have that prickling sensation as if something isn't quite right."

They drove higher up the mountain and when Kane pulled to a halt and jumped from the truck, she followed him. "What's up?"

"See that?" Kane pointed to a flattened bush and strange marks dug into the dirt road. "Something happened here." He moved closer to the edge of the ravine, and grabbing hold of saplings, dropped onto a narrow rocky outcrop.

Heart in her mouth, Jenna followed. "Be careful, it's not safe here. The sides are giving way."

"There's a pickup down there." Kane turned his head toward her, his eyes filled with regret. "It looks like the old vehicle Mrs. Darvish was driving yesterday." He pulled out his binoculars and called out the license plate. "Got it?"

Sick to her stomach, Jenna nodded and used her phone to run it. "It's her."

"There's no way we can recover that vehicle." Kane rubbed the back of his neck.

Jenna slid down the crumbling side of the ravine but Kane's back was blocking the view to the swollen river below. "We have to get down to her. She might be alive." She tried to go past him and he turned and grabbed her arm. Shaking her head, she glared at him. "We have to try, Dave. She's all alone down there."

"Jenna. Look at me." He gave her a little shake. "There's no way down by foot. It's a sheer drop over this ledge. Don't you figure I'd be heading down if I could?"

"She might have been thrown clear." Jenna took a step closer to the edge sending a cascade of gravel tumbling down into the ravine.

"Stop right now. This is suicide. Don't move and I'll take a look." He turned and scanned the area looking up and down side to side and then back to her. "She wasn't thrown clear. The side of the ravine is a sheer drop. She's still inside the pickup. The cab is submerged and she wouldn't have stood a chance even if she'd survived the fall, which is doubtful." He gave her a little push up the slope. "There's nothing you can do to help her, Jenna. Climb back up. Take your time and grip hold of the bushes. I'll be right behind you."

Alarm gripped Jenna by the throat. Had she made a fatal error by not escorting the old woman home last night? She had to find out what had happened to her. Biting back a sob, she nodded and slowly climbed back to the road. Following her, Kane stood for long moments staring back and forth along the road. As a cold wind buffeted her, she watched him with interest. She understood what he was doing. Kane had the ability to track a bullet's trajectory, so making sense of what happened would be a walk in the park. Her gaze followed him as he paced up and down, back and forth, bending to examine the dirt. She went to his side. "What do you see?"

"Here, there's chips of paint and glass. Someone rammed the passenger door and pushed her pickup sideways over the edge." Kane turned and stared down the road, hands on hips. "There's one set of tracks back and forth over the disturbed soil. I'd say that's Rio looking for his brother, so we know Mrs. Darvish went over the edge before four or five yesterday afternoon. I figure this happened on her way home. She mentioned a GMC truck causing her trouble yesterday, right?"

Dragging on her professional cloak, Jenna used her phone to take images of the evidence Kane had pointed out. "Yeah, with a silver grille and a bull bar, like a ton of vehicles in town. She didn't even make out the color." She pushed hair under her woolen cap and frowned. "How come Rio didn't see the evidence of an accident and stop to take a look? You spotted it the moment we turned the bend."

"Unless he's covering for his brother—it's not unusual for siblings to do that. It could have been either of them. Cade and Rio have similar vehicles. Likely the same tires as well." Kane gave her a long considering stare. "Both were on the mountain when Mrs. Darvish went into the ravine." He sighed. "We'd better head up to her cabin. She might have livestock that need tending, and I'll call the general store to cancel the supplies I ordered. We don't need anyone else coming up here and disturbing evidence."

# FOURTEEN

As Kane drove up the mountain, Jenna considered the situation. The thought of that poor old lady dying like that made her sick to her stomach. She'd seen the sides of the ravine. There'd be only one way of retrieving the body and that would be by dropping a team down by chopper. "Wolfe will need a search and rescue team to get him down to the retrieval site. There's no way up the river at this time of the year. The water is too deep and moving too fast."

"Do you figure the local search and rescue pilot has enough experienced to negotiate a deep ravine?" Kane climbed back inside the Beast. "It takes skill, with the wind and all, to drop a rescue team down and retrieve them in a limited space."

Concerned, Jenna stared at him. "I don't know. You know as well as I do that Wolfe is capable, but they'll need him on the ground. I'll call it in and see what they say." She made the call and explained the situation. "Well, if Doug is sick, I'll find someone else, but we'll still need a retrieval crew. There's no way down to the bottom of the ravine by foot or boat. Okay, I'll call you back when we've arranged another pilot." She glanced at Kane's frown and disconnected. "The pilot they have is sick, but they'll have their crew on standby."

"Call Ty Carter. He has combat experience, and he'd be the only person apart from Wolfe I'd trust in that ravine." Kane headed up the mountain and they turned into the driveway with the sign DARVISH posted on the open gate.

Jenna called the FBI field office in Snakeskin Gully to speak to ex-navy Seal Special Agent Ty Carter. Carter and behavioral analyst Agent Jo Wells had become friends and often assisted the team in difficult cases. She explained the situation.

*"Sure, I can handle that with my eyes closed. Glad you called. We're staring at the walls going crazy with boredom here. I'll have wheels up in twenty."* He mumbled something Jenna missed and then came back on the line. *"I'll hand you over to Jo. She'd like to know more about the case, I'm sure."*

As Kane pulled to a halt outside the old cabin, Jenna looked around. All was quiet apart from the chickens. She frowned. "Can I call you back, Jo? We're at the assumed victim's home and I need to take a look around."

*"Sure, but from what Ty said before, this case is complicated if you have someone killing old women and in different ways. I'd like at least to come with Ty so we can discuss it. Do you mind? I won't interfere with your case, Jenna, but I'll be there to consult with if you need me."*

Jenna smiled. Having an FBI behavioral analyst as a friend was a real bonus. "I'd love to see you both again. If you want to stay, Kane's cottage is free."

*"Well then, we'll see you soon."* She disconnected.

She followed Kane to the front door. The house was locked up tight. "Best we check on the chickens."

They went round the house with Duke sniffing all around but he gave no hint of smelling a bear in the area or anyone else. The chickens looked just fine. Jenna frowned. "If Mrs. Darvish died in the wreck, what happens to her chickens? She doesn't have any relatives." She wrinkled up her nose. "Don't suggest we take them home. I really don't want chickens, Dave. It's just another thing we have to have cared for if we go away."

"The good thing about chickens is they can care for themselves." Kane refilled the water and sprinkled pellets on the ground. "We could let them out to fend for themselves. There's water and they'd scratch around for food. At night they'd return to the coop but the eggs would go to waste."

Horrified, Jenna stared at him. "What about the wildlife around here? They'd end up being eaten by something."

"Call Father Derry. He'll have someone pick them up." Kane stood hands on hips surveying the area. "They have a chicken coop out back of the shelter. The eggs will come in handy." He walked away toward a shed made of granite and examined the lock and the ground all around. "This looks like a robbery. This lock was forced using a crowbar or similar. As far as I know, bears don't carry crowbars." He pulled out his phone. "I'll call Wolfe and give him the details. Did Carter give you an ETA?"

Jenna shook her head. "He said wheels up in twenty is all." She checked her watch. "I'd say he'll be landing in an hour and a half."

She followed Kane back to the Beast, listening as he gave Wolfe a concise description of what had happened. When she climbed into the passenger seat, she turned to him. "We'll have time to drive up the mountain and hunt down Cade."

"He could be anywhere." Kane headed out the driveway. "You know as well as I do there are trails and fire roads all over this part of Bear Peak. Cade's girlfriend could live down any one of them." He shrugged. "We'll need to meet Carter and get things rolling."

A rumble came in the distance and, alarmed, Jenna stared out the window. "What was that?"

"I'd say another rockslide higher up." Kane pointed to a curl of dust rising into the air. "Atohi was concerned about the chances of road blockages, remember?"

Jenna frowned. "Yeah, I called the mayor and told him. He has the opinion that a rockslide is nature running its course and his job is to make sure the roads are passable, but he did say he'd pass my concerns along to the department involved." She shrugged in frustration. "I might as well have saved my breath."

"There's a truck coming." Kane slowed at the driveway as two white GMCs drove past and headed down the mountain, going way too fast. "That's Cade and there are two women in the truck behind him." He pulled out slowly onto the road and waited as the trucks disappeared around the next bend. "I'll keep back to avoid the rocks spinning away from their wheels. I don't know about Rio's ability to get through to his brother for acting like a jerk but as a cop, I can come down hard on him for reckless driving." He glanced at her. "Unless you have other plans?"

Jenna shook her head, but after seeing Cade drive by, the nagging feeling he was involved somehow in Jolene Darvish's road rage incident, if not her death, would not go away. "I want to speak to him, that's for sure, but the lecture would come better from you. He looks up to you, especially when you agreed to rebuild his motor."

"Well, it's no more Mr. Nice Guy, after seeing that display of driving." The nerve in Kane's cheek twitched in obvious anger. "We had an understanding, or so I thought, that he'd drive the truck like a responsible adult, not like a spoiled child."

As they arrived at the bottom of the mountain, Jenna made out Rio's truck blocking the road. Cade and Rio were out of their trucks and standing nose to nose. At seventeen, Cade was, without doubt, a strong and powerful man. It looked as if he had no intention of listening to Rio and was shaping up for a fight. As Kane backed into a driveway, they sat and watched for a few seconds. Jenna blew out a long sigh. "Maybe we should wait and see if Rio can sort things out."

When Cade let fly with a blow to Rio's face and his brother just took it, Kane nodded toward the other truck. "I figure the problem is right over there."

# FIFTEEN

Jenna moved her attention away from the fight. Two women, one maybe sixteen and the other in her twenties, stood leaning against the front of their truck, watching with interest. They were dressed the same, sweaters under denim jackets, blue jeans, and dusty cowboy boots. The girl wore her dark hair in a straight bob with long thick bangs cut in a severe straight line and black lipstick to match her fingernails. The woman had a mess of long dark curls swirling unrestrained down her back. Thick lines of kohl surrounded her dark eyes, giving her the surreal look of a cartoon. Long dangly brightly colored beaded earrings seemed to be the flavor of the day. Raising an eyebrow, Jenna turned to Kane. "Try to diffuse the situation and I'll go talk to the women."

"I'll do my best." Kane gave the women a quick once over. "The older one is carrying. She's wearing a shoulder holster. Don't trust them... not yet anyway." He moved past the trucks, one hand on his weapon.

Keeping her distance but getting close enough to speak to the women, Jenna kept her expression neutral. "Hi there. Are you Cade's friends? We've been searching for him. Zac was convinced he'd wrecked the truck."

"Cade's been stayin' with us." The older woman pushed long black curls behind one ear and smiled. "His brother is suffocatin' him."

Nodding, Jenna moved a few steps closer. "I'm Jenna Alton and you are?"

"Amber and Kara Judd–I'm Kara." The older woman lifted her chin. "Cade is seventeen, a man by the look of him, and yet his brother figures he can rule his life." She moved her dark gaze onto Jenna. "Now he's ridiculing him by calling out the sheriff to hunt him down like a lost kid. Zac needs to step back and leave him alone. He's not doin' anything wrong."

Moving her attention back to the men in the middle of the road, she frowned as Rio's vehicle drove away. Kane had taken a nonchalant pose and was talking in hushed tones to Cade, but she hadn't missed the young man's clenched fists. She held her breath, hoping that Kane would make him see reason, because, if he made a huge mistake and punched Kane, all bets would be off. Beside her, a few rocks slipped past her feet and she turned to look back at the two girls. Her gaze slid past them and to the shotgun in a rack at the back of their cab. She cleared her throat. "Do you have to be somewhere?"

"Amber needs to go to school. Cade was going to drive her, but he needed to drop by home for a spell." Kara gave her a slow smile. "He'll be packing his things and moving in with us this afternoon."

"Oh, I see." Jenna chewed on her bottom lip. "All this trouble would have been averted if Rio had known where he was staying. Where exactly is your cabin?"

"Up yonder–we like to keep our whereabouts private." Kara's brow wrinkled. "We're not doing anything illegal."

Taking in the old truck, Jenna pushed a little more. "You live up here all alone?"

"What's wrong with that?" Amber's eyes narrowed. "We like it up here."

Jenna smiled. "I like solitude too. I live in an isolated area myself. What do you do to get by? I haven't seen you around town."

"We trade most times." Kara shrugged. "And I get work when the rodeo comes to town. That money is all we need to get by."

The crunching of boots on the gravel caught Jenna's attention and she turned to see Cade walking toward them. He gave her a nod and she smiled at him. "I'm glad you're okay."

"How could I not be okay, Jenna?" Cade folded his arms across his chest. "I have two beautiful women to care for me." He snorted derisively and glared at Kane's arrival. "I'm not a darn kid. Zac is trying to come between me and my woman. He's jealous is all, because he can't keep a woman interested in him." He turned and took Kara into his arms in a passionate embrace. "Take Amber to school. I'll call you later."

Jenna blinked. She'd assumed the teenager was Cade's girlfriend but said nothing as Cade climbed into his truck and pulled it over to allow Kara to drive past. She turned to Kane. "I didn't see that coming."

"Hormones." Kane shrugged. "Add that to a woman who can tie a young guy around her little finger and that's what happens." He sighed. "I've seen kids of Cade's age throw their lives away for raging hormones. He can't see straight right now and he figures he's in love, but I'm not sure how he'll handle sharing her with the rodeo cowboys when they hit town. She is what they fondly refer to as a buckle bunny, and no doubt she'll have her sister following right along behind her soon enough." He raised an eyebrow. "She's a hooker, Jenna."

Shocked Jenna gaped at him. "Her, really? I thought they all left with the rodeo. Do you recognize her?"

"Oh, yeah. Kara Judd has been working the rodeo circuit for

a time." Kane watched the women drive away. "Rowley pointed her out to me over two years ago. He asked me plain if we could book her for prostitution, but as she's as smart as a whip, there's not a chance of her approaching a deputy. I've seen guys push bills down the front of her shirt, but there's no law against that or what they do in the privacy of their own trailers."

"Yeah, I recall you mentioning it at the time. So that's what she meant about working at the rodeos." Jenna narrowed her gaze at him. "You never thought to mention this to me before now?"

"Jenna, these things go on at all festivals and rodeos." He shrugged. "This goes way back hundreds of years to the camp followers who followed the troops during the civil wars, and even the railway workers. Trust me, buckle bunnies go back to the first rodeo. Many follow the circuit. Not all ask for money. For some, just bedding the local champion is all the payment they need." He laid a hand on her shoulder. "Don't beat yourself up about it, Jenna. Most times you're hunting down the bad guys." He waved a hand after the dust cloud vanishing along the straightaway. "You shouldn't worry yourself about something there's nothing we can do about." He scratched his chin. "Unless you can convince Carter to ride a few broncos and do well enough to get her attention. He's the only cop I know who'd be able to pass as a rodeo cowboy."

Jenna grimaced. "That wouldn't be worth the risk... although he has been bored lately." She checked her watch. "We need to move things along if we're going to meet with him and Wolfe before they head out to view the wreck."

"I'll do the retrieval. I'm fitter than Wolfe. Are you coming with me?" Kane raised both eyebrows and stared at her.

Jenna shook her head. "I know my limitations and I'm not trained in body retrieval. I'll likely get washed away in the rapids and you'll be searching for my body next. I'd only get in the way. I'll head up to the other side of the ravine. I'll be able to see from there and the road is safer." She wet her lips. "You'll trust me with the Beast and Duke, won't you?"

"I guess." Kane scratched his cheek considering. He indicated toward Cade, sulking in his truck. "We'll need to follow him home. I sent Rio to get some sleep and I don't want any trouble." He glanced at his watch. "We'll have time."

"I'd like to talk to him." Jenna pushed her hands into the back pockets of her jeans. "Maybe I can get through to him."

"I doubt it." Kane flicked Cade a glance and then looked back at her. "He's angry, maybe see how he responds if you tell him to hand over his keys. It would be safer if you drove down the mountain, and I'll be in front of you all the way."

Straightening her spine, as if readying for a fight, she nodded. "Okay. Drive slowly."

# SIXTEEN

Taking her time to gather her thoughts, Jenna strolled to Cade's truck and held out her hand. "Move over, I'm driving."

"Think you can handle her?" Cade gave her an amused look, but climbed into the passenger seat.

Meeting his gaze, Jenna nodded. "My cruiser could eat this for lunch." She climbed inside the truck and started the engine.

Ahead, Kane moved off slowly and Duke looked back at her through the open window with a wide grin. She moved down the bumpy mountain road and cut him a quick glance. "I'm not telling you how to live your life, Cade, but Dave told me about—"

"Yeah, yeah, I know." Cade blew out a breath. "First, it's Mrs. Jacobs. I mean, she's employed by us... she started on me about dating a hooker. That old biddy doesn't have the right to interfere in my life. She's worse than my grandma and that's saying something." He slammed his fist down on the edge of the seat. "Kara swore to me that she's not seen another man since we met. Mrs. Jacobs is wrong about her and so is Dave." He barked a laugh. "The pious Dave Kane is living a lie, Jenna. If he knows all the hookers around town, he isn't as old school as he's led you to believe." He pushed a hand through his hair. "Kara told me she did it a few times to make money, but that's in the past now. I get my inheritance when I turn eighteen in two weeks. Kara and I will be married. It's all planned. I'll be able to look after them. They won't need to sell their bodies to survive."

Rio had mentioned how smart his brother was, but right now he was acting like a jerk. "How do you plan on getting by once your inheritance runs out? You should finish school and get a decent job."

"My share is around $30,000." Cade grinned like a wolf. "It's a fortune. I won't need a job."

Jenna drove the truck with care around potholes, going way too close to the ravine edge, and gritted her teeth. Once on another straightaway, she relaxed a little and snorted. She'd tell him like it is in the real world. "That won't last a year. Your girlfriends will need clothes and they're expensive. They need to visit the beauty parlor about every six weeks and then there's food, gas, bills, taxes. Amber still attends school and you'll have to pay for that too. Nope, you'll be working seven days a week hauling manure or sweeping up after people to keep them unless you find a decent occupation." She shrugged. "Then what if kids come along? How are you going to manage, Cade? Or do you want them living with your grandma? You know darn well welfare will take them from you if you can't feed them and send them to school."

"Hey, you're getting way ahead of yourself, Jenna." He pushed a hand through his hair in an agitated manner. "I'm not planning on kids."

Going for the jugular, Jenna shrugged. "Well, if you can't keep it in your pants, and it's obvious that's the only reason you're planning on moving in with them, then you need to face facts. These things happen and with DNA paternity tests these days, you can't just walk away from your responsibilities. That's eighteen years of support, Cade. Are you sure you're ready for that?" She cleared her throat. "Kara might look good now, but how will you feel when you're twenty-one and she's starting to show her age? The smoking and drugs take a toll on a woman's looks. They age them by ten years or more. Will you walk out on your kids when you're tired of her and find someone younger?"

"You're messing with my head." Cade scrubbed his hands down his face. "Talk about something else. Why are you on the mountain?"

Jenna watched the Beast disappear around the next bend and, keeping in the tracks followed him, it was taking all her concentration to negotiate the road. Rocks had tumbled down since they'd driven up earlier and the sound of dust and gravel hitting the roof sounded like rain. She chewed on her bottom lip. "We were coming to check on Mrs. Darvish. She reported a road rage incident yesterday."

"The old lady in the beat-up old truck?" Cade chuckled. "I'm not surprised she upset someone, she drives at, like, five miles per hour, and if you're behind her, it takes a long time to get anywhere."

The hairs on Jenna's neck bristled. "You know her?"

"Not to speak to, no." Cade turned in his seat to look at her. "Has she said it was me?"

"Nope." Jenna chanced a glance at him and then looked back at the road. "Did you see her yesterday afternoon on the mountain?"

"I don't recall." Cade shrugged. "Why?"

Jenna stiffened, deciding what to tell him, but his reaction to Mrs. Darvish's death might be worth noting. "She's at the bottom of the ravine."

"Well, I guess shit happens." Cade shrugged. "There's a few people I'd like to see join her right now."

Ignoring his last remark, Jenna concentrated on getting off the mountain, she had other things to think about. Her stomach churned at the thought of seeing the most important man in her life lowered from a chopper into the deep boiling rapids, freezing cold from the melt and buffeted by strong winds. The ravine changed dramatically during the year. The river flowing from the mountain was usually calm, but the melt was sending gallons of water per second down the mountain, and the extended winter and freezing conditions had made parts of the mountain unstable. In the chopper, Carter would be battling high winds and falling rocks. On the ground, Kane would risk a freezing torrent sweeping him away to certain death. She had no idea how they could possibly retrieve the body of Mrs. Darvish without something bad happening.

As they hit Stanton, Jenna sucked in a deep breath and wiggled her numb fingers. She'd been white-knuckling the steering wheel all the way down the mountain. As they drove through the forest, she heard Cade mutter under his breath. She glanced at him. "Did you say something?"

"Nope, just thinking out loud is all." He gave her a long look. "I'm guessing Dave will be taking back my truck?"

Jenna shrugged. "I've no idea. He worked on the engine of that truck because he thought you were a responsible driver, but speeding down a mountain road has probably changed his mind —and that truck was for both of you. Seems to me it might be Piper's turn to drive it."

"Hah." Cade grinned at her. "Do you figure Piper will stop me from driving it? You don't know her too well, do you?" He crossed his fingers. "We're twins. Two sides of the same coin, Jenna. We even think alike."

Jenna pulled up behind the Beast and waited for Kane to take Duke from the back seat. She touched Cade's arm. "Maybe wait up and see what Dave says. I figure he'll want a word with you."

"A lecture, you mean?" Cade pushed his hands inside his pockets and hunched his shoulders. "Seems to me now I have three fathers. Zac thinks he can tell me what to do, and now he's enlisted Shane and Dave as his backup crew. My dad is dead. If they figure they can take his place, they're wrong."

"If they didn't care about you, they wouldn't bother." Jenna waited for Kane to walk over and then stepped away, but she could hear them just fine.

"You can't stop me seeing Kara." Cade stuck out his chin. "You're not my dad."

"I'm not preventing you from seeing anyone." Kane moved in closer eyeballing him. "I have experience with women and you'll learn in good time, but I need to ask you one simple question: Did you mention your inheritance to her or Amber at any time?"

"Sure. I mentioned it to Amber." Cade shrugged. "She's one of Piper's friends and we mentioned it a time ago. What's this got to do with Kara?"

"Kara has a hankering for tough hardened cowboys—men who can show her a good time and give her money." Kane raised an eyebrow. "Why would she hook up with a seventeen-year-old inexperienced kid? Maybe you should think on that for a time. Zac tells me you're real smart, so you'll work it out. I sure hope you do. I'm holding on to the keys to your truck until you grow a pair and stop acting like a spoiled brat." He turned and looked at Jenna. "We have to go. Are you ready?"

"Yeah." Jenna walked to his side. "Think that will work?"

"Hope so." Kane shook his head slowly. "Blind Freddy could see she's only interested in his money. Poor kid. At that age they're easily manipulated by an older woman. Kara would be an expert too, so he wouldn't stand a chance."

"You sound like you're talking from experience." Jenna climbed into the Beast. "Come on, don't leave me hanging."

"Nah, not this time." Kane flashed her a broad grin. "Some things must stay in the vault."

# SEVENTEEN

As they drove into town, Jenna's phone chimed. It was Wolfe, and she put the call on speaker. "We're on our way, Shane."

*"Drop by your office. Search and Rescue have left a set of gear there for Dave. If he changes now, it will save time."* He paused a beat. *"Carter did a flyby on the way here. He's only prepared to take two men, so it looks like me and Dave."*

"What exactly did he say?" Kane pulled up outside the sheriff's department and looked at Jenna.

*"It's a wind tunnel and he'll be dropping us from higher than usual. From the weather report, we have a window of about one hour to get in and out."* Wolfe cleared his throat. *"There's a search and rescue guy here more than willing to go, so you don't have to risk your life out there. It's not your job to retrieve bodies."*

Jenna caught the nerve twitching in Kane's cheek and she met his blank gaze. "What are you going to do?"

"Is the guy married with a family?" Kane stared into space for a beat and then rubbed the back of his neck.

*"Nope."* Wolfe sounded annoyed. *"Oh no, don't pull the kid card on me again, Dave. I'm the ME. I have to go."*

"No, you don't." Kane blew out a long breath. "It's gonna be me, Carter, and the single guy. You can wait at the top of the ravine for me to retrieve the body if you must. You have the girls to worry about, and if Carter has concerns, it's going to be a rough ride. I'm going and that's final." He turned away and climbed out of the truck, unclipped Duke, and walked inside.

Swallowing the rising fear of knowing Kane was heading into a life-threatening situation, Jenna stared after him. "He's made up his mind and you know darn well there's no stopping him. We'll be there soon." She disconnected and followed Kane into the office.

As Kane grabbed the gear left at the front counter, Jenna followed behind him and waited until he came out of the changing room. "Dave, is it really worth risking three lives to recover a body? There must be another way."

"I'm open to suggestions." He handed her a backpack with his clothes and boots.

Wracking her brain for answers, Jenna took the bag as Kane shrugged into a brightly colored lifejacket and strapped on a helmet. "Can't you blow out the windows and let the water wash her out? We can pick her up downstream." She grabbed his arm. "If Carter is worried, it's too dangerous."

"I'm not worried. I've done worse rescues hundreds of times and with guys shooting at me. I'd be in the water anyway. I'll need to be down there to blow out the windows. Really, shooting out the window isn't an option. A bullet could bounce all around in there destroying evidence and the body could get caught up or torn apart by the falls."

Stomach churning, Jenna shook her head. "Rather a dead body than you."

"Nah, I'll be attached to a harness. I trust Ty to pull me out if I get into trouble. We'll work as a team." Kane pulled her close, kissed her, and then gave a nonchalant shrug. "I've got the easy job. I'll be on the ground. It's Ty and the other guy you should be worried about in the wind tunnel. Let's go. We have a small window of opportunity to do this and it's closing fast. I'll leave the Beast at Shane's office. You can ride with him in the van. From the Bear Peak lookout, you'll have a firsthand look at the retrieval." He bent down to rub Duke's ears. "Duke will be fine here with Maggie." He glanced around. "It looks like Rowley is still out hunting down our suspects."

Jenna headed back to the counter and raised her eyebrows at Maggie. "Has Rowley been checking in?"

"Yeah, he's fine." Maggie took hold of Duke's collar. "He's on his way to speak to Archie Bueller. We found him working out of Pine. He'll check in when he arrives."

Jenna nodded. "Keep me in the loop." She followed Kane out the front door.

Concerned by Kane's silence on the way to the ME's office, Jenna figured he must be preparing himself for the dangerous task ahead. It was so like him to make light of things, when she knew darn well he'd be risking his life. When they arrived, they greeted Carter and a young man introduced as Stevens. She noticed Jo outside Wolfe's office and went to her side. "Are you coming to watch the retrieval?"

"Not this time." Jo smiled at her. "I've asked Shane if I can look over his files. I want to make sure I haven't missed anything."

"Okay." Jenna headed back to the men and leaned against the counter in the vanilla-scented foyer of the morgue, listening intently to their plan to recover Mrs. Darvish's body.

"We'll take the FBI chopper." Carter crossed his arms over his chest. "The wind gusts up there are brutal and I know my bird. I'm not risking everyone's lives by taking the search and rescue chopper. Mine is fitted out with everything we need and it's more powerful."

"If I fall into the water, don't try and haul me out." Kane looked at Stevens. "Wait until I surface or my weight combined with the current and wind gusts will destabilize the chopper." He smiled. "I've done this a thousand times."

"If you don't surface in three minutes, I'm hauling your ass out of there. The wind and current be damned." Carter gave him a long stare. "You're not dying on my watch."

"Let's get at it then." Kane pulled on gloves and headed for the stairs to the roof.

As they ran up the steps, she bit back the overpowering need to call out. She so wanted to say, "Be careful," but Dave had slipped into combat mode and had shut off completely. As the chopper took off, Jenna's stomach dropped to her boots. The wind gust details and the chill factor alone frightened her.

As she drove with Wolfe up the mountain road, taking Stanton and then the cut through to Bear Peak Lookout, they passed the entrance to the parking lot and ended up on a high plateau with a good view of the ravine. From here, she could make out the edge of Black Rock Falls. The thundering water had filled the air with a freezing mist that clung to everything. Jenna turned her head forty-five degrees to the left to search for a smaller waterfall. Swelled by the melt, it tumbled down the mountain, filling a pool before crashing down into the ravine. Behind the ravine the mountain climbed in dripping-wet steps of rugged black granite to form the head of a grizzly.

The chopper was already in position high above the ravine, the sound of the engine muffled by the noise from the falls. Jenna gripped the edge of her seat in the van as the chopper dropped slowly and then swayed dangerously close to the edge of the ravine. Too darn close. The next moment, Carter took it higher and held its position as Kane dropped out onto the skids. The chopper turned slowly, and above the noise Jenna picked up the increased roar of the engine. It was obvious even from where she was that Carter was fighting the updraft. She gripped Wolfe's arm. "Oh, that can't be good."

"Carter has flown under fire and saved a ton of men from

the pits of hell." Wolfe looked at her. "He's the best there is, Jenna."

His words didn't stop her heart thundering. Jenna climbed from the van and, dragging her hood over her head against the freezing damp swirling air, she moved closer to the edge and slipped one arm tightly around a sturdy pine. Terrified for Kane's safety, she pushed her lips together to stop them trembling. High above, Kane jumped away from the chopper, dropped, and then clung to a rope as Stevens lowered him into the ravine. He might as well have been hanging from the tail of a kite. The wind spun him in all directions, taking him from one side of the ravine to the other. Jenna let out a small cry as he hurled toward the sheer rock face and, just at the last second, used his feet to repel himself away from certain death.

Rigid with fear, Jenna clung to the tree as Kane dropped lower and lower toward the raging torrent. The chopper above him swaying back and forth to get him into position. He seemed so small against the thundering waterfall at his back, and every so often, a cloud of water vapor hid him from view. Below him the river had changed in the last hour. Jenna stared in dismay at the swirling frothy water flowing over the hood and front of the cab of the wreck. The truck sat wedged between two boulders and sat nose down with its back wheels high in the air. From what she could see, most of the windows had amazingly survived the fall. It was as if Carter had lowered Kane into a bubbling cauldron with the skeletal remains of the wreck just visible above the water.

How could he possibly get to the body with the water dashing by so fast? If he slipped, the fast-flowing water would pummel him to death against the boulders. Biting her bottom lip, she held her breath as Kane landed legs spayed apart on the back window. He indicated above to slacken the rope, and slid on the slippery metal, his hands just catching the edge of the pickup before the current swept him away. Holding with one hand, he pulled something from his pocket and struck the glass. It shattered and Jenna gaped in horror as a rush of water took Kane's feet from under him and he tumbled into the raging torrent. "Dave!"

# EIGHTEEN

A bolt of searing pain hit Kane, tumbling him into a world of misery. Sharp freezing knives of agony sliced into his brain, as he fell deeper and deeper into the swollen river. His waterlogged boots dragged him down like an anchor to secure his certain death. The raging currents had him in their unforgiving grip, hurtling him into boulders and thrusting the air from his lungs. He opened his eyes, only to shut them again as the chill threatened to freeze his eyeballs. The shock of submersion made his heart race. The need to escape and fight against the raging torrent gripped him for a second or two. To panic now would mean he'd die here alongside Mrs. Darvish. As his back slammed against a huge boulder, he forced his body to relax and slowed his heart rate. The fast-flowing river pinned him to the flat surface with tremendous force and debris slammed into his chest like shotgun pellets. He could hold his breath for at least three minutes underwater, but the pain in his skull was screaming at him, clawing at his eyeballs, and shooting through his head as if lightning had struck him.

Water rushed past him and a quick glance showed him daylight above. He slammed his eyelids shut and, lungs bursting, used all his strength to turn and grasp the slimy boulder. He ran his hands all over the smooth exterior searching for finger holes and, dragging himself toward the light, headed for the surface. Gasping freezing air into his burning lungs, he held on as water splashed over him. Blinking rapidly to clear his vision, he stared around to get his bearings. The river hadn't taken him as far as he'd imagined. The back of the pickup was only a few feet away but fast becoming submerged by water. He wouldn't have much time to retrieve the body before the river claimed it. The metal plate in his head was affecting him more than he'd expected. The pain had become an unwelcome burden and the combat safety zone he'd wrapped around him was fraying dangerously around the edges. How long would it take the shooting torture in his brain to hammer through his mental defenses and destroy him? He slammed the thought away. He'd carried a wounded member of his team on his shoulder through enemy fire, swamps, and rivers for over five miles and never once thought about giving up.

He glanced to the top of Bear Peak and could almost feel Jenna's eyes on him. She'd be worried for his safety, not knowing he'd been in worse situations many times. Although, that had been before the metal plate in his head had become an unknown complication. He'd use what tools he had on hand to defeat this unexpected enemy and embraced the pain. He refused to fail.

High above, Carter battled to keep the chopper rotor blades from hitting the sides of the ravine. The rock face wasn't smooth here, this ravine had formed during an earthquake, the sides craggy and jutting out in all directions, but others on the mountain came about from glaciers carving a smooth path down the mountain over millions of years. A shower of rocks tumbled down hitting his helmet and shoulders, the melting snow had released another small landslide and it rolled down the side of the ravine to disappear into the bubbling water. He gave himself a mental shake. *Move now or die.*

Gritting his teeth against the searing pain, he lifted one arm and waved at the chopper. The line attached to his harness tightened, supporting him to the surface. He coughed water from his lungs and climbed on top of the boulder. Muscles frozen, he shook out his hands and legs, but a cruel wind plastered his wet clothes to his flesh. Face stiff as his exposed flesh froze, he slapped his cheeks and felt nothing. The cold had seeped into him, slowing him down, but now his brain was working just fine. Judging the distance between the boulder and the truck, he bent his knees and leapt into the air. He missed by a foot, but as the water washed him past the truck, he grasped the tailgate and clung for a few seconds before hauling his aching body into the tray. Vision blurry, and using the side of the pickup to guide him, he dragged his body to the broken window and peered inside. The pickup groaned and shifted under his feet, the raging water's sheer weight would soon lift the vehicle and send it down the river to tumble over the falls. His time was running out fast.

# NINETEEN

Jenna cried out as the pickup slipped and a huge rush of water submerged Kane again. He was in deep trouble. How many times would he be able to survive the waves of incredible pain as the freezing cold water hit the metal plate in his head? She'd seen the effect a winter's day had on him, and the way his face paled as he battled with the agony. Her stomach tightened and she lifted her head to the chopper. "This is crazy. You'll kill him. Haul him out. What are you waiting for?" Her words soundless on the wind.

Digging her nails into the bark of the tree, she stared in terror. Where was he? Why wasn't Carter doing anything? It seemed like hours, but it was only a minute or so before Kane surfaced from the freezing water again, shook his head, and hauled himself into the back of the pickup. He stood for long minutes, examining the interior through the broken window, and then looked up. Water streamed from his helmet, as he signaled to the chopper. The next second an orange stretcher dropped from the open door of the chopper and lowered, twisting precariously in the wind. When it arrived, Kane made three attempts to grasp it before tying it to the back of the truck.

Water was up to his chest and he had to dive into the raging torrent to haul out the frail body of Mrs. Darvish through the broken window. Jenna bit down on her cheek as Kane balanced precariously to strap Mrs. Darvish into the stretcher.

As the body lifted into the chopper, Kane went with it, spinning and swaying high into the air and over the trees. The sight of him so high up made her stomach clench. She had no idea where he'd gotten the strength to hold on. How had he survived such an ordeal? Eyes glued to the chopper, she waited for the stretcher to vanish inside the door and breathed a sigh of relief when a hand came out to haul Kane to safety. Without waiting, Carter took the chopper high into the air and it disappeared over the mountain peaks. Jenna stared after it and then turned and spewed in the bushes. She couldn't remember a time she'd been so terrified. Trembling and knees weak, she slumped against a tree, trying to gain her composure. Sensing Wolfe behind her, she turned to look at him, dragged a tissue from her pocket, and self-consciously wiped her mouth.

"They'll take the body straight to the morgue." Wolfe gave her a compassionate look and patted her on the back. "I have coffee in the van. You look like you need one."

She shook her head as her stomach heaved again. "I'll be fine but Dave's going to be in agony. That freezing water will bring on one of his headaches."

"You shouldn't worry so much about him. He's tougher than you think and only five minutes away from a hot shower and his meds." Wolfe touched her arm, his gray eyes sympathetic. "He's a combat machine, Jenna. That was a walk in the park for him and he probably got a kick out of it. He's an adrenaline junkie and works well under extreme conditions. It's what made him the best in his field. His mental abilities under pressure are second to none. The only downside would be retrieving the body. I've seen him lose his cool twice: once was when he lost Annie and the second when he thought you'd died. I've seen him walk through hell and not flinch." Wolfe narrowed his gaze. "Don't let him see you upset, Jenna. You're his Achilles heel. If he starts worrying about you when he's risking his life, he'll lose his edge and that could be fatal."

Understanding completely, Jenna nodded. "Okay, but I'm only human."

The idea that Wolfe considered Kane as part of his arsenal, rather than his friend, concerned her. She walked beside him back to the van. "I know he might be a machine to you, but I've seen agents killed and I'm sure you've seen many fine men killed in the line of duty. I don't want him to become collateral damage. I want him here beside me in Black Rock Falls." She waved a hand toward the ravine. "That was a senseless risk. The pickup will wash down the falls before long and we could have retrieved the body without risking everyone's lives. Did you see how Carter had to fight the wind up there? Three lives could have been lost to collect a dead body."

"The risk was acceptable because it's a homicide and we have a possible psychopath killing old ladies. Time is of the essence. We need any evidence we can find to stop this killer." Wolfe shook his head. "All three men wanted to see an end to the carnage. I needed the body before the water destroys any evidence and trust me if that truck went over the falls, there wouldn't be much for me to look at." He turned her around to face him. "Love is a powerful influence, Jenna. You're one hell of a good sheriff and you know as well as I do that solving the crime, preventing murder, and protecting the townsfolk comes first. It's your sworn duty. Don't allow anything to cloud your judgment."

Jenna climbed into the van and picked the splinters out of her fingers. "I'll do my best."

The trembling hadn't subsided. If Kane or any of the others had died retrieving a corpse, she would have been responsible. No matter what Wolfe said, she'd keep her humanity and look out for the ones she loved. Protecting people in danger was one thing, but she'd never allow her team to risk their lives again to gather evidence. It was a fool's errand and a complete disregard for life. Keeping her rising anger from showing in her face, she turned to him as he slipped behind the wheel. "I think I'll have that coffee after all."

# TWENTY

Kane pressed both hands flat against the shower tile and allowed the hot water to pour over his aching head. When he'd hit the river, the brain-numbing pain had stunned him. He thought he'd gotten over the nerve damage caused by a car bombing and the recent bullet wound to the head, but the freezing river had sent a searing-hot rod of misery through his temples and blurred his vision. He stared at the white tile, allowing the heat to soothe the pain. The sight disturbance hadn't lasted long but was something he needed to speak to Wolfe about before it became a problem. The retrieval had been what he expected, a thrill ride, until he hit the river. The body of Mrs. Darvish had been floating face down in the water and she hadn't been wearing a seat belt. Not that it would have helped her, but it made him wonder if she'd tried to escape the pickup before it went into the ravine.

As the meds kicked in and the hot water thawed out his frozen limbs, Kane stepped out, toweled off, and dressed. He could hear voices as he left the bathroom and walked into the hallway and found Jenna chatting to Emily. They both turned and looked at him at the same time. He smiled. "Emily, it's good to see you again. How is the new semester shaping up?"

"It's great!" Emily led the way to Wolfe's office. "Dad is unpacking the body. Sit down and I'll make coffee. You both look frozen. Was it terrible on the mountain? The retrieval must have been hair-raising."

Shrugging, Kane dropped into a chair. "Not for me but it was darn cold up there. The water was freezing. If it had taken any longer, I'd have ended up a Popsicle." He looked at Carter's Doberman, Zorro, sitting like a statue on a mat in the corner of the room, and then moved his attention to the hallway. "Where's Carter and Jo?"

"He's refueling the chopper and doing whatever he does after a flight." Jenna sat beside him. "Jo went to get some takeout from Aunt Betty's. Shane figured you'd be starving by now."

"He knows me so well." Kane chuckled. He looked at Jenna. "Mrs. Darvish wasn't wearing a seat belt, which I find strange. I wonder if she tried to get out of the pickup before it went over the edge."

"If someone was pushing her toward the ravine, it makes sense, but why didn't she get out? I sure would have tried and there is a small ledge just below the edge. She would have known that surely." Jenna took the cup from Emily with a smile. "Unless the truck rammed her faster than we figured?"

Kane shook his head. "On an incline like that and with the pickup sideways, it would have been slow not fast. A shunting forward by the damage I saw on the door. It was caved right in."

He wrapped his hands around the cup and allowed the scene to fill his mind. For a moment he stood on the mountain road, looking back and forth. What had he seen? What had he felt? The sensation of being there, the cold wind blowing up from the gully, filled his mind. He blinked. "The wind gusts coming up from the ravine would have pressed against the door, making it difficult to open. She was a frail old lady and didn't stand a chance."

The door opened and Jo walked in laden with packages. She dropped them on the table with a sigh.

"Wolfe didn't say what to buy, so I asked Susie, she sent burgers, fries, and peach pies." Jo pulled up a chair and looked at Jenna. "What have we got here? Not an accident, from what Wolfe was saying."

"No, Mrs. Darvish had a run in with a GMC truck before she went over the ravine. Someone wanted her dead but decided to play a little with her first." Jenna pulled a face. "What sort of a person bullies a sweet old lady?"

Biting into a burger straight from heaven, Kane chewed and swallowed. "Someone who finds old people a threat maybe."

"From what I heard from Cade Rio this morning he had a problem with his grandma." Jenna nibbled on fries. "He was at the right place at the right time. Is he capable of murder, do you think?"

Unable to consider Cade, who he'd come to know well, as a cold-blooded killer, Kane looked straight at Jo. "He and his sister are twins, and they were placed with their step-grandma after their parents died. They didn't cope with her at all and ran away. Zac Rio has custody of them now. I figure they weren't young enough or there long enough to cause that type of deep-seated emotional damage."

"Hmm." Jo peered into a bag. "It depends on many factors. Remember, they'd just lost their parents. They were emotionally traumatized before they went there and then something significant made them leave. You'll need to investigate their circumstances a little closer. Some people only require a small trigger to set them off on a path of destruction." She glanced at Jenna. "I've come to the conclusion that coincidences don't happen in Black Rock Falls. What links has Mrs. Darvish to the other victim?"

Kane opened his mouth to reply, but Jenna touched his arm. He exchanged a look with her, noting how her face had drained of color since this morning. "Jenna has that info in front of her."

"Thanks, well they're both elderly, live alone, and belong to the quilting circle. The women in the town are very involved in everything, so there could be more crossovers." Jenna pushed both hands through her hair. "What's the deal with someone scrawling a note on our door? Did the killer of Agnes Wagner want us to find her?"

"She's the one they mutilated, right?" Jo nibbled at a burger. "Face and eyes and then dragged into a closet?"

"Yeah, what's that all about?" Jenna reached for her coffee and sipped. "How could that possibly be the same person who pushed Mrs. Darvish into a ravine? The MOs are completely different."

Wanting to jump in, Kane looked from one to the other. "That's because our minds want to put things in neat packages. You only need to look at some of the most notorious serial killers to know that not all of them kill in the same way. Agreed, some follow a pattern, but it seems to me the more we deal with these people, the more diversity we encounter."

"I have to agree with Kane." Jo smiled. "You mentioned Mrs. Wagner was attacked from behind, as if she was trying to get away from her assailant?"

"Yeah, same as Mrs. Darvish." Jenna snapped her fingers. "Fear. The killer wants to inflict fear but again... why the note?"

"Yeah, fear seems to be the common denominator." Jo put down her burger and paused a beat. "I figure the reason they left the note on the glass door was to direct you to the crime. Mrs. Wagner's home was isolated, so it would be doubtful someone would miss her for a time." She stared into space for long moments, and then nodded as if making up her mind. "Hmm, two reasons both juxtaposed to each other. Either they wanted to show you what they'd done or they want you to stop them from killing again."

"We have a couple of suspects, men who have been in contact with both women." Jenna leaned back in her chair and shrugged. "I'm waiting on Rowley to get through interviewing them. Well, two of them at least. We've included a plumber in the mix as a person of interest as well, mainly because he installed new furnaces in both houses recently. I haven't been able to hunt him down yet. His phone goes to voicemail, so I'll try and call him after hours. The other two are contractors the quilting circle use and both recently employed by the victims."

"You have something else on your mind though, don't you?" Jo leaned forward taking a confidential pose. "There's someone else, apart from Cade, you believe is involved, isn't there?"

Kane shot a look at Jenna. "Not that I know. Do you have someone, Jenna?"

"Not really, but have you noticed how distant Rio is of late?" Jenna met his gaze. "Missing from work, not finishing his shifts, not answering his phone, and then we find him parked up the mountain almost hidden in the bushes, waiting for his brother to pass by." She rolled her eyes. "Oh, don't give me that look, Dave. Rio was unaccounted for the night Mrs. Wagner died and then he's up the mountain, by his own admission, when Mrs. Darvish dies." She snorted in derision. "We've hauled people in for questioning on less information than that and you know it. We can't look the other way because he's a deputy."

Trying to get his mind around Rio and his brother having the ability to kill old ladies, he shook his head. "Zac Rio? No way. I did a psychiatric workup on him, and Bobby Kalo, the FBI whiz kid who can find out dirt on anyone alive, went through him from the ground up. There's no way, he could have hidden psychopathic tendencies from me." He sighed. "I've been one-on-one with Cade working on his truck for weeks. We talked about his time with his grandma. Yeah, he had some resentment, mainly because she made them work so hard around the place, they couldn't keep up with schoolwork. I didn't get the vibe from him that he'd like to murder her or anyone else."

"What if you're wrong, Dave?" Jenna blew out a long breath. "One thing is for sure. Something isn't right with either of them and we need to make sure they're not involved."

Kane held up his hands in surrender. He'd rarely seen Jenna so riled. "You're the boss." He shook his head. "I'll see what I can do."

# TWENTY-ONE

Deputy Jake Rowley pulled up outside a house on Pine and sat awhile, regarding the man cutting back the dead branches from a bush and dropping them into a wheelbarrow. He glanced at the photo ID of Archie Bueller: a gardener, forty-five years of age, and of robust build. The man wore a woolen cap to cover his hair and a plaid shirt, which he'd rolled up to the elbows to display muscular forearms. From inside his truck, Rowley couldn't miss long scratches on both arms running from above his work gloves to at least his elbows. He picked up his mic and called Maggie. She acted as the sheriff's office dispatch and he checked in with her on a regular basis, especially if he was out on his own. "Hey, Maggie, I'm outside where Archie Bueller is working. He appears to have scratches on both forearms, but I'm parked some ways away from him. I'll go and speak to him now. I'll check in when I'm back in the truck. Out."

*"Copy that."* Maggie sounded cheerful. *"Kane retrieved the body and everyone is at Wolfe's office. I'm sure glad that's over. When they called in Agent Carter, I started worrying. I'm sorry for Mrs. Darvish but so happy everyone has gotten down safely from the mountain. Out."*

Rowley smiled. "That's good to know. Out." He hung up the mic and slid from behind the wheel, grabbing a statement book from the console.

He made a point of whistling as he approached Archie Bueller. He figured any tune would do rather than walk up behind a man using a lethal pair of pruning shears. When Bueller turned and glanced at him over one shoulder, Rowley observed him for any hint of guilt. Some suspects would tense their shoulders, or even blush when a law enforcement officer approached, but Bueller just went about his work and ignored him. He stood some distance away. "Archie Bueller?"

"That's me." Bueller dropped the sheers to one side and raised his eyebrows in question. "You didn't mention why you wanted to talk to me. What's up?"

Rowley pushed back his Stetson and took a nonchalant pose. "I'm just following up on anyone who worked for Agnes Wagner out of Snowberry Way."

"Yeah, I've worked for her." Bueller wiped the end of his nose with the back of his gloved hand. "Last week. She kept hearing noises around the house." He smiled. "Many of the old folk hear bumps in the night. I guess they feel vulnerable when they're alone."

Rowley tucked the statement book under one arm and opened his notebook. "So what did you do for her?"

"Pruned a few trees back away from the house is all." Bueller shrugged. "There's still snow in patches up there, so there's not much for me to do right now."

Taking a closer look at the scratches on Bueller's arms, Rowley cleared his throat. "When was this and was it the last time you saw her?"

"Late on Sunday afternoon." Bueller rolled his eyes. "She was in full panic mode, hearing things. She said she'd thought it was the old furnace and had Trey Duffy replace it and the noises kept on happening. So, I got up there around four and did what I could to clear the branches away from the house. I explained to her that when it's windy the trees will brush against the walls." He pushed the pruning shears into his leather belt and lifted his chin. "She asked me to do a walk-through with her and I did to make her feel better."

Rowley's ears pricked at this information. "The cellar as well?"

"Yeah, I told her I'd close the window for her but she wanted to air the place. Duffy found a dead critter in there." Bueller leaned casually against a tree. "I was there until about five-thirty, maybe six, I guess."

"Okay." Rowley made notes and then looked up at him. "You've also worked for Jolene Darvish out of Rocky Road, Bear Peak, I believe?"

"Not often." Bueller stared into the distance and then moved his gaze slowly back to him. "Why?"

Rowley strolled over to Bueller's truck and cast his eye over the bull bar noticing many scratches. He smiled at him. "I was thinking about getting a new one of these for my truck. The rockfalls on Rocky Road are becoming a problem."

"Not only there, the melt has pulled trees clean out by the roots." Bueller scratched his head and frowned. "You never know what you might need to push out of the way."

Nodding, Rowley turned back to face him. "When was the last time you saw Mrs. Darvish?"

"I don't rightly recall." Bueller paused a beat as if thinking. "She did call me asking if I could cut back the rose bush around her porch. Said it was getting out of control. I told her to wait until after the melt."

"Were you anywhere near Rocky Road yesterday afternoon?" Rowley lifted his pen and waited.

"I was all over yesterday. Maybe." Bueller looked at his feet and waved a hand toward the house. "I gotta go. These folks pay me by the hour and won't appreciate me jawing with you on their time."

Thinking better than to push him anymore as he'd been cooperative, Rowley closed his notebook and slipped his pen back inside his pocket. "Okay, thanks." He turned and headed back to his truck.

After calling in, Maggie transferred him to Jenna. She was still in the morgue. He gave his report. "They both could be involved."

*"Yeah, it wouldn't be the first time a killer has admitted to being close to the murder scene. Head back to the office and update the files. Wolfe wants to give us a preliminary report on Mrs. Darvish. It's been a long day. We'll follow up on Trey Duffy in the morning, unless I catch him at home later."*

"Okay." Rowley drummed his fingers on the steering wheel. "Any news on Rio?"

*"Yeah, we found him on Rocky Road, waiting for his brother to show. He's been there all night. I sent him home to get some rest."* Jenna mumbled something to someone and cleared her throat. "Wolfe's ready for us. I'll speak to you back at the office." She disconnected.

Rowley started his engine, shaking his head. *So, Rio was close to the crime scene all night and didn't see anything—yeah right.*

# TWENTY-TWO

Wolfe waited for Jenna and the rest of the team to join him in the examination room. He looked at the concerned or blank expressions on all of them. Jenna always started with a concerned expression and seemed to gather herself and turn to stone once he'd completed the preliminary examination. Jo showed interest but her eyes showed great sorrow. Kane and Carter never gave a flicker of anything—no compassion, remorse, or anything else. Both had the training to turn off emotions and did so the minute they entered the room. He understood the reason. Allowing their innermost feelings to cloud their judgment could have meant certain death if captured behind enemy lines during a tour of duty. The marine training he'd received had been tough but he'd not come close to their standard. It took a special person with exceptional capabilities to push past or ignore the triggers that turn ordinary men into heroes. Only one or two percent of soldiers had the mental and physical capabilities to be good enough to join the elite forces. Wolfe welcomed his compassion. Having that empathy for the people who came to his table by peaceful or violent means meant he left no stone unturned to find their cause of death. Everyone he examined in the morgue needed him to tell their story.

He turned on the screen to display the X-rays of Jolene Darvish and caught Jo's sharp intake of breath. All eyes had moved to the screens and it didn't take a doctor's eye to see the damage the fall had inflicted on the frail old woman. "Okay, as you can see, we have multiple fractures. I will categorize the damage sustained and add it to my report but from my preliminary examination of the body. Jolene Darvish died before she hit the water. I've yet to establish cause of death but due to the lack of hematomas around the skull fracture, it's likely she had a coronary before the pickup hit the water."

"She died from her truck being pushed over a ravine. We know that wasn't an accident, but that doesn't establish a cause of death, does it?" Jenna peered at him over her face mask.

Wolfe shook his head. "I have to be more specific. We say someone died due to blunt force injury or a gunshot wound, but we must establish what actually caused the death of the victim. Did the bullet explode the heart? Enter the brain or sever a major artery, for instance."

"I understand, but with all the injuries, will you be able to give a cause of death?" Jenna cleared her throat. "There is so much damage."

Wolfe nodded. "Yeah, but it will take a long time to list every injury. I'll check her heart and I've taken blood to check for a protein called troponin. This indicates if a person has suffered a coronary. If I find evidence of heart damage, the test will confirm my diagnosis."

Before anyone could ask another question, Kane's phone chimed. He glanced at the screen and headed for the door without saying a word. Wolfe raised one eyebrow. "Questions?"

"Anything under her nails? Rowley noticed Archie Bueller had scratches on his arms." Jenna peered at him over her mask.

Wolfe turned to her. "No, nothing under her nails and no evidence she was in a physical altercation with anyone."

"Could she have drowned?" Carter's green eyes matched his scrubs but gave no indication of his inner thoughts. "Wouldn't water in the lungs indicate she was alive when she hit the river?"

Moving his attention to Carter, Wolfe shook his head. "I couldn't imagine with head trauma to this degree—" He pulled back the sheet to display the battered remains. "—that she could have possibly been conscious when she entered the water. Taking into account the fact the windshield hadn't smashed, there would have been a few seconds before water engulfed the vehicle. It would be impossible to prove death by drowning in this instance as the laryngospasm—the gag reflex as you'd call it —relaxes during unconsciousness, allowing water to enter the lungs. If we consider this a possibility in still water, then as a raging torrent had submerged the body, mouth open, the possibilities increased tenfold." He sighed. "In fact, drowning is really a generic term because I could give you a list of possibilities for cause of death due to lack of oxygen. However, allow me to use my judgement in this case until I can prove otherwise. I suggest that Jolene Darvish died from a coronary induced by a traumatic event and, from the evidence found at the scene, was caused by person or persons unknown pushing her pickup into a ravine."

"We'll stay until you examine the heart and lungs." Jenna leaned against the counter and folded her arms across her chest. "I want to know."

Surprised by Jenna's insistence to remain during a harrowing autopsy, Wolfe picked up his scalpel and went about making the Y incision and cracking open the chest. After dissecting the heart and collecting fluid from the lungs, he turned to Jenna. "I'm going to wait for the results of the blood and fluid samples before I make a finding, but from what I see here, she died from a trauma-induced coronary."

"Okay." Jenna straightened. "We'll work on that for now." She looked at Kane as he came back inside the room. "Is there a problem?"

"Nope." Kane lifted his chin to Wolfe. "Did you find anything?"

Wolfe explained. "That makes two homicides this week."

"I'll send out a press release to alert the elderly women to lock their doors." Jenna frowned. "I know one murder might be personal, but two usually tells me that number three is just around the corner."

# TWENTY-THREE

Outside the examination room, Jenna turned to Jo. "Are you staying?" She dragged off her scrubs and tossed them into the basket and then used a wipe to remove the mentholated salve from under her nose. "You can stay in the cabin for as long as you like." She took in a breath, glad to be out of the stink of rotting flesh.

"We'd love to." Jo smiled at her. "This case is very interesting. Unless you'd prefer we didn't get involved?"

More than happy for the assistance, Jenna shook her head. "Not at all. I have so many conflicting factors spinning around inside my head that I'd appreciate your input. The cottage is yours and you can drive my cruiser if you need a ride while we're out doing the grunt work."

"Perfect." Jo leaned her back against the wall. "It's been a long day."

Jenna pushed a hand through her hair. "It's not over yet. Rowley has been interviewing suspects. I'll send out a media release and then get a report from him. Unless anything else happens, we can go home."

"Our bags are in the foyer and I'll just grab Zorro." Carter headed toward Wolfe's office, opened the door and whistled for his constant companion. He glanced back at Kane. "Where's Duke?" He set out for the foyer, the dog's nails click-clacking on the tiles behind him.

"He's at the office." Kane bent to pick up Jo's bag and headed out the door.

Jenna stared after him, knowing instinctively something was on his mind. A subject he didn't want to speak about in front of Jo and Carter. As she climbed into the Beast, her phone chimed. She stared at the caller ID, surprised to see it was Mayor Petersham. "Sheriff Alton."

*"I received a request out of Cedar Canyon for a deputy transfer, and as Sheriff Tom Griffin is a good friend of mine, I agreed that Deputy Anderson could work alongside your team to gain experience in homicide investigation. If you consider her a fit, she can take one of the two extra deputy positions you requested."* Mayor Petersham chuckled. *"You see, I do listen, Sheriff. This deputy will be an asset to your team. Look, I've even arranged a place for them to stay. Surely, you're not going to complain about getting another pair of hands?"*

Annoyed the mayor had overstepped his mark, Jenna sucked in a breath and stared out the window as Kane drove back to the office. As sheriff, it was her job to hire and fire the deputies. The mayor had no idea what qualifications she required for her team. She wondered why his good friend was trying to unload a deputy on her office. What was wrong with them? Obviously not enough to fire them. "Okay, but I can't babysit a rookie. We're in the middle of two homicide cases. It will be a desk job at best right now." She cleared her throat. "I'll decide if they're good enough to join my team. One inexperienced deputy can put everyone at risk right now."

*"I understand completely. Just humor me for once, okay?"* The mayor disconnected.

Keeping her expression blank, she climbed from the Beast

and headed for her office. She gave Maggie a wave, patted Duke as he did his happy dance at seeing Dave, and went to speak to Rowley. "Can you come up to my office and bring us up to date with the interviews? Any luck at locating Trey Duffy?"

"Yeah, he was working out of the industrial area and his phone hit a black spot." Rowley gathered his things and stood. "He'll drop by tomorrow around noon and you can speak to him. I mentioned it was about the furnaces. I got the impression he figured something was wrong with the installation, so I didn't say anything about the murders."

Still thinking about the new deputy, Jenna shrugged. The name Cedar Canyon was familiar. She focused on the job at hand. "At least we don't have to hunt him down."

"Something else." Rowley glanced down the hallway to the room that housed the CCTV screens for around town. "There's been a buzzing from the conference room. I went inside but I can't find anything wrong."

Jenna nodded. "I'll ask Kane to take a look after the briefing." She waved him upstairs.

She followed him into her office. The room hummed with conversation, and Kane was at the whiteboard adding information. Sitting behind her desk, she looked at Rowley. "Okay, what did you get from Archie Bueller—he's the gardener, and Colby Hahn is the local handyman." She glanced at Jo and Carter. "Both of these men had contact with our victims."

She listened with interest as Rowley brought them up to date. "What were your impressions?"

"They had the opportunity to be involved, and as the two women lived in remote locations, witnesses would be few, if any. It seemed unusual that these men worked for both victims. Hahn lives out of Bear Peak and uses Rocky to get into town, and then we have the furnace guy, Trey Duffy. The women had contact with at least two of these men in the last week or so." Rowley glanced at his notes. "The suspects cooperated, same with Duffy. The two I interviewed could be innocent or great liars."

Wondering which way to take the investigation, Jenna stared at the whiteboard, and rubbed her temples. "All of the potential suspects drive GMC trucks. I'm at a standstill." She looked around the room. "Any suggestions?"

"Maybe we can discuss the case over dinner tonight?" Carter pushed back his Stetson and leaned forward in his chair. "It's been one hell of a day. We'll all think better after an hour or so rest. If we head home in Dave's truck, I'll help him with the chores and give you both time to freshen up. I'll leave the bird at the ME's office."

Jenna opened her desk drawer and pulled out the keys to her vehicle. She tossed them to Carter. "You have the code to my gate on your phone. Your fingerprint will open the cottage door. Go make yourself at home. Come by to eat at our place tonight. We have a ton of steak and Dave will cook." She nodded to Kane.

"Sure, why not?" Carter grinned. "As long as I can help."

"You can handle the horses. The kitchen is my domain." Kane's phone chimed and he glanced at it and pushed to his feet. "I need to take this."

*More private calls?* Jenna frowned at him. This was so unlike Kane. "Go check out what's buzzing in the conference room while you're at it." As Kane disappeared through the door, she looked at Rowley. "You should head off home and kiss those beautiful twins for me. Hopefully Rio will be back tomorrow to help, and we have a new deputy arriving sometime." She'd been so annoyed at the mayor she'd forgotten to ask him when to expect the new deputy.

"Okay, I will, thanks." Rowley smiled. "They're growing so fast. They'll be heading off to school before I know it." He collected his things and headed for the door before turning back. "Do you want me to tell Maggie to go home?"

"Yeah, sure. I'll lock up." Jenna leaned back in her chair and twirled her pen in her fingers. She needed the assistance of the FBI's IT whiz kid, Bobby Kalo, one of the team out of Snakeskin Gully. She moved her attention to Jo. "We need super-fast background checks on our suspects. Will Kalo mind if we call him this late in the afternoon?"

"I doubt it. He rarely goes home and has a cot in the interview room." Jo chuckled. "He lives in a different world to us. He works very well but the rest of the time he's in a game with a ton of people. It's strange working with someone so young, but I admire what he does." She pulled out her phone. "I'll call him."

"I'll send him the files." Carter pulled out his phone. "He lives for finding dirt on people."

"Great, thanks." Jenna made a few notes and emailed a press release to the local media. By the time she'd finished, Kane was still missing. She stood. "I'll go and see if Kane needs any help in the conference room." She headed out the door.

As she reached the bottom of the stairs, she couldn't help overhearing Kane's conversation. She kept on walking. What he was talking about was none of her business, but she didn't intend to conceal the fact she'd overheard him.

"I'll figure something out." Kane's back was to her. "It's difficult to get away right now." He spun around to look at her. "I've gotta go." He disconnected and pointed to a blank screen. "The CCTV camera outside the office is out. The buzzing was a warning. I'll call someone to look at it in the morning."

Jenna stared at him for a long moment but he said nothing about the call. She met his gaze. "The mayor called me before. He's sending us a new deputy. Transferred out of Cedar Canyon. It seems we have no choice. They're coming and staying unless I fire them."

"Yeah, I gathered as much from what you said in the truck." He walked back to his desk and picked up his laptop. "Are you ready to go? I'll wait for you down here."

Jenna turned around and headed back to the stairs. "Sure, I'll grab my things."

Behind her, Kane hummed a tune. She turned to watch him bend and rub Duke's ears, wondering what the heck he was up to.

# TWENTY-FOUR

Over the years with Jenna, Kane had figured saying nothing was often the best thing for him to do to avoid a misunderstanding. Her silence on the drive home meant only one thing: she'd overheard part of his conversation and, knowing how her mind worked, she'd be conjuring up all types of scenarios. He gritted his teeth and went to work preparing a meal. Living with Jenna was certainly different. His wife, Annie, didn't have a jealous streak but she wanted him close at all times. She enjoyed his protection; Jenna was the complete opposite, fiercely independent and hated him to coddle her, which bruised his need to keep her close many a time. He understood her better than she realized and would make her happy whatever the cost. As the smell of the savory biscuits he'd slipped into the oven filled the room, he tossed the salad and placed it on the table.

"How come someone hasn't snapped you up yet?" Jo walked into the kitchen sniffing appreciatively. "Need any help?"

Kane dropped steaks into a pan. "Yeah, if you can set the table, it would be good." He smiled at her over one shoulder. "You like your steak well done, right? Same as Jenna?"

"Yeah, thanks. Burned to a crisp for me. I've never been able to eat bloody steak." She pulled plates from the shelf. "You're obviously living with Jenna, so is there a relationship going on here or is it platonic? You both hide your emotions so well, but I pick up things. It's part of my job."

"Uh-huh." Kane checked the potatoes in the oven with a fork and grinned at her. "Let's say it's a work in progress."

"Well, I guess that's better than saying 'it's complicated.' That's such a cop-out." Jo chuckled. "Ah, here's Jenna now." She stared into the hallway. "Well, she was here. I guess she went to take a shower." She laid out the silverware and looked at him. "Anything else?"

"There's sour cream and coleslaw in the refrigerator." He flipped the steaks. "We'll sort out the drinks when everyone arrives, but I have a nice bottle of pinot noir breathing over there with glasses if you'd like a glass?"

"Oh, that smells like heaven." Jenna came into the kitchen wearing her PJs and glanced at the table. "It looks like you have everything in hand." The front door opened and closed, and footsteps echoed down the hallway with the unmistakable noise of Zorro's claws. "Ah there's Carter."

Kane dropped two more steaks into a second pan. "I'll have everything ready in a few minutes." He looked over his shoulder at Jenna. "Can you get the drinks?"

"Sure." Jenna stood and went about her task. When she sat down, she looked at Kane. "How did you do all this so fast? It takes me ages just to make toast."

"Practice." Kane, pulled the biscuits out of the oven, dropped them onto a plate, and placed them on the table. He went about filling plates with food and handing them around. He sat down and looked at Jenna. "Heard anything back from Kalo?"

"Yeah." Jenna cut into her steak, took a bite, and hummed in contentment. "His first look-see gave no history of criminal behavior, so he's digging deeper. Checking for sealed juvi files, and other states. He'll send a report in the morning."

"Let's lay the cards on the table, Jenna." Carter sipped from a bottle of beer. "I know these three guys are suspects and, looking at all of them, I agree any one of them could be our man. So why would you even consider Rio and his brother? Trust me, when Rio's name came through our office, Kalo found out everything about him. He is solid. I read his file today. There's nothing in his background to suggest he could turn rogue."

Kane cleared his throat. "I figure he's solid too, but we know he went through two traumatic events before coming here. His parents died and then his siblings vanished for months. He discovered that the step-grandma hadn't been treating them very well. He probably blamed himself and I've seen people turn to crime for a lot less than that."

"That's true." Jo took the glass of red wine that Kane handed her. "With a mind like his that never forgets anything, all the memories would be swimming around in endless torment. He can't turn them off. I can't imagine how difficult it would be not to have the defense mechanism that can block or compartmentalize disturbing memories." She let her gaze rest on Kane and then shift to Carter. "Some can shut down emotion completely and not have any psychopathy at all. With Rio, unless I can speak to him and see what's happening inside his head, we won't know."

"Man, you guys see psychopaths crawling out from under the beds." Carter shook his head. "So what if Rio took some personal time to sort out the twins? So what if he let his phone run dry? He did what he had to do and put his family first." He looked squarely at Jo. "You'd walk out in the middle of a case if Jamie was in trouble and don't say you wouldn't freak out some. Your daughter is your life and you know it. I figure we concentrate on the suspects, the guys who were in the vicinity of the murders at the time. All this speculation over Rio is just wasting energy."

"Okay, okay." Jenna let out a long sigh. "It's not Rio."

Seeing Jenna's eyes flash, Kane swallowed hard and looked at Carter. "Jenna is just being careful."

"I still think it wouldn't hurt to check up on him." Jenna looked at Kane. "Can you make an excuse to call him when we're done here?"

Kane shrugged. "Sure."

After eating he made the call. "Hey, how are things? Has Cade settled down some now?"

*"Nope. Now he's giving me the silent treatment."* Rio sounded annoyed. *"Thanks for taking his keys. He needs to be brought back to earth. Taking the bus to school for a while will hopefully make him see reason."* He let out a long sigh. *"That woman is way too old for him. He figures the sun revolves around her. She's just using him. The idiot told her about his inheritance. I can't watch him twenty-four/seven and I'm concerned he'll take off from school with her. I spent hours trying to find her cabin. Bear Peak is like a maze and driving around there is dangerous."*

Kane scratched his head. "The bears are one thing but the guys living off the grid are a little nervous of law enforcement snooping around. They shoot first and ask questions later, so you'll need to be careful." He thought for a beat. "Next time he goes missing, call it in and we'll work together. Wolfe has a drone he is planning on using for aerial shots of crime scenes. Maybe we can use it to track Kara's truck back to her cabin."

*"Thanks, I'd appreciate your help."*

"So, I guess you're staying home to watch Cade tonight?" Kane rubbed the back of his neck thinking what to say next. "Do you figure he'll run off again?"

*"I hope not. I'm his brother and there's not too much I can do. I wanted to take his phone but it would have ended up in a*

*fight. He's seventeen. I can't force him to stay home either, but if he heads out, I'll follow him."* Rio cleared his throat. *"Thanks for calling, I'll see you in the morning."*

Kane stared into space. "Yeah, sure." He disconnected and headed back to the family room. "Rio's home watching Cade. I don't figure he's going anywhere."

"See?" Carter relaxed in one of the leather chairs beside the fireplace. "Everything is fine."

"That's a relief." Jenna shook her head, allowing her bangs to spill over her forehead.

# TWENTY-FIVE

## THURSDAY

Deputy Zac Rio stirred at the sharp tone of Jenna's voice and inhaled the stench of death. Nausea gripped him and he forced open his heavy eyelids, blinking into the shaft of sunlight pouring from an open door. He lifted one hand to shield his eyes and stared in horror at the dried blood covering his fingers. Disoriented, he struggled to sit up, and gaped at the sticky mess of crimson smothering his jeans. His shirt stuck to his chest under the darkening red stain running from neck to navel. Footsteps came closer and he turned his head. Pain shot through his temples, as his gaze rested in horror at the blood covered floor.

"Stay where you are, Zac." Jenna moved closer with her Glock steady in her hand. "Give me your weapon. Take it out using finger and thumb." She held out her hand. "No sudden moves."

Confused, Zac removed his pistol and handed it to her. "Where's all this blood coming from?"

"Hands on your head." Jenna pushed his Glock into the back of her belt.

He complied. The room was unfamiliar and he had no memories of how he'd gotten there and for him that was impossible. He shook his head in disbelief and stared up at Jenna's stern expression. "What's going on here, Jenna?"

"I could ask you the same question." Kane crouched beside him. "What's the last thing you remember?"

Rio searched his mind. He'd been born with a retentive memory and could recall everything he'd seen at will and had the ability to process information at high speed, but right now he came up with a distorted array of memories. "I'm not sure. I answered the door around nine last night. It was a kid who said Flora Carson out of Buffalo Trail had sent them to tell me about a prowler. Her phone was out and the kid came by on his bike."

"Then what?" Jenna was moving around him snapping images with her phone.

Trying not to spew, Rio looked at Kane. "Nothing until I woke up here. Nothing at all. My mind is a complete blank." He turned to Jenna. "Can I put my hands down now? I'm gonna spew."

"Take a few deep breaths." Jenna pulled on surgical gloves and picked up a bloody Ka-Bar knife, dangling it between finger and thumb. "Does this belong to you?"

Focusing on the combat knife, Rio shook his head. "No, I've seen two people with them, one is Kane and the other FBI Special Agent Ty Carter."

"It's not mine." Kane slid his knife from a leather sheath on his belt and ran his thumb across the sharp blade before slipping it back. "And Ty was with us last night."

Rio shook his head. "I've never seen it before."

"Can you stand?" Kane pulled on surgical gloves and grasped Rio by the arm, pulling him to his feet.

Head fuzzy, Rio staggered before spreading his feet to gain his balance. "Yeah. I feel like I've been out drinking all night and then had a bull stomp all over me." He turned his head and caught his breath at the sight of a pair of feet sticking out from a doorway, one wearing a tattered bedroom slipper, the other clad in a pink sock. A trail of blood ran from one room to the other. He swallowed the rising bile. "Oh Jesus, is that Flora Carson?"

"There's every possibility." Kane's face carried a grim expression. "It's a bit hard to tell right now, seeing that someone took the Ka-Bar to her face." He narrowed his gaze on him. "The knife we found next to your right hand. Your blood-soaked right hand."

The sound of a vehicle came from outside, and the slamming of doors. The next moment, Shane Wolfe stuck his head inside the door, followed by Emily and his assistant and badge carrying deputy, Colt Webber.

"Morning." Jenna lifted her chin. "It's a bloodbath. Kane cleared the area. There's no sign of forced entry. The scene is concentrated to this area. We haven't been near the victim. It's obvious she's deceased. I didn't want to leave Rio and go get our forensics kit, but I've bagged the knife and recorded the scene." She cleared her throat. "The knife was located beside Rio's right hand. He was unconscious on our arrival. When Maggie arrived at the office there was another message on the door. It said, '*Zac Rio is a killer.*' She notified me at home and I gave Rio a call and got his machine again. I tried his house and Cade said he didn't come home last night, but he didn't know he was missing until this morning. I checked Rio's files. He'd logged the prowler complaint with the address before he went out at ten after nine. We came by immediately and found the front door wide open. The moment we stepped inside and viewed the scene, I called you."

"Okay." Wolfe went to work processing the scene.

"Zac, what happened?" Emily's face had drained of color. "Are you okay?"

"Don't question the suspect." Kane raised an eyebrow. "He hasn't been Mirandized."

"He's my friend." Emily's eyes flashed with annoyance.

"You can't possibly believe he'd do something like this?" She looked at Rio. "Tell them, Zac. This is crazy."

Rio lifted his gaze to her. "I didn't hurt anyone, Em."

"Do your job, Em, and let us deal with this side of things, okay?" Jenna touched Emily's arm.

Horrified, Rio stared at Kane. "I'm not a suspect. Have you lost your mind, Dave? I didn't kill anyone."

"It's not looking very good for you right now." Kane still had hold of his arm. He looked at Wolfe. "What do you need?"

"His clothes but just cover them and his boots for now, bag his hands." Wolfe turned to Webber. "Go get him a suit." He looked back at Kane. "We'll get him covered up for the trip back to my office. Don't allow him to wash." He took booties and gloves from his kit and pulled them on and then walked over to Rio and examined his head. "Just one minute."

Still dizzy, Rio waited as Wolfe peered at him. He blinked at the flashlight aimed at his eyes. "My head hurts and I feel nauseous."

"You don't have any head trauma." Wolfe's face was unreadable. "Do you often have blackouts, memory loss?"

Rio snorted. "You know darn well my memory is unique and no I don't suffer blackouts, never until now." He glanced at the prone figure of the old woman. "What motive would I have for killing her? I came here to help her. This is crazy. I'd never hurt anyone."

"Roll up your sleeve." Wolfe turned to Jenna. "I'll need to take blood, but if he's been drugged, it could already be out of his system." He bent to collect the necessary equipment.

Annoyed, that no one believed him but willing to cooperate, Rio stood motionless as Wolfe extracted blood. "Now what?" He looked at Jenna.

"You know the drill, Zac. Now you'll be locked in a cell until we can sort out this mess." She read him his rights. "I'm holding you for questioning, for the murder of Flora Carson.

You'll be held in custody pending further investigations. Do you want me to call you a lawyer? Sam Cross?"

Rio shook his head. "Not yet, but I'm going to insist on being examined by an independent doctor. A forensic pathologist from the California State Medical Examiner's Office, Dr. Susie Cooper."

"Okay, I can arrange that if I find anything incriminating but don't you trust me to give an unbiased opinion?" Wolfe frowned.

Rio shook his head. "It seems to me you've all made up your mind I murdered that poor woman. I figure if this goes to court, I'll need all the help I can get."

# TWENTY-SIX

Noting Rio's obvious disorientation was a double-edged sword. Kane had seen the confusion following date rape drugs and he'd witnessed the disbelief when someone realized they'd taken a life in a fit of anger. Both scenarios displayed the similar shocked, bewildered expressions, but he'd never seen any similar behavior from a psychopath. Most, if caught in the act of murder, would try and excuse their actions by concocting a very reasonable excuse. One thing was for darn sure, they wouldn't be sheet white, trembling, and needing to vomit. Wanting to remove Rio from the carnage and alleviate the shock a little, Kane took him into a hallway and patted him down, removing everything in his pockets and dropping them into evidence bags. He stared at the surgical gloves they all carried in their pockets, and back at Rio's bloody hands. Rio was a darn good cop and understood everything there was to know about forensic evidence at a crime scene. If he'd intended to kill someone, why not wear a pair of gloves? If he'd happened across the crime scene, following procedure before stepping inside the house and wearing gloves was as natural as breathing.

He'd seen Rio at the practice range and noticed that, like

him, he could shoot with accuracy using either hand, but casting his mind back, he recalled Rio favored his left hand. He balled up a pair of booties and tossed them to him. When Rio's left hand shot out to make the catch, Kane chewed on the inside of his cheek. They'd found the knife beside his right hand and no doubt Rio's prints would be all over it. He had a hunch and needed to speak to Wolfe. He handed Rio the coveralls. "Can you manage to get into these okay?"

"Yeah." Rio took them with a shake of his head. "Trust me, if I'd wanted to kill someone, the last thing I'd use is a knife. Someone of her size would go down with one punch, no noise and no mess." He waved a hand toward the victim's body. "I'm not a killer, Dave. You know darn well I didn't kill that woman." He hopped on one leg getting his feet into the coveralls. "If someone is scrawling lies about me on doors, it screams of a setup."

Unable to comment on his personal thoughts about the case, Kane played it by the book and shrugged. "You know I can't comment. It's in your best interest to allow me to investigate. You of all people should understand how crucial visual observations are at this point of an investigation. Suit up and I'll bag your hands. It's only until Wolfe takes a few swabs. Cooperation will get you home sooner. You know that as well as I do." He walked over to Wolfe and led him away from the others. "Can you tell if a set of fingerprints on a knife are a result of a knife being used as a weapon or pressed on by a third party?"

"There are many clues to deciding if a knife was placed in a suspect's hand after the fact." Wolfe kept his voice low and his gaze kept flicking to Rio. "One set of prints on a bloody knife isn't an indication of guilt. You have your fingerprint scanner on you. Hand it to me."

Kane took it out of his pocket and dropped it into Wolfe's palm. "What does this prove?"

"Take out your Ka-Bar knife. Clean it." Wolfe handed him a

wad of cotton. "Place it back inside the sheath. Remove your gloves, take out the knife, and then position it in your hand to kill someone. There is a ton of blood so that knife is getting slippery. How many times during an attack would you reposition your hand?"

Kane complied. He pulled out the knife, moved it as if to attack Wolfe and then shrugged. "Okay so what's your point?"

"Give it to me and I'll show you." Wolfe held out one gloved hand for the knife. He ran the fingerprint scanner over it and showed Kane the results. "See, every action can be accounted for. The knife doesn't remain limp in a hand during a murder."

The knife had a set of fingerprints from when he removed it from the sheath, more in a different direction as he settled it into the palm of his hand and a few smudged ones on the handle from where his fingers slipped slightly and repositioned. "All this and without the possible blood slip. Not that the design of a Ka-Bar allows a hand to slip in blood, but I see your point."

"Then there's latent prints. Those we can't see that carry oil and even DNA from a person." Wolfe met his gaze. "If someone placed that knife in Zac's hand, I'll be able to tell. I noticed the reflex test you did on him. He is left-handed but can be called ambidextrous. I figure in a rush of passion as in a kill like this one, he'd unconsciously use his left hand—unless he's smarter than we figured."

Pulling on a fresh pair of gloves, Kane scanned the room. Blood spatter was everywhere, the victim didn't go down easy. "Have you found Rio's prints in the house?"

"Yeah, on the doorframe of the front door so far, but we have a long way to go. All the bloody fingerprints you can see are smudged and that's impossible unless the killer was wearing gloves. The bloody footprints all look like a fit for Rio and the victim." He sighed. "Going on the rigor, I figure the victim died close to the time Rio left home around nine last night. When I take the body temperature, I'll have a better idea."

Kane nodded. "What can I do to speed things along?"

"It will take hours to process the scene." Wolfe cast a long look about the room. "It would save time if you could get Rio back to my office. Strip him down, bag his clothes, and give him scrubs to wear. Put him in one of the sterile rooms to wait until I get there. He can't get in or out without a keycard, so he won't be going anywhere." He paused for a beat. "I'll take swabs of his hands and then you can go." He frowned. "I'll need to get the victim's body on ice as soon as possible. I'll be sending Webber back to the morgue with the body. It's not usual to have a suspect in situ and right now I need to be in both places at the same time."

"Okay." Kane cleared his throat. "I'm not trying to tell you your job, but we've documented the scene. Once you've removed the body, you can complete the in-depth forensics sweep later. I need you to check over Rio and run what tests you need to do because, if someone drugged him to set him up, we need to know what they used and how they administered it."

"Yeah, well I've taken a blood sample, but some of the more easily accessible drugs are gone from the body in eight hours and we may have already missed the window." Wolfe's expression was grim. "But you do have a point. I can come back later with Webber. Emily has classes this afternoon." He waved a hand toward the body. "I'd better get at it."

Kane stepped around the blood-soaked rug, trying to avoid the footprints, and went to Jenna to explain. "Do you want to stay here or come with me?"

"I'll come with you." Jenna turned to the sound of Carter's voice and then looked back at Kane. "On second thought, take Carter with you and see what information you can pry from Rio. Having an FBI agent take on the case is an advantage and, as they're outsiders, there'll be no conflict of interest should it go to court. Now we have three murders, we have another serial killer on our hands. If Rio hasn't murdered this victim, we have a killer intent on manipulating our team, and I want Jo's insight into their mind. I'll let Jo do her thing and I'll get a ride back to the office with her when we're done."

Giving Jo and Carter a wave, Kane turned back to Jenna. "I'll be a time. I want to be there right through Rio's examination. Wolfe's not convinced he's involved."

"I'm following procedure and he was found at the scene with the murder weapon." Jenna's eyes flashed in annoyance. "I don't go easy on a fellow officer, not ever. For me, right now with all this evidence, it's hard to believe Rio isn't responsible."

Kane shook his head. "That's exactly what the killer wants us to believe, but I'll give you two pieces of solid evidence to prove his innocence. He's left-handed for one and, second, the prints on the Ka-Bar are too clean." He indicated with his chin toward Wolfe. "He put me through a series of tests just before to prove the number of prints that should be on a knife if it was used in a murder. One thing is for darn sure, Wolfe is the best there is when it comes to forensics. He sees the truth and not what someone wants us to see. I know Wolfe will find the underlying cause of it."

"For all our sakes, I hope you're right." Jenna shook her head. "Although, it will mean the killer is still out there, and none of them stop until we hunt them down." She sighed. "Before you leave, stop by Rio's cruiser and check it for fingerprints and see if he used his GPS to get here. The fact he left his vehicle by the gate and walked to the house suggests stealth. I want to know why he did that and, if he'd seen someone suspicious, why he didn't call for backup."

Kane pulled off his face mask and grimaced at the stench. "Copy that."

"Do you mind if I look at the victim?" Jo hovered anxiously on the porch. "Is that okay, Shane?"

"Sure. Keep to the outside of the room." Wolfe bent over the body.

"Wait there, Jo. I'll get you some coveralls and booties." Jenna looked at Carter. "I'll need the keys to my cruiser. Shane wants Rio taken to his office. Do you mind riding shotgun with Dave?"

"Nope. I figure there's enough people here contaminating the scene already." Carter fished the keys from his pocket and handed them to her.

"Thanks." She turned back to Kane. "Get Rio ready to leave. I need to discuss the MO with Jo and we can't discuss the case with him in the room."

Kane rubbed the back of his neck. "I think he pretty well knows what's going on, Jenna. He's no fool."

"Well, if what Wolfe said about the knife proves to be right, then setting Rio up is a diversion to keep us off the trail of the real killer." Jenna met his gaze. "Get me the proof, Dave, before someone else dies."

# TWENTY-SEVEN

As the temperature in the room increased from the heat of everyone's bodies, the smell of death became intolerable. Jenna pinched her face mask a little tighter over her nose. Books and movies rarely depicted a real murder scene. Sure, they gave the positions of the bodies and a liberal spreading of blood, but they didn't come close to the real thing. Only being on scene gave a true indication of the horror a victim had endured. She'd once arrived on scene during winter when steam still rose from the victim's blood. It swirled above the corpse and then dissipated into the air, giving the impression of a spirit leaving the body. The sight had disturbed her sleep for weeks. No one took into account the internal turmoil a law enforcement officer endured when finding a slaughtered victim or understood the hard physical challenge they faced to actually place one foot in front of the other, and walk into a life-or-death situation. Then there was the part of all murders that no one dare mention in fear of disturbing someone's sensibilities—the reek of urine and feces mixed with the stench reminiscent of the smell in the forest when a hunter dresses his kill.

Jenna ground her teeth and stepped around pools of

congealed blood to examine the body. The sight made her stomach roll, and a mixture of remorse and anger took hold of her in equal measure. With effort, she pushed her emotions into that tiny space inside her head that allowed her to look objectively at the victim. She could feel Jo moving close beside her and a sideways glance at her expression told her Jo was battling her demons as well. She stared down at the mangled corpse and shook her head in dismay at the damage. It made her sad and angry knowing that someone had once loved the victim and no amount of the undertaker's magic could ever repair her for a viewing. There would be no goodbyes for this grandma. She turned to Jo. "Facial damage similar to Agnes Wagner, but this one fought back."

"It's a similar MO to the Wagner murder, right down to the open front door." Jo met her gaze over the mask. "I wonder if someone disturbed the killer?" She stepped around the body of Mrs. Carson. "From the blood spatter in the family room, she died there, and looking at the way her arms are out in front of her and the trail of blood, someone dragged her here. Maybe they were looking for a closet to push her inside, the same as Mrs. Wagner."

Jenna tried to avoid looking at the unrecognizable face. "Maybe but we can rule out the kid who dropped by Rio's house... There's no way a kid could drag a body that far." She let out a long sigh. "If Mrs. Carson was a member of the quilting circle, we know where the killer will hit next. We can't watch all the women twenty-four/seven but we can warn them. I sent out a general press release last night. The townsfolks know to keep their doors locked until we catch this killer."

She stood to one side as Emily kneeled on a plastic sheet and tenderly lifted each hand and placed it inside a bag. The way she patted the old woman's arm as she stood to leave brought tears to Jenna's eyes. The compassion Emily showed for the victims who came through the ME's office astounded her.

She turned to Wolfe. "When you leave, we'll seal up the house. I'll go and search for the house keys. They must be here somewhere. I'll ask old Deputy Walters if he can watch the place until you return. You'll be back once you've processed Rio, won't you?"

"Yeah." Wolfe dropped a body bag onto the floor. "I'll leave the autopsy until tomorrow. I'll make sure we have everything we need from here, so you won't have to leave anyone outside. I'll need you to chase down the next of kin and notify them. I'm going to be too busy. It's only Webber and me this afternoon. I'll call you about the autopsy, but I figure with everything I have to do, it won't be until tomorrow afternoon." He rolled the victim inside and pulled up the zipper.

Jenna nodded. "Okay, I'll go find the keys. Don't worry, we'll lock the place up tight and Walters lives close by. I won't leave until he arrives."

"Thanks." Wolfe nodded to Webber and they lifted the body onto a gurney and headed for the front door. "I'll be back as soon as possible."

"I'll help you find the keys." Jo followed Jenna into the kitchen. "This is one tangled mess. I hope Rio isn't involved. I like him." She moved through the kitchen. "This woman has a place for everything. I'm betting there's a hook for the keys somewhere."

Jenna searched the walls and found a bunch of keys on a hook beside the kitchen door. "Got them." She pulled out her phone and called Walters. "I need you outside a crime scene: 3 Buffalo Trail. I'll wait here until you arrive. Wolfe is processing a suspect found at the scene and will be back to do a full forensic sweep in an hour or so."

*"I'll be right along."* Deputy Walters disconnected.

Jenna went about barring the door with crime scene tape and added some to the front gate before heading for her cruiser. She climbed inside and leaned back, letting out a long breath. It was good to be out of the stink. It was a smell that got into her hair and stuck to her clothes. She rubbed both hands over her face. "I sure hope Rio is in the clear but I still have a feeling something is going on around him. Maybe it's just the trouble with Cade?" She glanced at Jo in the passenger seat. "What's your take on it?"

"If you look at it logically, Zac being there doesn't make sense." Jo turned in her seat to face her. "I can see by the clotting of the blood how long he's been there, not to mention the smell. The blood on his hands and clothes was dry. I figure he's been there since last night." She narrowed her gaze on Jenna. "You're right, that feeling could be a reaction to his mood and his sudden change from being a reliable deputy. He must be at his wit's end with Cade."

Jenna placed both hands on the steering wheel and stared at the peaceful tree-lined road. "Maybe. I'll leave my judgment until Wolfe has examined him." She glanced up and down the road. "I live in isolation. It was a choice but I have security. Every one of the victims lives like I do, in houses far enough away from neighbors. If they screamed no one would hear them, and yet not one of them has as much as a deadbolt on their doors."

"There's no sign of forced entry." Jo flicked through crime scene images on her phone. "It's the same with all the murders. That would make me believe the victims knew their attackers."

Scrolling for Rowley's number on her phone, Jenna nodded. "Yeah. Dave always insists we look outside the box, and for me that would be Rio, but right now we have three suspects all known to the women, inside the box." She waited for Rowley to pick up. "Jake, we have another murder out of Buffalo Trail. I'll need you to go hunt down both suspects you interviewed yesterday. I need proof of their whereabouts from, say, eight last night until seven this morning."

*"I was waiting for Trey Duffy to show."* Rowley tapped

away on his computer keyboard. *"I'm the only one in the office right now. Rio is a no-show again and what's with the message scrawled all over the front door? Do you want me to wash it off?"*

After bringing Rowley up to speed, Jenna glanced at her watch. "I'll be back before Duffy arrives, and if he shows early, ask Maggie to take him down to an interview room to wait for me. Make sure you check in with Maggie when you arrive and leave the interviews. We have another psychopath out there. If anything doesn't sit right with you, get the hell out of Dodge and call for backup. I have Jo with me, and Kane and Carter will be back soon."

*"Copy that."* Rowley disconnected.

A pickup came hurtling down the road, throwing up dust, and skidded to a halt outside the house. A man jumped from the vehicle and ran toward the door. Jenna gave the siren a blast and the man stopped, turning to stare at her. Pulling her weapon, she slid from the cruiser. "Sheriff's department. Stop where you are."

"What happened here?" The man in his thirties ran toward her, his eyes round with alarm. "This is my grandma's house. Is she okay? A friend drove by to see her just before and called me after seeing the medical examiner's truck and your vehicle here."

Jenna holstered her weapon and pulled out her notebook. "Can I have your name and contact details?"

"Bret Carson." He rattled off his information and then his head turned toward the house. He took a few hesitant steps and then stopped and stared at her. "Is my grandma okay?"

Resting a hand on the man's arm, Jenna shook her head. Telling someone their loved one had died had to be the worst part of her job. "I'm sorry. She passed away."

"What happened? Did she take a fall?" Bret Carson scanned her face and his eyes flitted to the crime scene tape.

"Does that mean someone murdered her?" One shaking finger pointed toward the tape.

Feeling the man's grief wash over her, Jenna swallowed hard. The details of what had happened could destroy this man and have a domino effect all through his family. She nodded and kept a firm grip on his arm. "It would seem someone else was involved. We'll know more later."

"Can I see her?" Bret Carson attempted to pull away from her. "You can't just leave her there alone. She needs me to take care of her."

Under her palm, a tremble went through his arm and she gripped a little tighter. "She's not here and I can assure you she is not alone. Dr. Shane Wolfe and his daughter Emily are with her. They will take the greatest care of her and treat her with dignity."

"Oh, sweet Jesus." Bret Carson collapsed to the ground and buried his face in his hands. He rocked back and forth, wailing like a wolf at the full moon.

"Do you have someone we can call?" Jo came around the hood of the cruiser and gave Jenna a concerned look. "Your parents? A wife or minister?"

"My wife. My parents passed when I turned eighteen." He searched his pockets for his phone and thrust it at Jo and then dropped his hand. "No, maybe not. I don't want her driving after hearing the news and she'll insist on coming here." He scrubbed at his tear-streaked face and staggered to his feet. "Where is my grandma? Where have you taken her?"

Jenna took hold of his arm again. "She's at the medical examiner's office. He'll help me find out who killed her. It's best if you go home and wait for him to contact you. I'll drive your truck and you can show me where you live."

"My place is on Stanton, just past Pine." Bret Carson made an obvious attempt to pull himself together.

"Just sit for a while." Jo opened the back door of the cruiser and urged him to sit inside. "Is your wife at home?"

"Yeah." Bret Carson dashed a hand through his hair. "I come by as regular as clockwork every Friday. I was heading out to the grocery store when Harriette Jefferson dropped by and told me about seeing you here. After hearing the news about locking our doors, I came straight away." He clasped his hands together staring at them. "Harriette comes by on Thursdays to visit her. She lives two doors down from me. I told her I'd drive out and see what was happening."

Seeing Deputy Walters pull up behind her, Jenna sighed with relief. She looked at Bret Carson. "I'll be right back."

After bringing Deputy Walters up to speed, she took Bret Carson to his truck and slid behind the wheel. They drove in silence, with Jo driving the cruiser close behind. When Jenna pulled up outside Carson's house, she looked at him. "Will you be okay? Do you want me to come in and speak to your wife or call another family member to sit with you?"

"No, I'll wait by the phone for Dr. Wolfe to call." Carson gave her a red-eyed look. "We will be able to see my grandma, won't we? We'll have to identify the body."

"No, that won't be possible." Jenna blew out a sigh. "If you can give me the name of her dentist, Dr. Wolfe will use her dental records for comparison." She touched his arm. "It's really better if your last memory of her isn't at the morgue."

"Yes, I can understand that, and I thank you for considering our feelings." He climbed unsteadily from the truck.

Jenna followed him to the front door and stood in the hallway as he gave his wife the dreadful news. She left them and walked with leaden feet to the cruiser, more determined than ever to find out who was killing grandmas in her town.

# TWENTY-EIGHT

Bringing in a team member as a suspect concerned Kane. He'd interviewed Rio and found him to be solid. He'd given Rio the same background and psych tests he'd ordered for his team during his tour of duty. Living in serial killer central meant they needed to trust everyone—boots on the ground and men in the air. He'd not risked giving Jenna the wrong advice. He'd called the LAPD and spoken to Rio's superior, and had Wolfe and Bobby Kalo check him out to ensure they'd chosen the right guy for the job. Nothing in his background led him to believe Rio had any evidence of instability. His sudden change of behavior notwithstanding, it was obvious when Cade went missing that Rio placed his brother's welfare over his job.

He thought back to his own situation during the time after a car bomber had murdered his wife. He'd been a mess, but anger hadn't been a part of his despair. Could he, if he'd not been in a hospital with a metal plate in his head, been able to function in the field? He dropped into the zone and nodded to himself. He'd never lost the mental discipline to block emotion and control his body. He recalled the training to bring him to this state of mind. Submerged repeatedly in freezing water, the only way to survive was to relax and not fight the panic. It took a body ninety seconds to adjust to the shock—get through the first ninety seconds without panicking and a person should adapt to the cold. During his ordeal, his training officer would bark questions at him to test just how resilient his mind had become. Most normal people couldn't think straight but he never had that problem. They'd dunk him repeatedly and then on the point of hypothermia they'd allow him to climb out and run a mile or so to warm up before enduring the process again. This and waterboarding, being left in dark confined spaces, and other training exercises made his mind strong. It had given him the ability to drop into the zone at will and slow his heartbeat. In this state everything around him dropped into slow motion and he moved and processed threats in a blink of an eye. Jenna had asked him once why he needed to be in the zone before taking out a target with a sniper rifle. He'd explained how a flinch or the slightest movement could mean a bullet missed the target by a wide margin. There was no place for nerves in the world of a sniper.

He caught Carter frowning at him and snapped back to the now. Pushing off the wall he walked to the table and dropped into a seat opposite Rio in the sterile room. He allowed a smile to crease his lips at the sight of Carter dressed in scrubs, his hair tucked neatly under a cap. "We all look as if we're going to perform surgery."

"Well, if you're planning on dissecting me, go right ahead." Rio leaned on the table looking pale and drawn. "I wave my rights to an attorney. Let's get this shit over with."

"I wouldn't mind asking you a few questions." Carter looked at Kane. "If you don't mind?" He pulled out his phone, wrapped in a plastic bag. "We can record the interview on my phone."

Kane shrugged. "Fine by me but Jenna will want to be included."

"Jenna's not here." Carter raised an eyebrow. "Let's get this done. Wolfe has likely finished with all the tests he needs to do on him. We have a duty of care to Zac and he hasn't eaten since last night and he's sitting here covered in a victim's blood."

Leaning back in the uncomfortable plastic chair, Kane nodded. "Sure, get at it."

"You can't remember anything since you answered the door to a kid, right?" Carter drummed his fingers on the white plastic table. "So, if you were drugged, how was it administered? You were at home since leaving the mountain. Did anyone come by or did you order takeout?"

"Nope." Rio looked at his blood-soaked hands and shuddered. "I don't know what happened. I keep getting flashes of disjointed memories. Nothing makes sense right now."

"Okay, think back to when the kid came to the door." Carter sat back and inclined his head, looking at Rio. "Did you know him? Did he give his name? Would you recognize him again?"

"No, no, and no." Rio shrugged. "He was sitting astride a bicycle under the tree out front. "He called out, 'Flora Carson out of 3 Buffalo Trail told me to come get you. She's seen a prowler.' Then he took off in the dark."

Kane calculated the distance between Buffalo Trail and Stanton to be about five miles. "That's a long way for a kid to ride at night. Can you remember what he was wearing?"

"A ballcap and dark clothing. I didn't get a good look at his face. It was in shadow." Rio sighed. "I went inside and made a note in my daybook. I told the twins I was heading out and left."

"Did it occur to you that Buffalo Trail is an isolated area? Or what was a kid doing way out there alone at night for Mrs. Carson to ask them for help?" Carter opened his hands. "Can't you see how sketchy this looks? The prosecution would tear you to shreds. No one is going to believe there was a kid, let alone one that rode five miles to specifically get you."

"There was a kid. I called out for him to stop, but he rode off into the dark, and at the time I didn't know where Buffalo Trail was." Rio glared back at him. "You know darn well I've not lived here long. My priority was a woman in danger, not getting the name of a kid on a bicycle."

"If she had been living in suburbia, wouldn't she have run to a neighbor before sending a kid five miles to get help from you? And why *you* in particular? Why didn't she ask the kid to call 911? Most kids carry phones." Carter shook his head. "You're a smart guy. Think about it. Did you honestly believe an old lady ran down her driveway in the dark with a prowler hanging around, in the hope someone might happen by?" His brows met in a frown. "No, she'd have locked all the doors and armed herself. And for your information, Mrs. Carson's phone and cell were both working just fine when we arrived."

"I didn't think it through." Rio let out a long sigh. "I was exhausted and I guess I assumed the kid came from close by. With two murders in town, my focus was getting to the woman and keeping her safe."

Kane stared at Rio's confused expression. "Why didn't you call for backup?"

"The old folks are on edge since the media release. It could have been someone hearing things or a hoax callout for a prowler." Rio snorted. "Give me a break. I was planning on doing a drive-by, if everything looked okay. I would have checked on the woman." He shot a long look at Kane. "Her place isn't posted. It wasn't like she planned on shooting me when I drove in her gate."

"How did you know that her place isn't posted?" Carter flashed Kane a knowing look. "Have you been there before?"

"No, but I just had a memory. It was the flash of my headlights sweeping an open gate. There were no signs anywhere." Rio stared at Kane. "My cruiser was there, so I must have driven there, right? Maybe my memory is coming back."

"Yeah, you know darn well you parked just inside the gate."

Kane frowned. "You must have walked up the driveway. Why didn't you follow procedure and drive by the house using your vehicle for protection?"

"I have no idea." Rio shrugged. "Maybe I saw someone and wanted to get the jump on them."

Kane stared at him. "So, from that glimpse of memory, we can be sure you drove without any problems to the house. You know, I've checked your vehicle. All the prints are yours and the GPS has the victim's address as the last place you entered." He sighed. "Your prints are on the front doorframe, so you rested your hand there before entering the house. Unless you blanked out and murdered the woman, we must assume someone administered the drug as you entered the house."

"If I remembered, don't you figure I'd tell you?" Rio let out a huff of exasperation. "How much longer do I have to sit here? I have the headache from hell. I need coffee and something to eat."

Kane's phone buzzed. Wolfe was calling from just down the hall. "Yeah?"

*"Can you come to the lab. You need to see this."*

"I'm on my way." Kane disconnected the call and turned to Carter. "I'll be right back."

# TWENTY-NINE

Kane walked to the examination room with the red light glowing outside. He flashed his ID and the doors whooshed open. The drop in temperature hit him and he walked to where Wolfe was peering at a readout of tests on a computer screen. He peered over his shoulder. "Find anything interesting?"

"I have a ton of conflicting evidence." Wolfe spun his seat around to look at him. "It's very unusual. The victim has a few fibers on her clothes but not a great deal that match. I know she's in the quilting circle, so she might have handled different fabrics at any time." He frowned. "On Rio's clothes are carpet fibers, which match the victim's carpet as if he rolled around the floor or was dragged. Not what I'd usually see, especially as the same drag pattern is on the victim."

Kane scratched his cheek. "So that would tell us that both the victim and Rio were dragged over the carpet?"

"Yeah." Wolfe pointed to the images of bloody footprints. "This evidence added to everything else is enough to convict Rio. The prints were made by Rio's boots, there's no doubt." He took an evidence bag from a pile containing Rio's blood-soaked clothes and held up a pair of socks. "Rio was wearing his boots when we found him, so how did blood get onto the toes of his socks?"

Kane examined the evidence. "His boots were removed but he didn't walk in the blood, did he? There's no blood on the bottom of his socks or on his bare feet." He stared at Wolfe. "Are you saying, someone removed his boots, put them on, and then dragged the victim into the hallway?"

"From the lack of other footprints, it suggests Rio was unconscious before the killing. The killer put on Rio's boots and murdered the victim. Dumped her in the hallway and then dragged Rio through the blood. His feet were on the edge of the blood spatter when we found him. The killer replaced his boots and left. I found fluff from towels on the carpet, same as at the Agnes Wagner crime scene. The killer used them to leave the house without leaving a blood trail. They likely burned their clothes. I'll check the incinerator when I go back this afternoon and look for any blood spatter from the killer outside the house." Wolfe had a determined look on his face. "Talk to Jo. We've assumed that the killer gets his kicks from frightening the old ladies before he kills them. If this is what happened, then the killer had Mrs. Carson restrained or held at gunpoint when Rio arrived."

Processing all the information, Kane rubbed his chin. "This would mean Rio was set up. What else have you got?"

"Or he is a killer trying to hide his tracks. He could just as easily have killed the woman, dragged her into the hallway, and then removed his boots to fabricate the evidence to match the first murderer's MO." Wolfe brought up a blood analysis on his screen. "Rio is symptomatic to a date rape drug. What is available on the streets right now is gamma-hydroxybutyric acid, commonly known as liquid ecstasy. It's easy to transport and inject. I tested specifically for that and got a hit. I've run tests for everything I can think of, but the results will take time and are probably unnecessary." He shrugged. "I checked the victim for trace evidence and found nothing under her nails but the incisions to her forearms and hands indicates she faced a frontal attack and tried to protect herself. I'll be able to give you specifics after the autopsy tomorrow."

Kane blew out a long sigh. "So, we still don't know if he's in the clear?"

"We're dealing with a superior mind here, Dave." Wolfe met his gaze. "Let's just check out a few more things before we make a decision. Take him to the showers and when he's done, wrap him in a towel and I'll examine him from head to toe. If someone injected him, we'll find a needle mark. It would have had to have been a fast-punch type of jab, so they usually tear. Also, it will be likely on his back. I have to be sure he hasn't done this to himself to cover his involvement."

Thinking for a beat, Kane ran the possible scenario through his head. "Liquid ecstasy would drop him immediately, wouldn't it?"

"Going on the size of the dose, and the time he was unconscious, yeah, it would happen very fast. He'd likely stagger around and then collapse." Wolfe pointed to the results on the screen. "From the residue still present in his blood, it was enough to drop a horse. He's lucky to be alive."

"Okay." Kane stared at the screen. "So where is the syringe? He wouldn't have had time to dump it somewhere." He imagined himself in the same situation. "Unless he injected it and threw the syringe into the yard, then staggered back inside the house, or threw it out a window."

"He could have just as easily injected himself in the bathroom, flushed it, and then staggered into the family room. It was a few feet." Wolfe shrugged. "It's possible and what I'd do. But using this drug as an alibi is way too risky."

Kane stared at him. "How so?"

"It's life threatening in high doses and its use as an alibi is too dependent on the timeframe. We might not have found him for hours." Wolfe rested his head in the palm of one hand. "If this was a setup and we assume the killer is familiar with the drug, then they wouldn't expect me to detect it. Liquid ecstasy has a very narrow temporal window and they didn't bank on me taking a blood sample within eight hours of the drug's administration. Once that time has passed, there'd be no evidence to prove anyone drugged Rio, making him appear guilty. Same as if he used it for an alibi, he'd have to bet on us finding him within eight hours for it to work in his favor. If we find a needle stick injury in his back, it will prove someone else administered the drug."

"So, he can go for a shower and then we bring him in here?" Kane could feel the cold seeping through his clothes. "That would be barbaric. I don't know how you work in these low temperatures."

"I'm used to it." Wolfe smiled. "Not getting soft, are you? Maybe it's time to run you through another training session."

"The dunking in the ravine was enough for me." Kane chuckled. "Trust me, everything is working fine."

"Take him back to the sterile room. At least it's warmer in there. I'll roll in the equipment I need and be ready when he's finished." Wolfe stood. "If I find a needle mark, I'll know if he jabbed himself or not. Another thing, from the angle of the incisions on the victim's face, whoever did this was right-handed. It's just an observation currently, not conclusive. I'll look closer at the autopsy."

Kane hustled back to the sterile room, swiped his card, and stepped inside. He looked at Rio. "Well, some good news at least. Wolfe has collected all the samples and run the tests he needs to do on you for now, so you can take a shower. He'll be by to examine you once you're done and then we'll be taking you back to the office."

"Can I get some food?" Rio was holding his head. "Please?"

"I'll grab you something to eat from Aunt Betty's once we get back to the office."

"Can I get some of my own clothes?" Rio stared at his blood encrusted hands. "These scrubs don't do much to keep out the cold and I need a pair of boots." He shivered. "I have plenty of spare uniforms at home and boots. Mrs. Jacobs, my housekeeper, will bring them over. She's five minutes away."

Kane could see the goosebumps on Rio's arms, and his face had been sheet-white since they'd found him. "Sure, I'll call her." He looked at Carter. "I'll go and pick up his clothes if you can handle the shower?" He looked at Rio. "You'll need to use the nailbrush to get the blood from under your fingernails. Take your time. I'll be back as soon as possible."

Kane stripped off the scrubs and tossed them into the bin and headed out the door. He stopped outside in the sunshine and stared into a cloudless blue sky spreading out above the mountains. He took in a few deep breaths of pine-scented air and allowed the scenery to push away the horror of the morning. He climbed into the Beast and called Rio's housekeeper, only saying Rio needed a change of clothes and not mentioning the murder. He headed off and arrived at the house a few minutes later to find her waiting for him with a grocery bag filled with clothes and a pair of boots balanced on the top. He smiled at her. "Thanks, he'll be glad to be dry again."

"Did you bring his wet clothes for me to wash?" She eyed him dubiously.

Kane shook his head. "Ah no, I think we'll burn them." He took in her puzzled expression. "I'm sure he'll explain later."

He headed back to the ME's office and, once inside, delivered the clothes and headed to Wolfe's office to grab a to-go cup of coffee for Rio. He wandered back and his phone chimed. "Yeah?"

"*Where are you?*" Jenna sounded irritated. "*I expected you back by now. I have Duffy to interview at noon. Will you be back by then? Rowley is out on his own talking to our suspects. I need more boots on the ground here."*

Kane rubbed the back of his neck. "Wolfe is examining Rio again as we speak. Once we have him sorted, I'll drop by with him and Carter. I'll go by Aunt Betty's for takeout and be right back. Rio hasn't eaten since last night."

*"Do you figure he's involved?"*

"I can't say just now, but I doubt it." Kane juggled the coffee and phone to scan the door to the sterile area. "Gotta go. I'll see you soon."

He walked inside as Wolfe finished his examination. "What did you find?"

"There's a needle mark here, right between the shoulder blades." Wolfe pointed to the red mark. "It's impossible for a person to administer an injection there." He handed Rio two pills. "For the headache. You'll feel better once you've eaten and the memory should come back in sections. Write down everything you see in the flashes. It will assist with proving your innocence."

"I'm glad at least one of you believes me." Rio tucked the towel around his waist and shivered.

Kane handed Rio the coffee. "We're just following procedure. If we let it slide because you're a deputy, it looks as if we're covering up a possible suspect in a homicide. You'd do the same in my position and let's face facts here, finding you with a body and the murder weapon next to your hand is damning evidence. We had to be sure you hadn't killed the woman. All we did here protects you from being set up for murder one." He shrugged. "Get dressed and I'll drop you at the office." He looked at Carter. "I'll drive down to Aunt Betty's. We'll be too busy to stop and might have time to grab a bite before Duffy arrives for his interview. You can bring Jenna up to speed."

"That's fine by me." Carter removed his face mask and tossed a toothpick into his mouth. "Pulled-pork rolls for me, two, and pie—I'm not particular on what kind. I'm famished." He went for his wallet.

Kane held up a hand. "Lunch is on the department. We have a tab at Aunt Betty's." He pulled out his phone and headed for the door. "I'll call ahead and give them our order." He made the call.

Carter followed him out the door and peeled off his scrubs. He was shaking his head. Kane stared at him. "What's on your mind?"

"There's one thing worrying me." Carter moved the toothpick across his lips. "If Rio isn't responsible for killing the old lady, then Rowley is out there alone with two possible suspects. From what I've seen, this killer isn't going to worry about taking down a deputy. We need to have Rowley's back before he becomes the next victim."

# THIRTY

Shocked by Rio's drawn appearance when he staggered into her office with Carter, Jenna sat him down and pushed a cup of coffee in front of him. She trusted Wolfe's opinion and would act on it. She looked at him, needing to say something positive. "I'm sorry I was so hard on you, Zac. I'm glad Wolfe was able to clear you of any involvement so quickly. You should go home and rest. We'll find the person who did this to you."

"You followed procedure." Rio lifted his red-rimmed eyes to her. "I'd like to stay if you don't mind. When you discuss the case, it might trigger flashbacks of what happened. I'll stand down if it becomes a conflict of interest."

Considering the options, Jenna nodded somewhat reluctantly. "Okay." She turned to Carter. "What have we got?"

She listened as Carter updated her and shook her head when he voiced his worry over Rowley's safety. "I've trained Jake to be cautious. He wouldn't put himself in danger. These suspects are both working outside, in full view of the neighbors and homeowners, or I wouldn't have sent him out alone. He's fine. He called just before and he's on his way back to the office.

He's spoken to Bueller and Hahn, and neither of them had an alibi for any of the times of the murders, so they are well and truly still on our list of possible suspects." She dropped a pen into the old chipped cup with WELCOME TO HAWAII printed on one side and looked at him. "Hahn was within five minutes' drive of the last murder scene, and Bueller admits to being in transit between Stanton and Main around nine as well. Both men were in the vicinity of the murder scene. Neither has anyone to prove their whereabouts. Although Hahn dropped by Aunt Betty's at around eight-thirty. We can check that out."

"Any clues to who left the message on the front door *again*?" Carter placed one boot on his other knee and leaned back in his chair. "No prints and no CCTV?"

When Carter aimed his piercing green eyes at her, it sometimes made her feel like a rookie. It wasn't him. She liked him just fine, and away from the job he was a really nice guy. Like Kane, he shot straight from the hip and didn't sugarcoat anything. His investigative experience was mind-blowing and sometimes a little daunting. Jenna pushed the hair from her eyes with a sigh. "Nope. I assume they used a stick dipped in the mud puddle beside the door to write it. No prints and the CCTV camera is still out. I walked the streets with Jo when we arrived to ask everyone close by if they noticed anyone and got zip." She met Rio's troubled gaze. "Someone sure has it in for you, Zac. Is there anything we should know?"

"Not about last night, no. Wolfe told me the memory might come back in flashes and as soon as anything comes back, I'll tell you. It's about Duffy. I had him come by to check the furnace a couple of weeks ago. It makes a noise and keeps me awake at night." Rio scratched the dark stubble on his chin, making a rasping sound. "He recommended I put in a new one. He was real chatty and then went as cold as ice, as if he'd flipped a switch, when Mrs. Jacobs said I should get a few quotes before I asked you about replacing it." He shrugged. "Colby Hahn has worked for us as well. I had a few jobs for him to do around the house but he had a problem with Cuddles... Ah, that's Mrs. Jacobs' cat. The twins said they had an argument because he locked the cat in a cupboard to keep it from rubbing around his legs."

Jenna stared at him in disbelief. "Why didn't you inform us about your contact with the suspects?"

"Because I haven't been here and at the time they weren't listed as suspects." Rio sipped his coffee.

"Jenna." Carter raised both eyebrows. "He's likely in shock. I figure we get him something to eat and drive him home. He needs to get his head straight."

"I'm sitting here." Rio's dark eyes flashed. "My brain is working just fine. I'm just exhausted is all and have a drug hangover. You need me, in this investigation. We know Duffy and Hahn both had access to the inside of the victims' houses. They'd have had the layout, could've left a window unlatched, or could've made an excuse to drop by. The women would have opened the door to them at night. I'm wondering now if I'd asked Duffy to replace the furnace, would I have made my housekeeper, Mrs. Jacobs, a target." He swung his gaze to Carter. "Her part of the house is separate from where I live. She has her own front door but access to our part via an internal door. Although, we use the same furnace. If he'd dropped by when we were out, Mrs. Jacobs would have taken him through the connecting door. I don't lock it. She'd have been a sitting duck."

Considering Rio's thoughts, Jenna nodded. "Hmm, something to consider, but would a killer be so confident to murder a woman in a deputy's home? Most people know it's owned by the department. We've had deputies living there for years."

"It wouldn't be a first in that house, would it?" Carter raised one eyebrow.

The phone rang and Jenna lifted the receiver. It was Maggie from the front counter. "Yes, Maggie."

*"Mr. Duffy called to say he'll be here by one. He's finishing up a job. Ah... you might want to come down here. Kane's back and it looks like we have a new deputy."* Maggie disconnected.

Standing, Jenna glanced at Carter and Rio. "Do you want to join Jo? She's in the conference room going over some old cases for comparison. I'll meet you there. Kane's back with takeout and it seems we have a new deputy." She hurried down the stairs and through to the reception area and stopped dead. *Cedar Canyon, yeah, now I remember.*

Poppy was climbing out of Kane's truck, long blonde hair flowing over her shoulders, laughing and smiling like she'd just won a beauty pageant. Jenna pushed through the glass doors and walked to the Beast. "Need a hand with the food? We've moved to the conference room."

"Thanks." Kane's gaze moved over her face. "You didn't mention Poppy was joining us?"

Jenna shook her head. "I had no idea. I've never received her application."

"Hi, Jenna, nice to see you again. Mayor Petersham hired me." Poppy indicated toward Kane. "I just got into town and met Dave at the diner. He gave me a ride. I'm staying at the Cattleman's Hotel. Mayor Petersham said maybe I can stay with you for a few days until my rental is ready. I'll need a cruiser as well."

Jenna shot a look at Kane but got a blank stare in return and then moved her attention back to Poppy. "I'm sorry, I have two FBI Agents staying with me and we don't have any spare cruisers, ah, Deputy... Sorry, I don't recall your last name."

"Anderson." She smiled at Kane. "I'm sure Dave will give me a ride back to the hotel later. I'd like to start now, so I can get to know everyone. I haven't even bothered to unpack." She smiled at him. "You promised to take me to dinner. How about tonight? You can tell me all about the current caseload."

"I... ah... sorry, I'm too busy." Kane's Adam's apple bobbed up and down as he swallowed. "I'm in the middle of a case right now."

"Oh, come on." Poppy pouted. "You're not going to dump me here alone, are you? Have you any idea how difficult it was to persuade the mayor to allow me to come work with you?"

Wanting to throttle Mayor Petersham, Jenna took a deep breath. She didn't have the time to deal with a new deputy. "I'm sorry. I'll need Kane with me. Perhaps, our receptionist, Maggie, might be able to assist you with a ride." She took the carton Kane handed her. "Maggie will arrange a uniform for you and a badge, but you'll need to put up your hair. Long hair obscuring your view is a liability on the job. Maggie will give you a copy of our dress code. All deputies are required to adhere to the dress code, except for the deputy sheriff."

"Oh, Jenna, don't tell me you're going to be a stickler for every little rule?" Poppy's over-white smile almost blinded her.

Jenna heard Kane's low whistle and watched him shoulder his way through the glass doors, carrying a carton filled with takeout. He was heading for the hills. She turned her attention back to Poppy. "I play it straight down the line, Deputy, and my deputies refer to me as Sheriff Alton." She hoisted the box on one hip and climbed the steps to the office.

She dropped the carton on the front counter and met Maggie's surprised expression. "This is Deputy Anderson. Can you find her a uniform shirt and a rubber band for her hair? Oh, and a copy of the dress code? She'll be working desk duty. I'm sure you'll find her something to do. I'll be in the conference room. Call me when Mr. Duffy arrives." She glanced back at the door. "And send Rowley right along when he gets back."

"Sure thing, Sheriff." She smiled knowingly at Jenna and

then turned her attention to Poppy. "I'm Magnolia Brewster but you can call me Maggie." She opened the flap to allow Poppy behind the counter.

Pushing the new deputy from her mind, Jenna went into the conference room and placed the carton on the table. She noticed Carter grinning like a baboon. She rounded on him. "What?"

"Oh, don't let him rile you." Jo stood and laid a hand on her arm. "We had our fill of Poppy Anderson at the conference. Dave knows what she's like. What on earth possessed you to allow her to join the team?"

Jenna shot a glance at Kane, who was munching into a roll. "I had no say in the matter. She got into Mayor Petersham's ear."

"I should never have taken her to lunch all those years ago." Kane shook his head. "Now she figures we're best buddies."

"Oh, this is going to be classic." Carter's grin spread from ear to ear as he turned to Kane. "Haven't you told Jenna what a pain in the butt that woman is? We spent the entire conference in the men's bathroom trying to avoid her."

"I tried to." Kane gave Jenna an apologetic shrug. "We ran into her in Helena and she mentioned wanting to come here." He sipped a soda. "And no, I didn't encourage her." He tilted his head and his gaze flicked over her. "You don't have to keep her. You could give her a week's trial, and if you're not happy, send her back."

"That sounds like an option." Jo smiled. "From my impression of her at the conference, she doesn't have the stability you need in your team."

"She doesn't have a filter." Carter shrugged. "I know I had the same problem at one time but I knew when to keep my mouth shut. She never stops talking and could well leak information."

Considering everyone's opinion, Jenna paused a beat thinking before lifting her gaze back to Kane. "A week is a long time, Dave. I don't need the distraction right now, not with a killer murdering nightly—and neither do you. Maybe I should just fire her?"

"We'll be working in the conference room from now on and she's not on our team." Kane shrugged. "Give her the week—that's a fair assessment."

Nodding, Jenna glanced around the room. "Okay, but keep it professional and quit calling her Poppy." She sighed. "I'm over discussing Deputy Anderson. We have an interview at one and I haven't eaten yet."

She glanced up as Rowley came into the room and nodded to him. After sitting next to Jo, she hunted through the takeout for a bagel and cream cheese. It was a favorite and Kane usually included one or two in an order. The conversation in the room hummed around her and she listened as Carter gave Jo the details she'd missed.

"Did you find any similar murders?" Kane, leaned forward in his chair looking at Jo.

"Similar but not the same, no. We're assuming the killer has murdered three victims." Jo twirled her coffee cup in her fingers staring at the whiteboard. "You'd have reason to link them as they all had a fear factor. This is part of the killer's profile but so is the enclosed spaces. The pickup was an enclosed space and so was the closet. In the third case, it looked as if the killer attempted to drag the victim into the closet as well, but someone disturbed them."

"You think Rio arrived and they attacked him?" Kane raised both eyebrows. "Then how did they get the kid to ride by his house? They wouldn't risk getting the kid to relay the message and then go and kill Mrs. Carson, and we know they injected Rio in the back. They'd have to plan that move."

Jenna swallowed her last piece of bagel and sipped her

coffee. "We've established the killer wore Rio's boots. So he was down *before* the murder, or we'd have found bloody footprints." She placed her cup on the table. "Rio isn't a small man and Mrs. Carson must have weighed close to one hundred and fifty pounds. Have you considered that after dragging the victim into the doorway and then Rio into the blood, they might have been too exhausted to complete the fantasy?"

"If this scenario is correct, then we'll ask Wolfe if he found any ligature marks on Mrs. Carson. There's no way she would have just stood there and watched what was happening. She'd have run for the backdoor or grabbed a weapon from the kitchen. I noticed a knife block in there."

"There was an empty rifle rack in the hallway." Carter tossed a toothpick into his mouth. "They could have threatened her with the rifle and turned it on Rio for all we know. If it's not here they probably tossed it."

"If they'd had a rifle aimed at her, when I arrived, they'd have had to take it off her to aim it at me." Rio rubbed his temples. "If that happened, I figure she'd have called out to warn me. I'd have pulled my weapon and someone would be dead apart from the victim."

Running the conversation through her mind, Jenna nodded. "What if they drugged her as well?"

"Nope." Kane pulled a slice of peach pie from a bag. "She had defensive wounds on her arms. That wouldn't happen if she'd been unconscious."

Jenna's phone buzzed. It was Maggie. "Okay, thank you. I'll be right along." She turned to Jo. "Duffy is here. Do you mind sitting in on the interview? Over the phone, he sounds just too nice, and from what Rio said about him, he can change in the blink of an eye."

"Sure." Jo stood, gathered her empty wrappers and tossed them in the garbage.

After making sure the feed from the interview room was

playing on a screen, Jenna turned to the others. "You can watch from here. I want this to look like a casual interview. He'll clam up if he sees law enforcement officers waiting in the hallway." She headed out the door and stopped to speak to Rowley. "Good job out there this morning. Eat, and then write up your files."

# THIRTY-ONE

After waving Trey Duffy into the interview room, Jenna waited for him and Jo to sit down before pulling a statement book out of the drawer. She dropped into a chair and turned on the recording devices, stated the date and time, and turned to Duffy. "Thank you for coming in to answer our questions, Mr. Duffy. Can you please state your name and details for the record?"

"Trey Duffy out of 202 Stanton."

Jenna nodded. "I'm Sheriff Jenna Alton and I'm with Special Agent Jo Wells, who is here to observe." She glanced at Jo. "If you could state your name?"

"Special Agent Jo Wells out of the Snakeskin Gully field office." Jo smiled at Duffy. "Do you have any objection to me sitting in?"

"Not at all." The corner of Duffy's mouth twitched into a smile. "I'm interested to find out what happened to my clients."

Keeping her face impassive, Jenna took the pen from her pocket. "This interview is to establish a timeline before the deaths of Agnes Wagner out of Snowberry Way; Jolene Darvish out of Rocky Road, Bear Peak; and Flora Carson out of Buffalo

Trail. You have the right to have an attorney present. Do you wish to continue with the interview?"

"Sure." Duffy opened his hands wide. "I don't have anything to hide from you fine ladies."

Jenna read him his rights. "Okay. Let's start with Agnes Wagner. When did you do repairs on her furnace?"

"Let me see." Duffy pulled a notebook out of his pocket and flipped through the pages. "I worked there for a time. I finished on Thursday and dropped by on Friday because she complained of a bad smell in the cellar. It was a dead mouse. I took it out and opened the window to air out the place."

"Did you close the window before you left?" Jo leaned back in her chair.

"Nope, it needed a day or so." He raised both eyebrows. "I wasn't the only person up there. I had four guys from the warehouse to deliver the furnace." He chuckled. "You didn't expect me to carry the old one up the stairs and bring the new one down by myself, did you?" He shook his head. "I just repair them or fit them and make sure they're running right is all."

Jenna made a few useless notes in her book and lifted her gaze back to him. "How did you get along with Mrs. Wagner? Did you chat with her?"

"She was a clean freak." He narrowed his gaze. "She wanted me to remove my boots. I told her I must wear boots when I'm working. It's code. If I dropped a wrench on my toe, she'd be liable." He grimaced. "She followed us around with a cloth, wiping the floor, sweeping the stairs, but what can you say? Most of the old folk are set in their ways, and she always offers me lunch or a cup of coffee when I work there."

"Okay." Jenna watched his body language and came up empty. "So you're relationship with Agnes Wagner was cordial?"

"Yeah, I guess so." He rubbed his chin and tapped his bottom lip as if contemplating what to say. "You never know with the old folk. Some of them smell bad and act strange. I'm always worried they'll lock me in the cellar. I take my tools with me just in case I need to break out."

"Really?" Astonished, Jenna stared at him. "Did you do any work for Mrs. Darvish out of Rocky Road, or Flora Carson out of Buffalo Trail?"

"You know I did." Duffy leaned back in his chair and smiled ruefully. "I spoke to Colby Hahn this morning. He told me your deputy has been hounding him. Asking all sorts of questions, asking where he'd been. I can tell you now. I worked for both those women." He tossed his notebook at Jenna. "Check the dates. I've got nothing to hide and if you want to know where I was on the nights you asked Colby about, go see my wife."

Jenna made a note of the dates he'd worked for both women. "Okay, I'll need her name and where I can speak to her in private."

"Sally's at home." Duffy stretched his legs, looking supremely confident, and gave his details.

Jenna stared at the camera. "I'll get my deputy to go and speak with her without delay."

Seconds later her phone chimed. It was a message from Kane telling her he was on his way with Carter to speak to Sally Duffy. All she had to do was delay her husband a little longer. She glanced at Jo. "Do you have any questions for Mr. Duffy?"

"Yeah." Jo's gaze fixed on Duffy's face. "The quilting circle uses many of the same contractors for work. We know about Mr. Hahn and Mr. Archie Bueller. Are you aware of anyone else who might work for them? Do you often run into other contractors?"

"All the time." Duffy frowned. "The problem is with this question, Agent Wells. Giving out information like this goes against my ethics. It's like going behind someone's back. Most of my work in town comes from recommendations, from other contractors or from clients, and I don't want my business to suffer if the townsfolk believe I'm an FBI informant."

"If I'd wanted you as a CI, I wouldn't be speaking to you with Sheriff Alton present." Jo smiled at him. "Let's change the subject. Have you worked for many of the older folk in town?"

"Yeah, all the time." He folded his arms over his chest. "It's rare for one to call for just an estimate. They usually want the job done yesterday. Most of them want things replaced rather than fixed. It seems to be a new thing around town of late. They all want new furnaces, or new stoves, and they call me to get them for them. They're impatient and demanding but they're old."

"Have you always gotten along with your grandparents?" Jo's attention hadn't wandered from his face.

"Mine?" Duffy stared at his hands avoiding her gaze. "My grandpa died long ago and my grandma was a little crazy. She'd spend her time talking to him and set his plate at the table every night like clockwork. My parents couldn't see anything wrong with her, but when they died and left me with her, it was creepy."

"And how do you get along with her now you're older?" Jo flicked a glance at Jenna and then moved her attention back to Duffy. "Is she still a little creepy?"

"I try not to think about her. She died." Duffy raised his eyes and looked at Jo. "I was out there one day playing in the yard and she fell into the well." He shrugged and a slow smile creased his lips. "She probably heard Grandpa calling her and dived right in."

Jenna leaned forward. "Did you see her fall in?"

"Nope." Duffy shrugged. "The cops figured she'd wandered off somewhere, they found her down the well sometime later."

"Did that upset you... knowing you were there when she died?" Jo made a few notes in her book and then looked at him.

"Not really." Duffy shrugged. "Like I said, I figured she was crazy. I didn't like living there."

"Do you think your experience with your grandma makes it difficult to work for the older women in town?" Jo twirled the pen through her fingers. "Do they bring back memories, for instance?"

"The smell does, sometimes. The beeswax polish or the stale air in the house because they never open a window." Duffy picked at his fingers. "But I don't let it bother me. It's just a job. I don't have to stay there, do I?"

Jenna's phone vibrated in her pocket. She glanced at the caller ID. It was Kane. "I have to take this call. The interview is suspended." She gave the time and then pressed the pause button on the recorder. "I'll be two minutes." She flashed her card and stepped outside the door. "That was fast. What do you have for me?"

*"I have a statement from Sally Duffy that states her husband has been at home all night for the last month or so. I asked her if she's a light or heavy sleeper and she informed me she takes sleeping meds. She said, she goes to sleep around nine and sleeps through until seven like clockwork. Often she wakes to find her husband has already left for work."* Kane let out a long breath. *"His alibi wouldn't hold up in court. Did you get anything else?"*

Jenna stared through the one-way mirror at Duffy. "He had a problem with his grandma and she conveniently fell down a well when he was staying there as a ten-year-old."

*"That's not enough to charge him, but enough to make him one for us to watch."* Kane sighed. *"Try and get another look at that book he was referring to. If we know who he is working for next, we'll keep an eye on them."*

Trying to think up an excuse to make legal copies of the man's workbook, Jenna nodded absently. "Okay. I'll see what I can do." She disconnected and went back inside the room.

After pressing the record button on the video device, she

lifted Duffy's workbook from the table. She gave the time and people present again and smiled at Duffy. "Once I have a copy of your workbook, from the time you started work for Mrs. Wagner, you'll be free to go. Do I have your permission to make a copy of the last few entries?"

"Yeah, sure." Duffy lifted his chin and his mouth curled into a smile. "Sally told you I'd been home, right?"

Trying not to display her thoughts, Jenna pushed the statement book across the desk to him. "I'll go and make copies. If you'll write down when you last saw the victims and add your permission for me to make a copy of your workbook and sign it, you'll be able to get back to work." She glanced at Jo. "Agent Wells will be able to assist you."

"Anything to oblige." Duffy pulled the statement book toward him and took the pen Jenna handed him.

Jenna flashed her card across the scanner and went outside the door. She dropped the book on the small table under the two-way mirror and thumbed through the pages. Using her phone, she copied every page of the book from the week before Agnes Wagner's death right through to his future appointments. It didn't take her long. She smiled to herself. "If you are our killer, Mr. Duffy, you've just made your first mistake."

# THIRTY-TWO

It had been an interesting day and they sat in the truck gathering their thoughts, noting how the glass doors of the sheriff's office sparkled, with not a speck of dirt anywhere. They guessed that having a derogatory message scrawled across the front for all to see was more than the sheriff could stand. It was amusing to know the FBI had become involved and the great Sheriff Alton wasn't coping with the case. Calling in the FBI would be a last resort. This scrap of information confirmed that they already held the winning hand. Their string of perfect crimes was driving the sheriff insane. They'd left no clues and had an advantage that the FBI and sheriff hadn't considered, and yet it was right under their noses.

Achieving success at murder came down to intelligence because it didn't take a genius to plan a murder or to avoid leaving evidence behind. Everything they needed to avoid detection they could purchase at the general store, and those generic items were untraceable. Selecting the next person to die was a little more complicated and hinged on if the sheriff arrested Zac Rio for murder. If she did, it would be time to cut and run. They'd be free to find another small town, set in the forest with an old ladies' quilting circle. It would be game on and they'd have so many old biddies to choose from. So many all alone and living in isolated areas just made for them to exact their own special justice.

Ideas pooled inside their head, the concepts so sweet they rolled around like a piece of candy, each idea landing on a taste bud and spiraling into a macabre delight. Nothing came close to seeing the sudden realization on the old women's faces that something was terribly wrong. The uncertainty in their eyes and the questions all delivered with a harsh tone as if they were kids for them to discipline. So, they'd turn the tables on them and laugh and call them useless, or weak, and stupid. In fact, they were all these things. It had been all over the news to keep their doors locked, and yet they'd opened them without question. After waving them inside, they'd offered them refreshment. The houses always had the same smell. The musty odor that unlocked the memories and triggered the anger, but once inside, they'd had to be patient. The old women would leave them to shuffle around the kitchen and that time was all they needed to prepare. When the women returned, the fun began and the plan would unfold just as it had in their minds.

After, blood-soaked like a wild cat after its first kill, satisfaction had filled them, but like the finest steak dinner, who could stop at one? They wanted more from the quilting circle to be afraid—and needed more to suffer—for every darn terrifying second they'd spent locked inside the dark closet with the spiders—and for every meal they'd missed. Could they stop when they'd taught the last old lady on the list a lesson? No, they'd just gotten started and next they'd remove everyone who'd stood by during their punishment and said nothing—and that list was endless.

It was fun watching Sheriff Alton running in circles, and she'd ride that carousel forever before finding them. People from every walk of life interacted with the quilting circle and up to now, the sheriff had only skimmed the surface. Many Black Rock Falls residents lived alone, and in isolated areas. They figured only one in three could possibly have a suitable alibi for the nights of the murders. A word here, and a push in the right direction there, and the sheriff would find herself with a list of possible suspects a mile long.

They smiled to themselves. They'd achieved the perfect crime and wanted to sit and gloat but, of course, someone had to spoil the moment. One of the quilting circle ladies waddled past, basket filled with groceries and smiled at them. They waved back, gritting their teeth to fight the rising need to spring from the truck and sink a knife deep into her neck. They sucked in deep mountain-fresh breaths and calmed the rage. They must stick to the plan, even as the need to kill became intolerable. Being in control and selecting the women who'd had many visitors to their homes was the charm. In this way they spread the risk of discovery. Sheriff Alton didn't stand a chance. Their superior intelligence could outwit her time and time again.

# THIRTY-THREE

Kane high-fived Carter as they headed back to the Beast and grinned. "Oh, you did the best, concerned expression I've ever seen. You had that woman eating out of your hand."

"Well, Mrs. Duffy's pupils were a little dilated." Carter tossed a toothpick into his mouth. "I figured she was on some type of tranquilizers, and most who take them rely on sleeping meds as well." He swung into the truck and stared at him. "It's just looking for the signs."

Snorting with laughter, Kane slid behind the wheel and glanced at the dogs in the back seat. "Man, you could charm the skin off a bear." He patted Duke. "I'll drop the statement into the office but Duke needs to stretch his legs. He's been cooped up for hours."

"Sure, I took Zorro for a run earlier." Carter shrugged. "I'll check with Kalo and see if he's hunted down any more info on the suspects. I asked him to run them through every database he could think of, so if they're dirty, he'd find out all the details."

"Ask him about service records as well." Kane scratched his chin, thinking. "The Ka-Bar knife found at the scene looked like government issue to me. If not from the killer, it had to come from a close family member. It's not the type of knife I usually see carried in these parts; regular hunting knifes are more popular. Although, people can buy anything online these days."

He walked into the sheriff's office and went to the front desk to wait to speak to Maggie. As Carter moved past him, with Zorro sticking to him like glue, he smiled at him. "Tell Jenna I'll be back soon."

"Sure." Carter stopped walking. "I'm heading down to Antlers for a steak tonight with Jo. You coming?"

The thought of an Antlers house special filled Kane's mind and he groaned. "A steak sounds tempting but I'll need to head on home and tend the horses." He glanced back around, but Maggie was still speaking with someone.

"Do you want something, Dave?" Poppy leaned on the desk and smiled at him.

Kane smiled back at her. "Ah, no, I need Maggie to file this statement as soon as possible and get a copy into the murder book."

To his relief, the man speaking to Maggie turned to leave. He pushed the statement across the counter to her. "This is crucial evidence. Can you get this into everyone's files ASAP?"

"I sure can." Maggie took the paperwork and sat at her desk.

"Thanks." Kane turned away. "I gotta go walk Duke." He headed for the door.

"I'll come with you. Wait a second, I need to tell Maggie I'm leaving." Poppy turned away but soon caught up with him outside on the steps. "I was hoping we'd be able to talk but you've been so busy all day."

The last thing he needed was Poppy for company. Her constant chatter ground at his nerves, especially when he wanted to take the time walking Duke to think through the current caseload. He glanced at Poppy. He had to admit she couldn't have arrived at a worse time. "Talk about what?"

"I want to look over some old case files with you." Poppy

bounced along beside him, her face animated. "We could work in my hotel room. The mayor arranged a suite. It's very comfortable and there's room service... or we could wait until I move into my apartment. That would be cozy, wouldn't it?" She slipped her hand through his arm and pulled him to a stop and leaned into him. "I could learn so much from you, Dave."

Annoyed by her flirting, Kane shook her hand from his arm. "I'm sure you could learn from being here if you took the time to study the files. Right now, we're on duty and I'm your superior. So the first lesson is to start acting like a deputy." He patted his leg to get Duke's attention, walked to the curb, looked both ways, crossed Main, and walked into the park. "There you go, Duke. Run around and have fun."

He grinned when Duke looked at him, sniffed the grass, sneezed, and then waddled off at a snail's pace. He heard Poppy behind him and followed Duke, plastic poop bag in hand.

"Was it something I said?" Poppy fell into step beside him. "I thought we had a connection. I was so excited about starting work I didn't even unpack. I flew here ready to join the team." She tugged at his arm again. "Aren't you pleased to see me? I mean you seemed friendly enough at the convention. You did take my phone number."

"Because you insisted." Kane snorted through his nose. "I was being polite is all. It wasn't my intention to encourage you." He turned to look at her. "If I gave that impression, I'm sorry."

"But in Helena, you offered to buy me a meal." Poppy looked abashed. "What was I to think?"

"I have no idea." Kane rubbed the back of his neck. "I don't have a clue what's going on inside your mind. The lunch we had together years ago wasn't a date. It was two people sharing a table is all." He tipped back his black Stetson. "When I first met you, I'd just lost someone special to me. Maybe you noticed a vulnerability in me you wanted to exploit."

"Exploit!" Poppy rounded on him. "Really?"

Dumbfounded, Kane shook his head and followed Duke. "Uh-huh."

"Don't you dare walk away from me." She ran after him tearing the elastic band from her hair. "Why did you think I came here?"

*This is getting way out of hand.* Kane whistled Duke and turned his combat face on her. "I figured to learn about profiling. That's the only offer on the table right now." He walked away, leaving her staring after him.

He hated arguing with people, it was something he avoided like the plague. The idea of hurting Poppy's feelings stung his conscience, but it would only mean avoiding her for a week. He had little doubt, she'd remain in Black Rock Falls or secure the position. He'd keep their misunderstanding to himself and allow Jenna to make the call but after Jo and Carter's assessment of her, Jenna would never trust her and a team without absolute trust was worthless.

# THIRTY-FOUR

Dumbfounded, Poppy stared after Kane. How could she possibly go back to the office now? She turned and walked in the other direction, needing to get her head around what had happened. As she entered the playground, she noticed someone sitting on the carousel. She turned to go and heard him call her name. She looked over one shoulder and frowned. The man had been in the seat beside her on the flight to Black Rock Falls and had offered her a ride into town. They'd chatted and he'd been nice. She smiled at him. "Hey. Fancy meeting you again."

"I was opposite Aunt Betty's Café and noticed the argument with the deputy. Is he the guy you mentioned coming here to be with?" The man stood and pulled up his hoodie against the damp misty air. "He didn't seem too happy to see you."

Poppy shook her head. "I had it all wrong about him. To think I dashed into work without bothering to unpack my things. I was so excited to be here."

"Hero worship, if you ask me." The man shrugged. "Him and the sheriff think they're all that, but the truth is they couldn't catch a real serial killer on their own if they tried. They always call in the FBI. I could murder ten people and they'd never catch me—not that I would. Just sayin'."

Poppy smiled. "You could be right. There are women being murdered and they don't have a clue who is responsible." She looked around the park as the mist swirled around her feet. "What are you doing here?"

"I came to stretch my legs and thought I heard someone crying." He scratched the stubble on his chin. "It could have been a bird or maybe a cat but it played on my mind some. I was on my way to speak to you and the big guy when you started in on each other." He stared into the trees. "I heard it again just before. Has there been any kids going missing today?"

Staring into the darkening woods, Poppy shook her head. "Not that I know about. Where did you first hear it? Maybe we should take a look?"

"Up there a ways. I came down here because of the gate. The kids use it to access the park from a road on the other side of the woods. They ride their bicycles here after school some days." He shrugged. "I was planning on calling the sheriff's office if I heard it again. Being a guy, I didn't want to go into the woods alone, looking for a kid."

Poppy frowned. "What's being a guy got to do with it if someone is in trouble?"

"Oh, come on. This is Black Rock Falls." He snorted. "If I came across a kid in the woods and they started screaming, that deputy you were with would shoot me without a second thought."

"I'm sure he wouldn't." Poppy heard a sound. It could have been a bird but she wasn't taking the chance and turned toward the gate. "I'm going to see if anyone is there. If I find anyone, I'll call it in." She looked at him. "Are you coming?"

"Sure." He smiled at her. "Lead the way."

Poppy went through the gate and the forest enclosed her in dusk, under her feet a pillow of white mist, covered the narrow trail like a white linen tablecloth. As she moved deeper into the forest, she could only make out the night calls of animals. Low-hanging branches caught in her hair as she peered into the darkness. It was so creepy goosebumps rose on her arms. As she edged between trees, cobwebs touched her hair. "Are you sure people use this path? It's covered in cobwebs."

The next moment pain seared through her head and her hair was pulled so hard it tilted her head back exposing her neck. The cold steel of a knife blade touched her exposed flesh and she froze in terror. "What are you doing?"

"Move and you die." The man pressed hard against her and his rancid smell climbed up her nostrils. "Use your thumb and finger and undo your belt. Let it drop to the floor."

Trembling with fear as the sharp blade pressed into her skin and the warm trickle of blood ran down her neck, Poppy complied. "Okay. Why are you doing this? I'll be missed and they'll be out looking for me soon."

"I'm not worried about the sheriff or her deputies. I've been watching them for a long time. I know everything about them. I don't want to hurt you but I will if necessary. Cooperate and you'll be fine." He tugged at her hair again tearing it from the roots. "It makes no difference to me. You are the means to an end and I wasn't expecting you to fall right into my lap. The word is the sheriff will be hunting for new deputies in June. The mayor mentioned it in his speech and the sheriff is asking for women to apply as well as men. I was planning on waiting for a female rookie but you'll do just fine. Having you come along now, was a bonus."

In his type of situation, the only plan was to survive. Trying to control her quivering lips, Poppy stood perfectly still. "Okay. What do you want me to do?"

"You didn't have time to unpack, right? Give me your room key." He held her firmly, the knife pressed against her throat as she dragged out the keycard and handed it to him. "See that was easy, wasn't it? Now I want you to call the Cattleman's Hotel. Tell them you're checking out and to bring your bags down to the foyer, you're sending a cab for them." He tightened his grip on her hair. "Say just that and put your phone on speaker. One wrong word and I'll kill you. Understand?"

Keeping her voice as steady as possible, Poppy made the call. "Okay, now what?"

"Use your phone to send an email to the sheriff's department. Don't send it to anyone in particular, just send it to the general address. Say it was all a big mistake and you're leaving. You've gotten a ride with a truck driver to Colorado. Say that you don't want to be a cop anymore. Tell them you're tossing your phone, so don't bother contacting you. Your mind is made up and you don't want to speak to anyone about it." He chuckled. "That sounds like a woman scorned. After the public display in the park. You've sealed your boyfriend's fate. Show me before you send it."

She frowned not understanding his game. "What do you mean by that?"

"All this... meeting you on the flight. Watching you in the park and when you came over to talk to me. Wow! It was like the planets aligned or something." He chuckled. "Man, I couldn't have planned anything so perfect. It's like I'm dreaming." He tugged at her hair again. "When I'm done, I'll be famous." He laughed. "I wonder what name they'll give me? I hope it's spectacular. Write the email or you'll spoil everything."

If complying meant she stayed alive, she'd do anything. Poppy gripped the phone but her hands shook so hard, she kept making mistakes but finally he was satisfied and she pressed send. Not sure why all this meant something to him and how she'd become entangled in his delusions, she breathed in through her mouth to avoid his stink. "I've done everything you wanted. Now can I go?"

"Nope." He moved her forward still holding her hair. "Lock

your phone and drop it. Pick up your belt and then walk nice and slow that way." He pointed with the knife.

She walked slowly moving through the damp-smelling woods. As the path widened, a gravel-coated clearing emerged with a road leading off between the trees. In the middle sat an old sedan. They walked toward it and the man stopped. "Open the trunk."

Poppy popped the trunk and the smell of oily rags and gasoline wafted over her. "What now?"

"Like I said, we're going for a ride to Colorado." He grinned at her. "You'll love it there and I'll bring you back real soon. You'll find out my endgame soon enough."

Unable to believe the man figured he'd just pranked Sheriff Alton, she rounded on him. "If you think for one second, I'm climbing in there, just for a joke, you're mistaken. I'll scream."

He didn't reply, but the next instant, her head snaped back as a punch smashed into her temple. Pain shot through her eyes, and the world closed in around her in a sea of black.

# THIRTY-FIVE

Jenna waited for Kane to return to the office and then looked over at Carter, who sprawled in a chair opposite. "What did Kalo find on our suspects?"

"Duffy is the most interesting, apart from having no solid alibi, he admitted to living with a crazy grandma." Carter pushed back his Stetson and stretched his long legs. "His attitude in the interview about her death made me curious, and Kalo discovered he'd been bounced from foster parent to foster parent until he was old enough to leave. From what information he could find, most of the people were in their sixties and had more than one foster child. He wasn't a good student but had intelligence and once out of the system put himself through trade school. He is a plumber by trade, but continued his studies over many years."

"I think Jo will agree with me that he is showing psychopathic tendencies." Kane had removed his hat and sat curling the rim with his fingers. "It's a reasonable assumption he pushed his grandmother down the well."

"Maybe." Jo stared at the screen of her tablet. "I did find the overconfidence and attitude a little unusual for someone being questioned about the death of three women. Most people exhibit some form of tension for just being in a room with law enforcement but he volunteered to come in, gave us a statement, refused a legal representative, and admitted to finding some of the old folks intimidating." She shrugged. "We know confinement is an issue with the killer and he mentioned being concerned one of them might try to lock him in a cellar."

Jenna nodded. "Yeah, I figure it's unusual for a fit healthy man carrying a bag of tools to be worried about a frail old lady."

"And we know how many kids suffer trauma being moved from one foster home to another." Kane dropped his hat onto Jenna's desk with a sigh. "Most end up there because of a traumatic incident. It's not surprising they have an attitude against the system or fall into lives of crime when they get out or run away. How many of them end up on the streets? Kids need attention and they sure as hell don't get any in the places I've seen of late. I figure the system needs an overhaul."

Kane bristled with an undercurrent of anger and Jenna raised her eyebrows at him in question. "Well, I admit we have had our share of serial killers who suffered abuse as kids but I'm sure many get through the system just fine." She looked back at Carter. "Okay, so the odds are stacking up against Duffy. Do we have anything but circumstantial evidence against him? We can't arrest him on a hunch. We need physical evidence. Anyone else show up in Kalo's searches?"

"Yeah." Carter moved his toothpick to the corner of his mouth. "Hahn's brother was killed in the line of duty, that would be a connection to the Ka-Bar knife. He lives at Bear Peak, has been working with all the murdered women. I'd keep him on the list as well."

Jenna looked around the room. "Yeah, both these men could be suspects but it seems strange to, as they say, 'cut off their noses to spite their faces.' All these women employed them at one time and, it seems, are in constant need of their assistance."

"Now you're thinking logically." Jo smiled at her. "Psychopaths don't think like we do. If our killer is a contractor, then he sees a constant supply of people who feed his need to kill. He's smart and organized with enough control not to leave clues behind. He planned the murders, from not leaving footprints and the disposal of incriminating clothes right down to setting up Rio for the killings. I figure, if we'd arrested Rio, the murders would stop. Maybe start up in another county or state. Think about it. With him to take the fall, they'd have outsmarted law enforcement, and you know as well as I do that's the prize they seek."

"So maybe you should pretend I'm under arrest." Rio rubbed a hand down his face. "You brought me here in the back of a cruiser. If they'd been watching, they'd believe you'd arrested me."

Jenna shook her head. "You mean make this killer someone else's problem? Allow him to go on a murder spree in another town? No way. We have three people of interest, two are very possible suspects. We are that close." She held her thumb and forefinger an inch apart. "Another thing, with the press hanging around, any hint of you being involved will ruin your career." She looked at Rio. "You may want to leave after the way I treated you, but I did follow protocol. In the circumstances, I had no choice. You must admit, you haven't been acting normal these last few days and then we find you in a pool of blood with a murder victim. In my shoes, would you have handled the situation any differently?"

"Nope. I would have hauled me in as well." Rio gave her a tired smile. "I'm not planning on leaving, believe it or not. Being treated like a killer aside, I like it here."

"That's good, we like you being here too." Jenna closed the folder on the desk. "That's all we can do today. We'll see what the autopsy shows tomorrow. You might as well all head off home. Jake, can you tell Maggie and Deputy Anderson we'll lock up on the way out?"

"Sure." Rowley headed for the door.

"We're heading to Antlers and then Jo wants to video-call Jaime." Carter looked at Rio. "That's Jo's daughter. I'll keep in touch with Kalo but I'm hitting the sack early tonight."

Jenna nodded. "We can't do dinner. We must go feed our horses and I need to wash the stink from the crime scene from my hair. We'll see you in the morning. Breakfast is at six thirty."

"I'll help with the chores in the morning." Carter looked at Kane. "Chores and then a workout before breakfast? I need someone who's a threat to try some moves on. I've been encouraging the local sheriff at Snakeskin Gully to work out with me, but a Seal he ain't." He grinned around his toothpick.

"Sure." Kane grinned. "I can make you suffer."

"You can try." Carter chuckled. He turned to Jo. "Ready?"

"Yeah, see you in the morning." Jo picked up her things and headed for the door.

Jenna stood and went to push the folder into the file cabinet and locked it. She looked at Kane. "Ready to go?"

"Yeah, almost." Kane lifted his hat from her desk, smoothed his already immaculate hair and slid it on.

Concerned by his frown, Jenna leaned against the desk and looked at him. "Is it your head?" She cupped his face and ran her thumb over his cheek. "It must have been hell in the cold water."

"Freezing water and, yeah, it did hurt but I'm fine now." Kane cleared his throat. "It's not that. It's Poppy being here."

Jenna slipped her arms around his waist. "That bad, huh?"

"Yeah." Kane gathered her close. "I read her all wrong. I figured she wanted to further her career but she had an ulterior motive for being here. You were right, Jenna, and I'm sorry for not understanding. You know, I'm kinda set in my ways. I like helping people but she came from left field and slipped under my guard. When I'm out with Carter and get come-ons from women in bars I can shut them down before they get out of hand. Poppy... well I met her when I was just out of rehab and it was nice chatting to someone of like mind over lunch. Maybe she got the wrong impression? You know darn well it meant nothing to me. Not then, so soon after Annie had died. It was a onetime thing—a twenty-minute break between lectures."

Laughter bubbled out and Jenna couldn't stop it. She grinned at him. "I think Poppy needs to go back to Cedar Canyon."

"I think she does too." Kane smiled. "Oh, there's something about an understanding woman that melts my heart."

Grinning, Jenna tried to frown at him, but it didn't work and she giggled. "You caught me on an off day."

# THIRTY-SIX

Jenna headed down the stairs surprised to see Maggie still at the front counter. "You need to be off home. It's getting late."

"Well, I would but I promised to give Deputy Anderson a ride to her hotel." Maggie shrugged. "She mentioned taking a break and went hightailing it out of here when Deputy Kane took Duke for a walk and hasn't returned. Did you send her to do something? She hasn't called in."

"It's strange to need a break this late in the day. It's not as if she's working late on a case." Kane frowned. "Maybe she went to Aunt Betty's?"

"That deputy has been on a break all day." Maggie rolled up her eyes. "Has she ever worked in a sheriff's office before?"

Jenna nodded. "Yeah, out at Cedar Canyon. Why?"

"Nothing I asked her to do has been done." Maggie waved a hand toward the desk usually occupied by semiretired Deputy Walters. "She hasn't touched a thing all day but she was up at the desk quick-smart to chat to anyone who would talk to her."

Jenna pulled out her phone and recalled she hadn't added Poppy to her contacts. "I'll call her." She looked at Kane. "I don't suppose you have her number?"

"Yeah, I do." Kane gave her the number.

Jenna made the call and let it ring until it went to voicemail. She left a message to call her. "She's not picking up."

"I told her to turn off her phone." Maggie frowned. "She had her head down staring at it all day." She pulled a face. "I know for sure I riled her. She held up the screen to show me and said, 'There, are you satisfied now?' She didn't say another word to me until she left."

Concerned, she turned back to Maggie. "Can you stay for a little longer? We'll go and see if we can hunt her down. She's new in town and there's not many places she'd know about, so she's probably close by."

She hurried out the door with Kane and Duke close behind her. "For someone so highly recommended, she acts very irresponsibly."

"She's very immature and acting like a teenager if turning off her phone upset her so much." Kane moved beside her, his eyes scanning in all directions. "Where could she go? Where would *you* go if you were upset?"

Jenna shrugged. "I'd go visit a friend, but she doesn't have a vehicle or any friends in town. The library would be an option, the church. I guess it would depend on how upset I was. If being asked to turn off her phone is a major problem for her, she'll never handle the discipline needed to work on our team."

They walked down Main and peered inside Aunt Betty's. "Wait here and keep looking out for her. I'll go and ask if anyone has seen her." Jenna ducked inside and waved at the manager, Susie Hartwig. "Has our new deputy been in this afternoon?"

"No, I did see her in the park with Dave earlier." Susie's forehead wrinkled into a frown.

"Yeah." Wendy, one of the servers, wiggled her eyebrows. "She was acting weird and following Deputy Kane around waving her arms like she was trying to make a point. He walked off as cool as a cucumber and just left her standing there."

Clearing her throat, Jenna nodded. "Did you see where she went?"

"No, I had customers to attend to." Wendy waved a hand around the crowded diner. "It's been busy like this all day."

"Okay thanks. Give me a call if she shows." Jenna pushed through the door and looked at Kane. "She's not in there. Why didn't you tell me she followed you to the park? I had to hear it from Wendy."

"I handled it." Kane shrugged. "I didn't think it was necessary to tell you."

"Well, it is now. She'll be somewhere cooling her heels." Jenna pushed a hand through her hair. "Where did you last see her?"

"Across there, in the park near the tree line." Kane led the way across the road.

Jenna kept her eyes straight ahead. "Maybe you need to explain what happened to make her so upset she took off?"

"It wasn't that bad." Kane stared at her obviously uncomfortable. "When I went to walk Duke, Poppy insisted on coming with me."

Stomach cramping, Jenna dropped into step beside him and nodded. "Okay."

"I reprimanded her for coming on to me is all and she didn't take it too well. I walked away and left her and she yelled after me but I kept on walking." Kane slid his gaze over her and swallowed. "I didn't tell you because I prefer to deal with situations as they arise."

Inwardly sighing with relief, Jenna nodded. "What did she do? No, don't tell me. I don't want to know. You handled the situation and it's over."

"It might not be over if Wendy and others witnessed it."

Kane let out a long sigh. "It was vocal and unprofessional. Poppy was kinda loud and from the outside it could have been mistaken for a lovers' tiff." He shrugged. "There might be blowback from it."

Shaking her head, Jenna turned to him. "I don't believe for a minute that any of the townsfolk would figure you acted unprofessionally. If she comes to me with a complaint, which I doubt, I'll deal with it."

"As she has a habit for going over people's heads to get what she wants, I figure Poppy would go straight to the mayor." Kane snorted. "She has him tied around her little finger. She's probably in his office right now convincing him to fire me."

Jenna stopped walking and turned to him. "He's never in his office after four, and in any case, it will never happen. POTUS placed you here. Do you honestly believe the mayor has any say in the matter?"

"Nope." Kane stopped to scan the park. "But POTUS might transfer me somewhere else. He doesn't want me in anyone's spotlight." He frowned. "You'd never find me, Jenna."

Huffing out an agitated sigh, Jenna gripped his arm. "But you could find me."

"Unless they sent me overseas." Kane's brow furrowed. "I'm fit for duty. I could be sent anywhere and most of the places wouldn't be safe for you." He sighed. "Best-case scenario, we find Poppy and calm her down."

"Good luck with that." As they walked along peering into the bushes, Jenna turned to Kane. "I'll try calling her again."

She made the call and, in the distance, a ringtone played out a happy tune. "That's coming from the forest. Why would she go in there alone at dusk?"

"I'll go see." Instead of heading for the gate, Kane stepped over the wire fence and walked toward the sound. It stopped and he turned to Jenna. "Call her again."

Jenna watched him, moving through the darkening shadows, fearing the worse. "Have you found her?"

"Nope, just her phone." Kane pulled out surgical gloves from his pocket.

Jenna told Duke to stay and clambered over the fence. She hustled after Kane and stared at the phone lying discarded on a dirt trail. "See if she tried to call someone." She raised her voice. "Poppy, where are you?"

"This can't be good. She'd never leave her phone behind." Kane lifted his attention from the screen and looked at Jenna. "It's locked. Fingerprint-protected I think."

Peering in all directions and seeing nothing but trees, Jenna pulled an evidence bag from her jacket pocket and held it open for him. "If she doesn't show, we'll take it to Wolfe."

"She has to be here somewhere." Kane was scanning the area. "There's no sign of a struggle." He peered into the forest. "The mist is rising, if she's fallen or worse, we'll never see her. I'll go back and get Duke. Her phone will have her scent and he should be able to follow it." He held his hand out for the phone.

Moments later, Kane returned with Duke snuffling along the soft ground. A thick layer of pine needles covered the trail, muffling the sound of their boots. The ground was so springy their footprints vanished after each step. "There's no visible trail to follow." Jenna searched all around, peering between trees and into shadows. "I can't imagine why she came in here."

Mist swirled around her feet with each step closer to the river. Once the sun had dipped in the sky, the mist from the river crept through town in a sea of dampness. As Duke headed through the trees, head down and tail wagging, Jenna followed behind Kane and then stared at a tree alongside a narrow pathway. She snagged a few strands of hair and held them out toward Kane. "Hey, she came this way. This must be some of her hairs. Where is she going?"

"There's a fire road on the other side of these woods and

Duke is heading straight for it." Kane turned to glance at her. "She's new in town. How did she know to go this way?"

Recalling when she first came to Black Rock Falls, Jenna waved a hand toward the clearing opening ahead of them. "I studied the area before I arrived and I'd bet you did as well. If she did, then she'd know the fire road does cut right through to Stanton. She could walk to the Cattleman's Hotel from there.

"It's a long walk and do you figure her phone fell out her pocket?" Kane shrugged. "She could have run through the woods. It's not a nice place for a stroll this late in the afternoon."

Jenna stared all around but only the dead leaves of winter rustled in the light breeze. This deep in the woods spring was a long time coming. "Maybe. Let's keep following Duke even if it's all the way to the Cattleman's Hotel."

When Duke burst out into the clearing, he wandered up and down for a spell and then sat down and barked. Jenna pulled a face. "Hmm, if I'm reading this right. Poppy's trail ended here."

"Yeah." Kane rubbed Duke's ears. "When a trail goes cold on a road or similar, it usually means the person climbed into a vehicle or was carried from the area. She doesn't know anyone in town apart from the mayor. Maybe she called a cab and they arranged to pick her up here? She ran to meet the cab and lost the phone?" He crouched to examine the gravel and then straightening stared into the distance. "I'll call the hotel. She'd be back by now." He made the call and waited for some minutes before raising his eyes to Jenna. "When was that? Did a driver pick up her things? Did you see Deputy Anderson? Okay thanks." He disconnected. "Poppy checked out and had a cab driver pick up her things from the hotel. The driver handed in her key. The room had already been paid up for a week."

Jenna pushed both hands through her hair. "Okay. Well, I guess we'd better head back to the office." She shrugged. "It's too late to go anywhere. If she wanted to leave town, why not wait until the morning?"

"Your guess is as good as mine." Kane led the way back to the park and when they reached the fence, he lifted Duke over. "I figure she did this to have us running around chasing our tails." He held out his hand to her.

Jenna took his hand and he swung her over the fence and followed behind her. She followed Duke's wagging tail back to the office and walked inside. She leaned on the counter and rolled her eyes at Maggie. "It seems like Poppy has hightailed it out of town. How and why, we don't know. She's checked out of the Cattleman's Hotel and there's no buses out this late." She shrugged. "I have no reason to believe she's in any danger, so we'll head on home."

She waited while Maggie shut down the computer and gathered the things she'd left on the counter. "We'll see you in the morning. I'll be here before the autopsy."

"Just one minute." Maggie was frowning at the screen. "You need to read this. I'll print you a copy."

The printer whirred and Maggie stood to pass Jenna a copy of a document. She read the contents of the email and handed it to Kane. "It's from Poppy. She resigned and got a ride with a truck driver heading for Colorado." She shook her head. "How did she ever make deputy? That woman gives irresponsible a whole new meaning."

"Well at least that's one person we don't have to worry about anymore." Kane opened the glass door and ushered Jenna and Maggie outside. He waited for Jenna to lock the door and rubbed his stomach. "I knew we should have gone to Antlers with Carter and Jo. I'm starving."

Jenna pulled open the door to the Beast. "I'll get steaks out of the freezer and have them going before you've finished the chores."

"Ah... no." Kane slid behind the wheel. "I'll get the steaks out and you can come help me with the chores."

Giggling at his serious expression, Jenna fastened her seat belt. "I know you prefer to cook but will you at least allow me to make the salad?"

"Sure." Kane backed the truck out of the parking space and headed down Main. "But leave the dressing to me."

# THIRTY-SEVEN

It was dusk and the time of the evening Harriette Jefferson enjoyed the most. She liked the peace and quiet. By this time most folks had gone home, and in this part of Black Rock Falls, few people ventured out after dark. She sniffed the air and sighed. The rising mist brought with it the scent of leaf mold and damp soil. She wrapped her coat more firmly around her. The smell of ice and snow had almost gone and her daily walk had become a pleasure once more, as spring had arrived in a rush of wildflowers. As soon as the sun slipped over the horizon a new world emerged. The greens and yellows of day became the many shades of blue, black, and gray. It was as if she'd stepped inside a photographic negative, and she embraced the change with wonder. The only points of color came from the wild critters, their eyes, red or orange, peered out from the forest, running here and there trying to avoid the owls in the tall pines waiting to feed on them.

During winter, she'd avoided walking through the wooded area the locals called Wishing Well Park because slipping and breaking a hip wasn't an option. The last three weeks, she'd taken the bus into town, met with friends, or went to the library but always walked back along Stanton and took the shortcut through Wishing Well Park on the way home. The trees surrounding the park had unusual twisted boughs and it became a fairy grotto or a witch's lair over Halloween. Often people came from town and decorated it for birthday parties. The old well had been there for as long as she could remember, but a few years ago someone had encircled it with a brick wall. It now resembled a well from a fairy tale, with a wooden peaked roof and a bucket hanging from a center rung, complete with a handle. Nobody drank from the well but many tossed coins into the water and made a wish.

The sun had dropped low in the sky, and as she reached the end of Stanton, the houses became scarce. The open spaces between them were filled with bushes and natural alleyways. She heard a bus slow with a screech of brakes and a sigh to stop some ways behind her, and then it drove past, lights inside blazing. The disgusting smell of exhaust filled her nostrils. She moved slower now, the last part of her walk so exhausting she wondered how much longer she could walk this far. Old age was slowing her down and maybe tomorrow she'd stay home. It wouldn't hurt to miss her walk for one day. After all, she had walked around town but then she had eaten a large piece of pie at Aunt Betty's Café. Shaking her head, she pressed on.

Behind her, footsteps tapped on the sidewalk and she turned to look. The mist had risen to her knees and long shadows spilled from the forest and stretched across the road, making it hard to see. She blinked and listened but the footsteps had vanished. Turning back around, she ambled on toward the park, her mind fixed on making dinner for one and eating it in front of the TV. The *click, click, scrape, click* of footsteps came again. They seemed in a hurry and the temptation to look around to see who was behind her made Harriette stop again. She turned slowly and peered into the swirling mist but nobody was there. A shiver ran down her spine. Halloween was months ago, and in all her years of walking home, she'd never seen a ghost or anything spooky along this road. Maybe it was her imagination playing tricks on her or perhaps it was the trees moaning. They had been frozen for so long it would be reasonable to believe they'd creak and crackle as they thawed. She moved off again and had reached the park when the footsteps came again, running this time. Alarmed, she hurried toward the well. The footsteps pounded behind her, getting louder by the second. All the hairs on her skin stood to attention as a low chuckle came from just behind her. Spinning around, she stared at a masked figure, coming toward her flexing a long cord between gloved hands.

Harriette flung her handbag at them and staggered backward. She opened her mouth to scream but a strange breathless *woo woo* came out. Horrified, she stared into a hideous face and froze in fear. Her fingers trembled as she searched her pocket for her rosary beads and held them in front of her, mumbling a prayer. The monster lunged toward her and something squeezed and then cut deep into her throat. Unable to breathe she clawed at her neck, pleading with her eyes to make them stop.

"Are you praying for mercy? I've never forgotten what you did to me, and only God can forgive you for what you've done." Black pools of emptiness in the mask stared at her.

Unable to form words as pain shot through her head, she could only stare as the edges of her vision dissolved. Spots danced before her eyes and her sight faded to black. Her knees gave way and she hit the ground. Above her the chuckles increased to laughter. She'd heard once that the last sense to remain before a person died was their hearing but it was too late to tell anyone touch remained as well. Hot breath brushed her ear.

"Did I scare you? Did it hurt? Good. Now you know how it feels."

# THIRTY-EIGHT

## FRIDAY

Kane slapped his stallion's rump and watched him canter across the green grass. The three horses ran together, manes flying as they circled the fence, and then all rolled one after the other, legs flailing in the air. He loved to see them like this, out in the open, running and frolicking. Having them and Duke had created a part of life he hadn't enjoyed before. He'd cared for horses and dogs during his lifetime but never owned them. He'd ridden horses since he was old enough to sit on one and it had been an advantage many a time. Heck, he could even ride a camel. He heard footsteps on the gravel and turned as Carter emerged from the barn. He'd been surprised to see him show at five to help with the chores. Carter was a cowboy born and bred, which made having him around very useful, and Jo could cook, which meant, when they stayed over, Carter helped with the chores and Jo cooked breakfast. He checked the gate and then turned to greet him. "Thanks for the help."

"I'd like to own a horse but being away for days on end makes life difficult." Carter patted Zorro's head. "I'm content with Zorro, and if the need arises, I can always hire a horse from the local stables." He smiled. "I'm nice and warmed up and looking forward to that heavy workout you promised me. How did you feel after the dunking I gave you?"

Kane grinned at him. "Fine. I enjoyed it... well apart from the freezing water." He headed toward the house. "Jenna is a good workout partner but a couple of times a week I go down to Rowley's dojo for a tough workout."

"I know what you mean." Carter walked beside him stride for stride. "I've encouraged Jo to work out daily now. She learns really fast but I'm worried about hurting her. Not that she's fragile but you understand. One misplaced hit and people die."

Nodding, Kane followed him inside the house and, leaving the dogs outside to run, they moved silently down the hallway. They took the door to what was once the cellar but now held an extensive gym, with a separate room containing a hot tub. Working with Jenna's extension plans, they'd used the space below the footprint of the house to their advantage. Inside the gym, Kane stripped off his boots, sweatpants and sweater. He wore his workout gear underneath and so did Carter. He moved onto the mat. "Ready?"

Kane stood relaxed, hands at his sides watching Carter. In a fight he never struck the first blow unless he was in a combat situation. This wasn't the first time he'd worked out with Carter but before it was just the usual bag work and weights. This time it was different. Was Carter like him or was he a brawler? One thing was for darn sure, there were no rules and, as Carter had asked for no mercy, he wouldn't offer him any. He took in the man before him. Carter stood over six feet with a muscular build. He was also his junior by about five years. As a Seal, he'd be well trained in unarmed combat, and it had been some years since Kane had encountered a man of his ability in a fight. He'd figured Carter wanted to let off some steam after being holed up in Snakeskin Gully over winter. They stood staring at each other motionless, both waiting for the other to make a move.

Kane grinned. "Well, this is fun. You planning on just staring at me all morning?"

Moving like lightning Carter tried to sweep Kane's legs away but he jumped just before the kick to the side of his knee landed, and twirled to land a solid kick to Carter's back. The hit would normally flatten a man, but Carter rolled across the mat and sprung to his feet with ease. Then he danced around like an annoying mosquito, ducking and weaving with short jabs. Kane lifted his head just in time to avoid a headbutt. He didn't plan on hurting Carter, but his friend wasn't holding back. After a jab to his ribs, Kane used one arm to lift Carter and toss him across the room.

"Is that all you've got?" Carter rolled and grinned at him and then stretched out one cupped hand and wiggled his fingers. "Come on, old man, turn on the machine that Jenna is always crowing about—or is that talk to scare the townsfolk?"

Shaking his head but grinning back, Kane shrugged. "You'll be sorry. First blood and we stop. Agreed?"

"Deal." Carter moved to the right and started to circle Kane slowly. "But it will be yours. I don't bleed so easy and you have to catch me first."

Kane stood his ground waiting for Carter to attack. It was easy enough to bat away his punches, but a few that landed stung a bit. Carter was tough and he gave him a taste of his strength with a short fast jab to the shoulder. He smiled as the pain registered on Carter's face. He pulled back. It was just a workout, not a fight, although he could see the change in his opponent's eyes. Carter sure wasn't playing around now and tried a few times, with some impressive kicks, to knock him off his feet. It was never going to happen.

"Okay." Carter danced away shaking his head. "I've only met one other as good as you and he died when H Team went on a mission." He eyed Kane speculatively. "You know the drill and he never said a word to me about his team. None of us did about where or what we were doing, but I'd heard a whisper that not one of them returned. Legend says they made black ops look like kindergarten. When I left it was like, 'Mention the team and you die.' Those guys were taken away and conditioned. They returned like robots. I knew two who were selected. Well, I assume they were because they vanished from our team in the night. I saw one of them during a furlough between tours and he, like I said, was a robot." He moved around Kane with an inquisitive smile. "Just like you."

The detective in Carter was working overtime and Kane had to trust his integrity as a Seal would be good enough to stop this dangerous talk. Moving around to keep him in sight, he gave a shake of his head. "We've both been in the service and some things we don't discuss. People's lives may depend on it. So if I did know what the hell you were talking about, I wouldn't be able to say anything—would I?"

"Maybe not but I sure miss my team. They were like my brothers." Carter aimed a punch and missed. "I feel the same when I'm working here. The team Jenna has collected is professional... well apart from Poppy Anderson." He grinned.

Kane took a solid kick to the thigh and shook his head. "She's already gone. Packed up and hightailed it to Colorado." He sighed. "Now are we gonna talk all day or get down to business. It's like fighting a pesky fly."

"Really? Says the guy standing like a statue." Carter grinned. "Hit me, I won't break."

Kane shrugged. "You might."

Behind him, Kane could hear the door open and the smell of honeysuckle. Jenna had walked into the room. He didn't turn to look at her but kept his attention fixed on Carter. He had to admit Carter was fast and was coming in hot. Ducking and weaving to avoid the blows, Kane gave him a taste of the machine. One blow to the gut and a palm to the nose had Carter on the mat, dripping blood.

"What are you doing, Dave?" Jenna flew across the mat with a towel and handed it to Carter. "Are you okay, Ty?" She gave Kane a glare. "What is going on here?"

"It's my fault." Carter gave her a bloody smile. "I told him to turn on the machine. Holy cow, I figured you were exaggerating."

"Have you lost your mind?" Jenna stared down at Carter, her face incredulous. "I told you yesterday that Dave was a weapon. I wasn't making it up. I've seen him take down a group of guys and none of them got up again."

"Don't blame Dave. It's my stupid fault. I asked him for no mercy." Carter moved and let out a low moan. "I think my ribs are broken."

"How could you?" Jenna's eyes flashed with dismay. "Ty's your friend. It's all well and good to train, but fighting? Are you crazy?"

"It's something I've done in training many times." Carter smiled at her. "It shows we can fight anyone, friend or foe."

"That's great and if you get hurt, I'm another man down on the team." Jenna shook her head. "I guess I'd better call the paramedics."

Kane rolled his eyes. "His ribs aren't broken. If I'd hit him hard, I'd have broken his spine." He held out his hand and pulled Carter to his feet. "You'll be fine. I wasn't trying to hurt you, just keeping out of the way. You fight well. We'll have to train together tomorrow if you're up to it. I'd like you to show me some of your moves and I'll do the same. I don't figure brawling for first blood is a good idea. When I fight, I tend to hurt people." He shrugged. "Sorry."

"Are you sure there isn't metal under your skin?" Carter pinched his nose. "Or I must be getting soft." He winked at Kane. "It's just as well we're on the same team."

Kane snorted and slapped him on the back. "No metal. It seems I was born this way. That and training hard daily to keep my muscle strength is all I need—well, apart from food. I eat a ton of food a day." He turned to the punching bag and landed a few hard hits, sending the bag swinging. "I'll keep going. I need an hour a day minimum and if we're planning on getting into the office on time, I'll need to cut it short."

"I'm done here." Carter gathered his clothes and nodded to Jenna as he headed out the door. "Take your time, I'll be back soon to help Jo with breakfast."

"What is it about my cooking that makes everyone want to jump in and take over?" Jenna took a firm grip of the punching bag and looked at Kane.

Kane smiled at her and punched the bag. "Oh, I don't know. I guess not everyone has my love of burned toast."

# THIRTY-NINE

Jenna went through her exercise routine with Kane, concerned about what had happened between Kane and Carter. "You're skating real close to the edge with Ty. I figure he already suspects you're special forces."

"If he hadn't informed us about his background, I'd have picked him at the get-go for a Seal, same with you, Jenna. I knew by the way you moved and acted you had special training." Kane smiled. "Observation is what keeps us alive. Ty is solid or the best liar I've ever met. I'm not giving him any information but he can see me for what I am. A deputy in a small town wouldn't have the same skill set."

"Just be careful." Jenna's mind kept moving to Poppy. The woman had made such a fast exit it troubled her. She wiped the perspiration from her face with a towel and turned to Kane. "I'll follow up on Poppy today. I want to make sure she's okay. The first thing I'd do is replace my phone. She's likely got a plan with someone. So she'd get a new phone and SIM from the same company. We have the phone. Maybe Wolfe or Kalo will be able to help."

"Yeah, and she'll keep the same number." Kane shrugged.

"Most people do. It's a pain notifying everyone about a new number. Once the phone is unlocked, we should be able to discover what company she's with." He wiped down the weight bench and straightened. "But if she's gone off the grid to soak her head for a time, she might not return your calls."

Jenna collected the soiled towels and opened the door. "Well at least I'll have tried. I'll pop these in the wash and go take a shower."

She'd just finished dressing when her phone chimed. It was Wolfe. "Morning, Shane."

*"I've moved the autopsy back to the normal time. Emily is here. She doesn't have classes until this afternoon, so I'll see you at ten?"*

As she headed for the kitchen the smell of bacon and coffee greeted her and her stomach rumbled in appreciation. "Sure. We'll be there. We had a new deputy for a few hours yesterday. She took off and left her phone behind. I figure she dropped it. It's password protected. Can you get into it? I need to find her... well not find her, she resigned by email and said she was heading for Colorado but I'd like to check she's okay."

*"She'll pick up a new phone and SIM. Give her a day or so and call her number. My girls have lost phones and they never change their numbers."* Wolfe cleared his throat. *"Unless you figure she's been involved in a crime or is in mortal danger, I can't access her phone. You know as well as I do you'd need a search warrant to do that and you don't have the grounds to request one—not for a person resigning and losing their phone."*

Jenna shook her head. She didn't need to be reminded of the law but her concern had outweighed her judgment in this instance. "Of course, you're right. I'll give her a few days to cool down and try her number. We'll see you at ten."

*"I'll see you then."* Wolfe disconnected.

Taking a plate from Jo as she walked into the kitchen, she

smiled at her. "Thank you so much for cooking breakfast. I feel very spoiled, chores done and breakfast cooked."

"You can clean the table and stack the dishwasher." Carter looked up from his plate.

Sitting beside Kane she nodded. "That's fine."

"Please don't tell me that was Rowley calling with a 911 emergency for us to deal with this morning?" Kane cut into his pancakes. "If it is, can you ask him and Rio to handle it?"

Shaking her head, Jenna poured syrup over her pancakes. "It was Wolfe. The autopsy is at ten. He moved it so Emily could be there. She doesn't have classes this morning."

"So, nobody has died overnight?" Carter gave Jo a meaningful stare. "That's torn my theory to shreds." He nibbled at a strip of crispy bacon. "I figured the killer had lost control. The Flora Carson murder was messy... almost unfinished, as if setting up Rio was more difficult than they imagined. I thought maybe, as it didn't go to plan, they'd strike again as in a thrill kill random attack."

Jenna stared at him. "Really? They seem to be way too organized to risk a thrill kill."

"We discussed the case over dinner last night." Jo sat down and sipped her coffee. "I figured from the MO—as I'm convinced this is the same killer—that they had entered a heightened stage of frenzy. The need to kill is starting to overcome their judgment and they're getting reckless. At first, I thought this was the work of an organized psychopath... the reason being, the planning of each kill is meticulous. They leave no clues and use a variety of MOs that show a ton of thought, but unless the killer has a long-time plan, it's unusual for psychopaths of this type to kill so frequently."

"Everything about this case is unusual." Kane shook his head. "But these murders are linked and the differences is a deliberate ploy to mislead us. That's a mistake on their part as we've had many serial killers murder in a variety of ways. This isn't unusual at all. I know the minds of psychopaths are varied. Some kill the same way over and over, messy at first and then refining their art, but I've seen others consciously change their MO to outwit investigators. The thing is, most of them are super smart. The few who are completely out of control are usually caught because they make mistakes. So far this killer might as well have a degree in forensics. They know how to leave the scene and the victim without a trace of evidence."

Jenna pushed her plate away and reached for her coffee. "Yeah, and we have three possible suspects and circumstantial evidence at best. I can't even drag one of them in for questioning, I don't have any just reason. They all could be carrying on doing their usual jobs or one of them is a killer. There has to be a clue we're missing."

"The one I lean toward is Trey Duffy." Jo pushed the bacon platter toward Kane. "He has a suitable background that could trigger an episode and openly admits the old women scare him. This could be his excuse for killing them. They all have an excuse. I remember interviewing a killer who'd murdered his mother and her sister because they constantly belittled him. They drove him crazy with their constant chatter, so he beheaded them and then performed unspeakable acts on them... but he never killed again and handed himself in to the cops." She leaned back in her chair. "His excuse was they drove him crazy. Another, who worked for the mob, told me he killed because he was a contract killer, that it was just a job. When I asked him why he shot three kids in a truck, he told me they disrespected him... They all have an excuse."

"It is probably him." Kane pushed the strips of bacon onto his plate. "He could have had access to a military-issue Ka-Bar knife as well." He chewed slowly. "My problem is, why leave something with a connection to him behind, in an attempt to incriminate Rio? This goes against the organized psychopath theory."

Jenna sighed, stood, and collected the plates. "Maybe we leave a cruiser across the road from his house for a few days." She looked at Kane. "We could set up a camera inside and watch him to see if he leaves the premises?"

"Yeah, we can do that without a court order." Kane smiled. "We're just watching the road if it's not trained on his house."

As she packed the dishwasher, Jenna laughed. "That's one plan of action but we need a ton more if we're going to catch this guy before someone else dies."

# FORTY

At the office, Jenna called everyone for a meeting. She glanced around the room and noticed Rio missing again. "Where's Rio?"

"He called in." Rowley swiped at the tip of his nose. "Cade took off from school yesterday. Rio had to go in and speak to the principal. He should be back soon."

Jenna shook her head. "What is wrong with that kid?"

"Women." Carter smiled knowingly. "It's spring when young men's thoughts go to girls and baseball. I figure with two on his mind, school is the least of his concern. Now that he hasn't got a truck to go visit them, when they show up, he is blind to everything else."

"Oh, wonderful. You do know one of them is a buckle bunny?" Jenna pushed a hand through her hair. "And how long does this phase of a teenager's life last?"

"I don't know. Until summer, I guess, or until the right woman comes along." Carter grinned. "It's not just teenagers. It takes everything I've got to keep my mind on working a case right now."

"Oh, for goodness' sake." Jo glared at him. "You've never

mentioned baseball once." She turned to Kane. "What about you?"

"I love baseball but my mind is on the case." Kane opened his laptop. "Anything else come through from Kalo?"

"Nope." Carter peered at his screen. "If he finds anything, he'll call."

Collecting her thoughts, Jenna cleared her throat. "Okay, Kane, can you fit the old cruiser in the parking lot out back with a surveillance camera? Rowley, when Rio gets back, park the vehicle a short way from Trey Duffy's house. If you leave it opposite the intersection, it would be just about right."

"I figure you'll want to make sure the footage picks up his comings and goings." Rowley frowned. "Isn't that a little obvious? If you catch him doing anything, he'll challenge the illegal surveillance in court."

Jenna nodded. "Do you recall the two fender benders we had on that intersection just last month? I figured we needed to see how many run the stop sign. If there are a few over the next week, we'll ask the mayor to put in traffic lights." She raised both eyebrows at him. "That's what my daybook will read. If he just happens to show up on the footage, we can use it, and either way, it could save lives."

"Sometimes saving lives takes a little thought." Carter tossed a toothpick into his mouth and smiled around it. "That crossroads could be deadly."

A knock came on the door. Jenna looked up. "Come in." The door opened slowly and Rio poked his head around. "Oh good. Sit down. Is everything okay at home?"

"Not really, no." Rio removed his hat and ran a hand through his hair. "Cade's girlfriends were at the house when I got home yesterday. Kara had helped herself to my beer and I found her sorting through papers in my office. When I asked her what the hell she was doing, she took Cade and left with her sister. At least Cade was driving, and after what I'd been through, I was over chasing after him. He came back this morning and caught the bus to school. He refused a ride. When I spoke to the principal, I discovered Kara is always hanging around but has the excuse she's waiting for her sister." He shrugged. "I'm out of options. If I push too hard, Cade will move in with Kara and I'll lose him altogether."

Frowning, Jenna lifted her chin. "You can stop her from entering your house, but at seventeen, Cade is going to be a problem. I have no experience in raising teenagers, but unless he is breaking the law, maybe stepping back might work?"

"Until he turns eighteen and gets his inheritance?" Rio's expression soured. "I've always questioned the idea of releasing that much money to a kid. At twenty-one, he might have developed some brains when it comes to women."

"Are you his legal guardian until he turns eighteen?" Jo narrowed her gaze. "If so, you're in control of his property."

"Yeah, my parents mentioned it in the will but their grandma insisted on caring for them." Rio sighed. "At the time it was the best choice as I was working and living in a tiny apartment. The estate took a time to go through probate. My father had some outstanding bills, and being a plane crash, it was ages before the insurance came through. It wasn't until the twins took off that I discovered they were miserable."

"Okay." Jo smiled at him. "Who was executor of the will?"

"Me." Rio raised one dark eyebrow. "Why?"

"I gather you set up a trust fund for the twins?" Jo's eyes sparkled. "You would have included a provision to have the funds released according to your parents' wishes?"

"To the letter." Rio rubbed the back of his neck. "What are you getting at, Jo?"

"As their guardian, you have control over their money until they turn eighteen. So go and change the trust fund release date to until they turn twenty-one." Jo shrugged. "Seems to me you have more than a valid reason as Cade is acting irresponsibly, but you don't need a reason. If he challenges your decision when he turns eighteen, he won't have the finances to take it to court. In the circumstances, it would be my choice of action. When it's done, tell him and see how long his buckle bunny sticks around when she discovers it's a three-year wait before she can get her hands on his inheritance."

"Okay." Rio relaxed into the chair. "I'll get at it, when I'm free."

Jenna looked at Rio. "Make the appointment and go do it ASAP. We can work around you."

"Thanks." Rio blew out a long breath. "Why didn't I think of that?"

Rubbing her temples, Jenna dragged her mind back to the case. "We have an autopsy at ten." Her gaze moved over her deputies. "You have your orders, make it happen. Rowley, go help Kane set up the camera, and Rio, make the call." She waved them away.

She turned to scrutinize the whiteboard, trying to wring out one drop of useful information, when her desk phone rang. Maggie had a call for her from Bret Carson. Assuming Flora's son was asking after the autopsy findings, Jenna sucked in a long breath. "Mr. Carson. How can I help you?"

*"I'm concerned about Mrs. Jefferson, Harriette Jefferson. She's been very upset as we all have over my grandma's murder. I thought I'd drop by to see her this morning and she's not home. I called her and she's not picking up her phone."* He sounded stressed. *"I called some of her friends. I know them because they're the same acquaintances as my grandma's, and she didn't show up at any of their homes. They did see her yesterday. I took the liberty of looking around the house, just in case she'd taken a fall in the backyard. The chickens had no water or food and she loves her chickens. I'm concerned she might be ill inside the house. Or that something happened to her on her way home from town yesterday."*

Glancing at Jo and Carter, Jenna stood. "What makes you think something might have happened to her on her way home?"

*"She walks home every day from town as part of her exercise routine. She's always telling people about how her doctor insists she walks every day. So she does it Monday to Friday like clockwork. You can set your clock by her. The problem is, at this end of Stanton, the houses are spaced wide apart. Some four or five acres between. After what happened to my grandma, well, I'm worried about her."* Bret Carson let out a long breath. *"Could you drop by her house and check on her please?"*

Picking up a pen, Jenna pulled her notepad toward her. "Okay, give me her details. We'll come by now."

*"Thank you. I'll fix up the chickens and wait for you."* Carson disconnected.

In a few words, Jenna brought Jo and Carter up to date. "I'll need the keys to my cruiser."

"We'll come." Carter jumped to his feet, the action making Zorro stand and stretch luxuriously and stare at him. Carter glanced at Jo. "Right?"

"Yeah, we'll come." Jo gathered her things. "I'm out of ideas. I'm hoping Flora Carson's autopsy will give us something to go on."

Jenna nodded. "I'm hoping that too, we sure need a breakthrough in this case. Wolfe is the best, and if there's a clue to the killer, he'll find it."

# FORTY-ONE

As they made their way down the steps, Jenna noticed Maggie speaking to a boy wearing a hoodie. She was taking down his details and praising him for coming into the office. When she handed him a note, the boy scampered out the door, climbed on his bicycle, and rode away. Jenna walked to the counter. "I'm heading out to hunt down Harriette Jefferson. Let Kane know where I've gone when he comes in. The details are in my daybook."

"Harriette Jefferson?" Maggie's eyes widened. "You don't say? That boy just handed in her purse. He found it in Wishing Well Park on Stanton near the well." She looked from one to the other. "Oh, Lord, I didn't wear gloves. I just figured I'd look for ID and drop it into the lost and found."

*This is too much of a coincidence.* Jenna stared after the boy, making a mental note of his description, not that she could see his face. He could be any of the local kids. Hidden under ball-caps with hoodies stretched over the top, they all blended into one. *Could he be the same kid who told Rio about Flora Carson?* "Don't worry, we can eliminate the boy's and your fingerprints if needs be, but if it looks intact, chances are she dropped it. You did get his details?"

"I sure did, but he was wearing gloves, so no prints." Maggie indicated to the daybook on the counter. "I wrote him a note as well to explain why he was late for school." She frowned. "I'm not sure I could recognize him again. I wasn't paying too much attention."

"I didn't get much of a look at him either." Jenna pulled on gloves and took the bag from her. "Cash, house keys, and phone. So, it wasn't a purse snatching." She took the keys and dropped the purse on the counter. "Drop that into an evidence bag. I'll go straight to Wishing Well Park and see if there's any sign of her. When Kane comes back send him along. We'll wait for him."

Pulling off her gloves, she followed Carter and Jo to the cruiser. She climbed in the back seat, hoping that nothing had happened to Harriette Jefferson. She gave Carter directions to Wishing Well Park. "It's not in the GPS. It's a local name for a strange little clearing in the woods. People use it most times as a shortcut. It runs across a sweeping bend in the road and takes about ten minutes off the distance if you take the sidewalk."

It didn't take long to reach the grassy stretch beside Stanton and they pulled up beside a well-worn pathway leading into the woods. This area had been part of Stanton Forest before the town council built a road through it, cutting it off and leaving a wooded area with strange twisted trees. Some townsfolk believed the trees objected to being torn away from their families and had become ugly and angry. Although she'd discovered the town council at the time had poisoned the trees, but a rainstorm had soaked the area the same day. The trees had blackened and twisted from the poison. The outcry that followed from the townsfolk when they'd discovered what had happened, prevented any further intervention by the town council. In the eighty years since, the trees had remained a twisted reminder to everyone not to damage the forest.

She stepped out of the cruiser and looked around. "I guess we follow the path. The boy said he found the purse in the clearing near the well."

The three of them fanned out. Jo took the path and Jenna and Carter walked through the grass on either side of her. Zorro stuck to Carter's side like glue, lifting his long fine legs through the spiky grass like a prancing horse. Jenna sniffed, searching for anything unusual. The usual pine fragrance held an underlying damp smell as the forest recovered from the melt, but something else tainted the air. She turned to Carter. "Do you smell anything?"

"Yeah." Carter waved toward the clearing. "The wind is blowing toward us, so it's in that direction."

Scanning back and forth, Jenna searched the ground and found zip. As they moved closer to the dark grotto a shiver of apprehension slid down her spine. The smell was increasing and it was the stink she never forgot. Death lurked close by.

"It smells like something died recently." Jo peered into the gloom. "It's so dark in here." She pulled out her phone and a light lit up the area. "I can't see a body."

Jenna pulled out her Maglite and shone the beam around. Carter was doing the same, walking back and forth staring into the surrounding trees. She turned to him. "What about the well. Maybe she fell down there?"

"I don't figure an old lady could climb up there and jump in." Carter headed for the well and stopped to stare at the ground. "I have drag marks. I'll go in from the other side." He headed through the trees and emerged on the other side of the well. Shining a beam of light into the dark hole, he lifted his head. "She's here."

Jenna pushed her way through the dense undergrowth to his side and peered down the well to see a floating body of a white-haired old lady. "Oh, no." She reached for her phone and called Wolfe. "I'm sorry, the autopsy will have to wait. We have a body down a well. There are drag marks. It's a possible homicide."

*"Give me the details and I'll be right there. Is there room for a truck in there? We'll need to use the winch."*

Jenna swallowed hard. "Yeah, I think so. The well is narrow. I'm not sure how you're going to get her out."

*"Just leave that to me."* Wolfe disconnected.

Jenna inched around the well and bent to take photographs of the scuff marks. She turned to Carter and Jo. "We'll need to search this place all over. Collect and photograph anything you find that might give us a clue who did this. Even a single hair."

"I'm on it." Jo moved to her side. "Look around you. The scene carries many of the same traits we've seen in the other murders. It's an isolated place. I don't figure the victim dropped her purse. It was the only weapon she had and if it were me, I'd have thrown it at the killer, in an attempt to get away. The prolonged fear factor is evident in all the crimes. Here we have the confined space." She pointed to the well. "Look at the drag marks from her heels. To make them without the killer leaving a footprint took skill. The killer kept their feet on the gravel around the well, leaving no trace behind. I seriously doubt we'll find any evidence. This murder, like the others was a very sophisticated well-planned kill."

Jenna heard the Beast rumble to a halt on Stanton and the next moment Duke bounded toward her, the sheriff's department's badge hanging from his collar, reflecting in the sunlight. She smiled. As a tracker dog, Duke had become a valuable part of the team. When Kane came into view, she turned back to Jo. "There's something else." She glanced around and then waved Carter toward them. "Just wait until Dave gets here. I've noticed something significant."

She led them out into the sunshine and met Kane. She gave

him a rundown of what had happened. "Okay. Jo pointed out the connections between the crime scenes and how they link the cases together." She explained Jo's theory. "But there's something else that's waving red flags at me. All these murders happened in isolated places and chances are we wouldn't have found the bodies for weeks, but we did. Why? First, we followed a message that sent us out to Snowberry Way and the murder of Doris Wagner."

"Then Jolene Darvish tells me about the suspicious break-in of her food locker and someone running her off the road." Kane narrowed his gaze. "Both instances would warrant further investigation. The killer would know we'd roll up to Jolene Darvish's cabin to follow up."

Jenna rubbed her arms, suddenly chilled. "Then we had the mud message saying that Rio was involved. We discover a kid on a bike told him that Flora Carson had seen a prowler. A kid no one can identify. She could have already been murdered before Rio arrived."

"It was as if they'd left the mud message as a backup in case Rio didn't call in to tell us where he'd gone—as if they knew he'd left alone to check on Mrs. Carson." Jo frowned. "If you hadn't arrived when you did, Rio would have recovered from the drug. They wanted you to find him, sprawled out on the floor with the knife and body."

Chewing on her bottom lip, Jenna nodded. "Most folks would know that only one of us mans the 911 emergency line overnight. A call for a prowler wouldn't normally be a problem —a drive-by usually, as most times it's people's overactive imagination or tree branches rubbing against houses in the wind." She shrugged. "It has to be a local, with eyes on our usual procedure."

"Yeah, someone is playing us. It's not a coincidence when another kid shows up with the purse of a victim stuffed into a well." Carter scratched his cheek. "Right after you'd received a call from Bret Carson, a supposedly worried neighbor who just happened to show up at his grandma's murder scene—and the person who he claims saw Rio's truck outside can't be questioned because she's down a well. Yeah, it's as if someone is directing traffic. Not many people come here in spring and the smell wouldn't likely reach the houses. She could have been here for a long time before we discovered her body. Did Maggie ask the kid what he was doing here? She has his address as Maple. That's the other end of town, and not his usual route to school, is it? What was he doing here or was he delivering a message from the killer, so we'd find Harriette Jefferson down the well?"

"Which means they're watching us." Kane scanned the area. "And right now, they're one step ahead of us." He turned to Jenna. "When Rowley and Rio get back to the office, maybe send Rowley to drop by the kid's address and find him at the school. If he's not there, we'll know we're being played."

Jenna pulled out her phone. "Sweep the area for evidence. I'll make the call and when Wolfe finishes up here, we'll go and have a nice long chat with Bret Carson."

# FORTY-TWO

Kane ducked out from under the twisted tree branches and went to Jenna's side. "There's nothing, not as much as a footprint. What did Carson say when you called him?"

"Not much. I just told him to wait and we'd be along soon and that we had another call to attend to." Jenna shrugged. "He said he'd keep on calling her friends and would wait for us." She looked up at him. "I know where he lives if he decides to leave."

Pushing the Maglite back inside his pocket, Kane smiled. "He won't move, especially if he's trying to outsmart us. If he is involved, which is possible as he seems to know everyone in the quilting circle, he certainly slipped under our radar." He peered into the clearing. "Wolfe has pulled out the body."

"Let's take a look." Jenna pulled out a face mask and pressed it to her nose. "Oh, that stinks. I'll never get used to the smell."

The body with white wrinkled skin was in an advanced state of decomposition. Surprised, Kane lifted his gaze to Wolfe. "I always believed cold water preserved a body. This looks like it's been here for a lot longer than overnight."

"The water is stagnant and there's the remains of dead critters down there as well. It's a health hazard. I'll report it to the local council. It needs to be filled with cement to prevent the spread of disease." Wolfe met his gaze. "In normal circumstances, yes, you'd be correct, but in putrid water, filled with organisms and bacteria, a body's decomposition is increased." He pointed to the neck. "Ligature marks cutting deep. Strangulation using a cord of some kind and, from the crossed lines, I'd say it happened face to face."

Disgust rolled over Kane and he turned to Jenna. "Up close and personal. The killer wanted to see the victim's fear and feel the life drain out of her. It takes strength to make a sustained mark like that and the killer must keep up the pressure for at least four minutes to ensure their victim dies. That's a long time. Any shorter and the victim regains consciousness."

"If you wanted to make a quick kill and dispose of the body down the well, what would you do?" Jenna pushed a strand of hair behind one ear. "And looking at the scene, they didn't want to stab her. It would have been too messy. They'd have risked leaving evidence behind when they tossed her down the well."

Kane glanced away for a second or two. He disliked being asked how he'd kill someone. That part of his life was over... well, for now at least. "Breaking the neck is the cleanest way to kill, silent and instant." He met Jenna's gaze. "It takes strength and technique. It is also done from behind and that would rob the killer of watching the victim die. I know you're thinking military-issued weapon and now maybe this guy had military training, but none of these kills tell me military."

"Nope." Carter moved to Jenna's side. "What we've seen is inefficient ways of killing. Military is the opposite: a fast kill and move on. What I'm seeing is focused and brutal, for the killer's pleasure."

Nodding, Kane looked at Jenna and shrugged. "I agree. The

strength could come from drugs. Someone on crystal meth often has incredible strength and bursts of unreasonable temper. You need to cast your net over a wide area. This could be any one of our suspects."

"Okay, I'm done here." Wolfe stepped into the circle of people. "I'll do a preliminary back at the lab and put this victim on ice. We'll concentrate on the Flora Carson autopsy today." He looked at Jenna. "If I move it until three, will it fit into your day?"

"Yeah, thanks." Jenna smiled at him. "I have another person of interest to speak to, so that will work out fine. It's a shame Emily will miss the autopsy."

"She'll be back by three, so she'll be able to observe." Wolfe touched his hat. "See you later." He headed for his truck.

"Are you coming with us to interview Bret Carson?" Jenna looked from Carter to Jo and back.

"Yeah, I'd like to observe his body language." Jo turned to Carter. "You?"

"I wouldn't miss it." Carter strolled out into the sunshine. "Lead the way."

When Kane pulled up outside Mrs. Jefferson's neat house. He looked back down the long driveway and wondered why a woman of her age would walk so far each day. It must be three miles from town to her home and yet a sedan sat in a garage next to the house polished and clean. Another vehicle sat in front of the house, a white GMC truck with a man sitting inside. He walked up to the man. "Bret Carson?"

"Yeah." Carson opened the door and climbed out. "What took you so long? Harriette could be in trouble inside."

"We found Mrs. Jefferson." Jenna moved to his side. "I'm afraid she's dead."

"What do you mean?" Carson paled and ran a hand down his face. "What happened to her?"

Observing him closely, Kane flicked a glance at Jo, who was doing the same. "What makes you think something happened to her? She was an old lady. People die of old age."

"After someone murdered Agnes Wagner and then my grandma, not forgetting the horrible death of Mrs. Darvish, what else am I to think?" Carson looked at him wild eyed. "There's a crazy person running around town. You need to stop them."

The fact they'd considered Jolene Darvish's murder a homicide had never been released to the media. Finding her truck at the bottom of the ravine was described as "under investigation" and there'd been no findings in his grandma's murder pending an autopsy. Kane shook his head. "Those are wild accusations. Where did you get this information? The death of Agnes Wagner is still under investigation, the same as the others."

"Are you saying my grandma wasn't murdered?" Carson pushed a hand through his thick brown hair and glared at Kane. "Then why can't I see her? When I called the ME, he told me that I should remember her how she was, not how she looks now. They cut up her face, didn't they? Did they do that to the others too?"

"Mr. Carson." Jenna had a notepad and pen in her hand. "I need you to calm down. Were you home last night?"

"Yes, I'm home most times." Carson's cheeks reddened. "I'm on disability. I was in a wreck and hurt my spine. Why?"

"You mentioned Mrs. Jefferson likes to walk home from town and does so most weeknights." Jenna lifted her pen. "How do you know this?"

"I know because she is a friend of the family and mentioned her doctor told her to walk each day to improve her heart health." Carson stuck out his chin. "I was out walking my dog one evening and saw her walking out of Wishing Well Park. I told her it wasn't safe for her to be walking through there at dusk."

"Do you walk your dog every night around the same time?" Jenna bent her head to make notes.

"I walk him before supper, yes, every night." Carson folded his arms across his chest. "Why?"

"So you'd often see Mrs. Jefferson walking home?" Jenna lifted her gaze to him.

"Sometimes I did, not every night." Carson flicked a gaze to Kane and over Jo and Carter. "Why the interrogation?"

"Well, as she went missing and from your account the chickens haven't been tended, most people would assume she was either inside the house or something had happened to her on the way home." Jenna raised an eyebrow. "As it's obvious the house hasn't suffered a break-in, or one of the doors would be damaged, wouldn't any reasonable person retrace her steps to ensure she wasn't lying somewhere after collapsing or similar? Especially as you were aware she walked home the same way each night."

"I didn't think to." Carson shrugged. "I just called 911."

*To make sure we found her body?* Kane exchanged a look with Jenna. "Okay, Mr. Carson. What can you tell me about Mrs. Jefferson? Is that her vehicle in the garage?"

"It was her husband's. She doesn't drive." Carson glanced at the sedan. "She allows me to drive it to the carwash once a week."

"Do you know her family?" Jenna looked at Carson. "We'll need to notify her next of kin."

"She has none. She never had any kids." Carson shrugged. "She made me the executor of her will, same as my grandma did. They trusted me. I'll handle the funeral arrangements."

"Okay." Jenna cleared her throat. "I'd like to ask you some more questions. Would you mind coming down to the sheriff's office?"

"I suppose it's okay." Carson narrowed his eyes at her. "Is

there something you're not telling me about my grandma's death?"

"I'll know more in a few hours." Jenna looked at Carter. "Agents Carter and Wells will take you. I'll have someone drop you back for your truck later."

Kane waited for Carson to be placed in the back of the cruiser and turned to Jenna. "He could be a possible."

"My thoughts exactly." Jenna turned to Jo. "Can you take him back to the office and question him? Carter might be able to dig deeper. We'll check out the house."

Pushing his Stetson back from his forehead, Kane frowned. "We have four homicides and all but Mrs. Carson have no next of kin. What if Carson is executor of their estates as well? It's a group of people who've known each other for years. If so and he's the sole beneficiary, that's a darn good motive for killing them."

"Kalo will find out." Carter moved to their side. "Carson is acting suspicious."

"That's why I want you to handle the interview with Jo." Jenna smiled at him. "If you don't mind?"

"My pleasure." Carter touched his hat and headed for the cruiser with Jo close behind.

Kane looked after them and bit back a grin. "You've made his day."

"I find it difficult giving them orders." Jenna met his gaze with a frown. "I know this is our case and they're here as consultants, but sometimes it's strange. I mean, on the scale of things, they are higher up the chain of command."

Kane shook his head and followed her to the door of Mrs. Jefferson's house. He gave Duke the signal to stay and the dog sank down on the porch with a sigh. He turned to Jenna. "Nah, you're the highest-ranked officer here. The only person over you is the medical examiner at a crime scene. Jo and Carter are here not on a federal level. They're here to share resources so we can catch a killer. We needed their resources: Carter's flying skills, Jo's insight, and Kalo's IT expertise. They can't arrest anyone in your county unless they commit a federal crime. They understand what capacity they're in and won't overstep, even though the case is now a serial offender. Although they could step in if they considered the killer might be operating out of your jurisdiction."

"Well, I know that, but it's still strange." Jenna pulled on gloves and then took the keys from her pocket. "Let's take a quick look around and make sure nothing has been touched."

The house smelled of damp and stale rose perfume but inside was tidy. Kane moved through the downstairs rooms, clearing each one and taking his time to make sure nothing had been disturbed. He sucked in a deep breath and, with Jenna watching his back, ventured down into the cellar. "We'd better take a look."

"Is that a new furnace?" Jenna kicked at a pile of dust swept against one wall. "Hmm, if this is Duffy's work, he didn't take the time to clean up the mess he'd made." She pointed to an open window. "It looks like he makes a habit of leaving the window open."

Taking the time to examine the new furnace, Kane bent to pick up a wrench. "Seems he was in a hurry to leave. I think we need to have another chat with Mr. Duffy."

"If he admits to installing the furnace, it won't prove anything. I figure we wait and see what the CCTV footage shows after a day or two." She glanced back up the stairs. "Let's get out of here. I hate cellars." She headed for the steps.

Kane followed Jenna back into the main part of the residence. It was a large house with five bedrooms upstairs. He opened doors, finding four closets along one wall of the hallway. "This family must have been huge. Look at all the closets."

"Carson said she didn't have kids." Jenna frowned and

pulled open a closet door. "Dogs? Do you figure she kept dogs in here?"

The hairs on the back of Kane's neck stood to attention as he ran his Maglite over the inside of the empty closet. Cobwebs filled the corners and spiders ran from his light, but as he moved the beam around the small space, it picked out long marks dug deep into the door. On one wall someone had scratched a stick figure of a girl with a balloon on a string. He moved to the next door and then the next. All the empty cupboards had the same telltale signs. Turning slowly to take in Jenna's ashen face, he swallowed the lump in his throat. "She kept kids in here."

He pulled out his phone and called Kalo. "Bobby, can you check if Mrs. Harriette Jefferson out of Stanton, Black Rock Falls, had any involvement with kids, foster system, teacher, anything at all, and check out her husband too. He died. Go back as far as you can, twenty years if possible. Also, see if there were any reports of kids going missing around the same time. Check all surrounding counties. Thanks." He disconnected and looked at Jenna. "I guess we'd better go through the bedrooms with a fine-toothed comb. People like this keep souvenirs."

They moved through the house, checking out each room with care. Inside the master bedroom, Kane turned at Jenna's intake of breath. "Found something?"

"Yeah." She held out a cookie tin, the lid rusted with age. "A trophy hoard."

Kane peered into the collection of hair. Each strand held with a ribbon. Each ribbon had a name written in ballpoint pen. In the bottom of the box, a collection of earrings, necklaces, and bracelets, all costume jewelry or made of plastic—kids' things. His stomach tightened as his greatest fears for what had happened in this neat home rushed over him. "It's hard to believe that sweet old lady murdered kids, but it sure looks that way."

"Well, something sure happened here." Jenna shuddered

and pulled an evidence bag from her jacket pocket and held it open for Kane to drop in the cookie tin. "If she was involved with the foster system or not, we'd better get a team down from Helena to excavate the backyard. I'm treating this as a crime scene just in case."

# FORTY-THREE

As soon as Jenna climbed into the Beast, she called Jo and gave her a rundown of what they'd found. "Ask Carson if Mrs. Jefferson fostered kids. Wait for his reaction. He'd have been around if she'd been friends with his grandma. He'd know if she had kids in the house."

*"Hmm, interesting."* Jo sounded businesslike and Jenna assumed the interview had already started and she couldn't talk. *"I'll pass that on."* She disconnected.

Jenna shot a glance at Kane. "Okay, now what?"

"Call Wolfe and bring him up to date." Kane stared straight ahead as they sped along Stanton on the way back to the office. "He'll be able to arrange a forensic anthropologist team to search the grounds."

Jenna shuddered. "What is wrong with this town? I thought crime followed us, but the longer I live here, I discover terrible things have been happening here for decades." She pushed a hand through her hair. "Why in this beautiful place?"

"It's the vastness and the wilderness." Kane shrugged. "That's what attracts people both good and bad. It's the perfect place to escape the world and detection. That's why they sent us here, not to mop up the crime but to hide. Seems the more we dig, the more we find, and these cold cases are more chilling than the present crimes. Imagine what the town would have been like twenty or thirty years ago."

Jenna stared out the window as they moved through town. The place had changed dramatically since she'd arrived. In fact, it had tripled in size and gone from a sleepy backwoods town to a tourist destination. She pulled out her phone and called Wolfe. After explaining, she caught his sharp intake of breath. "So how do you want me to handle this?"

*"Four murders and now a cold case?"* Wolfe let his breath out in a long sigh. *"You do know there's only one of me working here? I can't possibly start an excavation with the bodies lining up here for autopsy. I deal with other cases as well. People die in hospital, at home, or have accidents and the cause is unknown. All of these come through my office."*

Swallowing hard, Jenna chewed on her bottom lip. "I know you're overworked, Shane. Just tell me who to call and I'll get right on it."

*"I can't call for a team from Helena to excavate without evidence, Jenna."* Wolfe tapped away on his keyboard. *"I could request a cadaver dog and handler. If he finds anything, you'll be able to get a team to do the excavation. It would be quicker to get your deputies down there to unearth anything that looks suspicious. It's unusual for people to bury children in deep graves. If they use my drone to search the area, they should be able to map any ground disturbances. Flowerbeds are popular places as well."*

"Okay, thanks for your help." Jenna frowned with concern. "We'll see you at three." She disconnected and turned to Kane. "Wolfe is swamped and I'm worried about him. He just about bit my head off when I asked him about excavating the Jeffersons' yard."

"Wolfe doesn't crack under pressure." Kane pulled up

outside the sheriff's office. "His wife was dying when I was in danger in Syria and he was as cool as ice. It must be something else." He snapped his fingers. "Oh, I bet I know." He turned and grinned at her. "The Helena medical examiner's department had a new professor join the team. She made quite an impression on Wolfe at the conference and I do believe he met with her for lunch when we went to Helena." He chuckled. "I happened to mention it as they had gotten along so well and he brushed it off by saying that any thoughts of moving on were out of the question as his girls would never allow another woman in the house."

Jenna gaped at him. "So, you're saying if a team arrives, she'd be in charge and working hand in hand with him, and he doesn't want to risk the girls finding out there's an attraction between them?" She shook her head. "No wonder he's cranky. Poor man."

"Knowing Shane as I do, he's the slow and steady type." Kane slid out and then opened the back door and stuck his head in as he unclipped Duke. "He was probably trying a long-distance relationship to see how things went before he mentioned her to the girls."

Jenna climbed out and went around the hood to meet him. "What would they have in common? You said she was a professor of forensic anthropology. He deals with the now and she deals with the past."

"Yeah, that's her specialty but she's an ME as well." Kane headed up the steps. "She's a very smart woman. I spent some time chatting with her at the conference."

Intrigued, Jenna stared at him. "What's stopping him, apart from the girls? Is she married or something?"

"Nope." Kane rubbed his chin. "Not that I asked her anything personal, but she did mention not having a man in her life because of her work. I think the problem might be her age."

Shrugging, Jenna walked beside him up the steps. "You

can't just say that without validating it. Why, is she a hundred or something?"

"Nope. The opposite." Kane opened the door. "She's under thirty, I'd say. Attractive and her family is Scandinavian." He shrugged. "She'd fit right in to the family with her blonde hair, but she has cornflower blue eyes."

Jenna bit back a grin. "She sounds perfect and why didn't you mention her before? You know, Dave, you're hopeless at gossiping. I never get anything interesting from you."

"That's not what I do." He grinned at her. "But I'm not sure why Jo didn't tell you. Maybe she didn't think it was interesting enough—or it slipped her mind."

Jenna followed him inside. "I'll be sure to ask her."

She walked into the lower office, glad to see Rio and Rowley at their desks. "Did you get the cruiser set up in place outside Duffy's house?"

"Yes, ma'am." Rowley looked up from his screen. "I've been watching the feed. Nothing to report."

Jenna nodded and moved her attention to Rio. "Did you get the trust accounts sorted?"

"Yeah, I was able to see the guy straight away and sign some paperwork to change things. It's all good."

Jenna explained what they'd discovered at Mrs. Jefferson's house and Wolfe's suggestion of using his drone. "Grab shovels and go get the drone. If you see anything suspicious, do a test hole. Be careful. If you find anything, bag and tag. Cover the ground and take what you have to Wolfe for identification." She let out a long sigh. "And keep me in the loop. We're heading out to an autopsy at three."

Both men stood at once and Jenna headed down to the interview room and joined Kane outside. She looked at him. "Do you want to go inside?"

"No." Kane's gaze was fixed on Carson. "I think Carter is doing a fine job. Carson looks a little intimidated, which for us is a good thing. If he were acting calm and in control, I'd be more convinced he was involved in the murders."

Jenna leaned against the wall. "You've taught me a ton of things about serial killers, but how do they react if they're accused of something they didn't do? Maybe the suggestion of being involved in a child's murder is making him defensive. If he can't be proud of what he's done, then we might not see the usual bravado."

"Yes, that's true and you could be right." Kane smiled at her. "I assumed they were still asking about the current murders. We'll find out soon enough." He indicated to the two-way mirror. "Carter has finished and stopped the recording."

They waited until Jo and Carter left the room and shut the door behind them. Jenna straightened. "Get anything interesting?"

"Tons." Carter pulled a toothpick from his top pocket and tossed it into his mouth. "I ran his whereabouts during the current murders and all but the one, where his wife told us she takes sleeping meds, check out. If he's our killer, it would be a remote chance at best."

"But he does remember the kids at Harriette Jefferson's house." Jo gave Jenna a triumphant smile. "And he got hostile when we suggested he was covering up something." She turned to stare at Carson through the window. "He looks nervous."

Jenna glanced at Kane. "I'm going to speak to him. Coming?" She looked back at Carter. "Did you read him his rights?"

"Yeah, and he waved his rights to an attorney." Carter smiled around the toothpick. "I grilled him hard and he only started to get jumpy when we asked about the kids."

"Okay." Jenna nodded. "I'll see what we can pry out of him."

She flashed her card over the scanner and walked into the interview room with Kane close behind. She turned on the recording device and sat down. "This is Sheriff Jenna Alton. I'm continuing the interview with Bret Carson." She gave the time and date.

"Deputy David Kane is present." Kane took a seat. "Okay, Mr. Carson." He leaned forward, resting his clasped hands on the table. "We've just come from Harriette Jefferson's home. Inside we discovered evidence to prove she kept kids in closets and we found a box of what we'd describe as trophies. You've admitted to Agents Carter and Wells that you were aware of the children at the Jefferson's home." He gave the man an earnest stare. "Now, as you seem to be the only person alive who has knowledge of what happened in that house, do yourself a favor and tell us what you know."

Jenna pulled a statement book from the desk drawer. "If you willingly withhold information about a crime, you will be charged and face jail time. Cooperate now, and if we can prove you were not involved, you'll be able to go home to your wife."

"I wasn't involved and it was a long time ago." Carson rubbed both hands down his face. "I mean like maybe fifteen or twenty years. The house I'm living in belonged to my folks. I inherited it when they died. Mrs. Jefferson has always lived in the next property. My folks had her and her husband over for cookouts and we went over there as well. The Jeffersons stayed home back then. It wasn't until Mrs. Jefferson had gotten older, that she went out. That was a long time after the kids left. I know she fostered kids way back, ten or twenty years ago. She must have been in her sixties then, I guess. She's always had white hair as far back as I remember."

Jenna made notes and looked up at him. "Did she bring the kids with her when you had cookouts?"

"No, never." Carson shook his head slowly. "She never allowed them to join us when we went there either. She'd always say they shouldn't get to like being with her because they'd be going soon." He moved around in his chair uncomfortably and met Jenna's gaze. "I went there one day, snuck over the fence and through the trees. She had two little girls outside washing their clothes on those old-fashioned washboards." He swallowed and his Adam's apple moved up and down. "She'd be raving on about how evil they were and how their parents died because of their sins, things like that." He clenched his hands on the table. "I told my parents and they said I was making up stories." He looked from one to the other. "I went back another day and she had a little boy standing out in the garden while she hosed him for wetting his pants." He shuddered. "I was hiding for at least an hour and she never cared for him. She just left him standing in the garden shivering."

Jenna winced. "How old were you then?"

"Oh, I don't recall, maybe ten." Carson thought a beat. "Yeah, ten. So twenty years ago."

"If she was so evil, how come you became close friends with her?" Kane was wearing his combat face. "You seemed awful cut up about her going missing, and from your account, she was a monster." He leaned closer. "What changed your mind?"

"She did." Carson leaned back in his chair. "She was nice to me, after my parents died. You do know her husband and my folks were out fishing and drowned? They were washed over the falls."

"They went fishing in the rapids above the falls?" Kane's brow wrinkled. "Really? Who would do a crazy thing like that?"

"Well, that's what she told me." Carson sipped from a bottle of water and cleared his throat. "She was there and tried to save them but they all went over. She managed to get to safety."

Wondering just how gullible this man was, Jenna scribbled down an abundance of notes. She raised her gaze to him. "You were eighteen when they died?"

"Yeah, I was away at college. I didn't come home then. I stayed and finished my studies. I couldn't cope with dealing with the house and all my parents' things. Mrs. Jefferson handled everything. She said she owed it to my parents. I didn't come back home until after I married. When we arrived here, Mrs. Jefferson had kept the house going for me, lawns mowed and the house clean. She'd even set up the master bedroom with a new bed." He looked from one to the other. "I guess, over the years, I figured I must have been wrong about her. She was a different person than I remembered." He opened his hands wide. "My grandma thought the world of her."

"Do you have kids?" Kane leaned back in his chair, making it creak.

"Nope." Carson shrugged. "My wife doesn't want any."

After reading through her notes, Jenna slid the book across the table to Carson. "Read the statement through. It's everything you've told us about the children at Mrs. Jefferson's house. If it's correct, sign and date it."

"Okay." Carson read the statement and moved the pen over the paper before handing it back to Jenna.

Jenna pushed to her feet and turned off the recorder. "Thank you for your cooperation. I'll give you a ride back to your vehicle."

"No, don't bother." Carson stood. "I need some fresh air. I'll walk some and then take a cab."

Jenna swiped her card and opened the door. She stood to one side as Carson passed. Jo and Carter came inside the room. She looked at them. "I believe him. He is mixed up but it sounded like the truth. I mean, who could make up a story like that on the fly?"

"Another thing." Kane leaned one shoulder against the wall. "See how he stood and walked out of here? I've hurt my back and I've walked like that when I've been in pain. I can't see him dragging Rio or a dead woman across a room. I say we watch him, but I figure he isn't involved."

Carter's phone buzzed and he took the call and then smiled at them. Jenna stared at him. "Well, what is it?"

"Mrs. Jefferson was removed from the list of suitable foster parents after a complaint about mistreatment from her neighbors the Carsons. The investigation ground to a halt when the Carsons and Mr. Jefferson drowned in the Black Rock Falls rapids." Carter smiled. "How convenient for her."

Jenna led the way out of the interview room and back to her office. She glanced at her watch. "I'm starved." She looked at Kane. "Can you order something from Aunt Betty's and get them to deliver?"

"Sure." Kane pulled out his phone and walked into the hall.

"I'll get the files up to date and check on what Rowley and Rio are doing." Jenna thought for a beat. "Can you guys split the list of Mrs. Jefferson's friends and see if we can get a time she was last seen. She obviously walked from town, but when?"

"I'm on it." Carter went to his laptop and looked at Jo. "I'll take the top four."

"Okay." Jo pulled out her phone and peered at the list of names.

After the conversations had stopped Jenna lifted her gaze to Jo and Carter. "What did you find?"

"Mrs. Mills said she was with Mrs. Jefferson on Friday and she left town just before five. So, at three miles an hour, she'd have gotten to the park by six maybe. Mrs. Mills said she walked at a good pace."

Jenna made a note. "Thanks. Are you coming to Mrs. Carson's autopsy?"

"Sure." Carter snapped his fingers and Zorro dropped like a statue of Anubis beside him. "Although I figure we have a pretty good idea about how she died." He turned to Jo. "No wonder you enjoy analyzing psychopaths. Whoever is doing this is breaking new ground. I've always found someone who fits the crime, but this time, I don't have a clue."

# FORTY-FOUR

Dr. Shane Wolfe arranged the image files for both the current victims. He'd had time to move ahead with Harriette Jefferson's autopsy and, having a badge-holding deputy at hand in the form of Colt Webber, his assistant, to save time, he'd completed the autopsy. When the rest of the team arrived along with his daughter Emily, he pulled back the sheet to display the old woman's body. "I went ahead with this one because it's straightforward. There is no trace evidence. The putrid water obliterated anything I could use. It was a soup of DNA down there. She had no skin or anything else under her nails. The hyoid bone was fractured, and from the ligature marks on her throat, the killer used a garrot made from nylon cord of a type found in any hardware store." He pointed to the images Jenna had taken at the scene. "Apart from the drag marks, there was no sign of a struggle, but a woman of this age wouldn't have been hard to strangle. The broken blood vessels in her eyes would add to my conclusion of suffocation due to strangulation by persons unknown. I've examined her organs and, apart from coronary heart disease, she was in reasonably good shape, although underweight."

"Time of death?" Jenna's pen poised above a notebook.

Wolfe smiled behind his mask. "As she was submerged in cold water it is hard to determine. What time was she last seen alive?"

"Mrs. Mills, spoke to her in town just before five and said that Mrs. Jefferson had set out to walk home. We figured she'd have gotten to the park by six, six-thirty, depending on how fast she went." Jenna sighed. "Does that help?"

Wolfe wiggled his eyebrows at her. "As the body temperature was inconclusive, time of death is between five last night and the time you discovered the body this morning."

"Anything else we should know?" Jenna blinked at him over her mask.

Covering the victim's remains, Wolfe gestured to Emily to return the gurney to the slot in the refrigerated wall. Nope, that's all." He indicated to Webber to move the second gurney covered by a white sheet under the light. "As soon as I've changed my gloves and apron, we can start on Flora Carson. I've entered all relevant details: name, age, height, and weight—into the file."

Carter's phone chimed and he held a finger up to Wolfe and hurried out the door. Wolfe stared after him as he changed gloves, scrubs, and apron. By the time he'd tossed his dirty clothes in the bin, Carter had returned. "Are you ready?"

"Yeah, but I have some good news." Carter's green eyes creased at the sides. "Kalo just called. He traced all the kids put into Mrs. Jefferson's care and they were all placed in new foster homes. Most of them are alive but none of them died in her custody."

"So she just terrorized kids by hosing them down and locking them in closets." Jenna shook her head. "No wonder someone wanted to strangle her. There's your motive." She sighed. "I'll call Rowley and tell him to abandon the search of her backyard. Do we have a list of the kids she fostered?"

"Yeah, but there's fifty or so." Carter moved closer. "Kalo is hunting down their whereabouts now but, you do know, foster kids often fall through the cracks when they leave the system. Many end up on the streets and change their names. They don't want to be found."

"Fifty?" Kane whistled. "She has a lot to answer for. I wonder how many psychopaths she created?"

"That's a classic scenario to create a psychosis in a susceptible personality." Jo frowned and looked at Jenna. "That might be a list we need to keep on hand for future reference."

Relieved that he didn't have to call in a team from Helena, Wolfe let out a sigh. He had developed a friendship with Dr. Norrell Larson and didn't really want to rush things along by having her in Black Rock Falls. He liked slow and steady. Any show of interest in her and he'd have some explaining to do to his very astute daughters. That could come later if needs be. He lifted his gaze to see everyone in the room watching him. He cleared his throat. "That is good news. The idea of wallowing in mud isn't my idea of fun and you know darn well I would have been expected to be there." He shrugged. "With all that's going on here, I really don't have the time."

"You know, when we solve this case, I might just take a closer look at that house." Jenna frowned. "I'm not convinced. People who hurt kids usually have an even darker side. I wouldn't mind betting this 'kind old lady'"—Jenna raised her fingers in quotes—"had something to do with her husband and her friends' deaths. Maybe they had questions she wasn't prepared to answer?"

Wolfe stared at her, watching her detective's mind run riot. "Sure, when we've solved this case, and if people stop killing each other long enough to give us some downtime, we'll go dig some test sites."

"I'd love to do that." Emily's eyes flashed with enthusiasm over her mask. "I want to be an ME like Dad, but forensic anthropology is so interesting I might keep studying and branch out."

"Oh, I'm sure if we find anything, your dad will find someone to drop by and give us a hand." Kane chuckled. "There are great teams just waiting to go in Helena."

Wolfe glared at him. "Right now, I'm waiting to start an autopsy. When you've all stopped chatting, we'll handle one case at a time. If there are bodies from twenty years ago buried in Mrs. Jefferson's backyard, they can wait until you catch this killer." He indicated to the still body on the gurney. "As sure as hell, she won't hurt another kid." He moved to the gurney and pulled down the microphone and gave the details of the victim. "We have the murder weapon. This morning I did a preliminary examination of the body to save time and to establish a cause of death. The notes are in the file. The incisions are consistent with the use of the Ka-Bar knife found at the scene. The direction of the incisions are consistent with a person using their right hand. I found no trace DNA on the knife or on the victim." He glanced up waiting for questions.

When everyone remained silent, he turned back to Mrs. Carson's body. "We've discussed the possibility that the victim may have been held prior to the murder. There is no evidence to support this unless the killer held a weapon on her, which would seem impossible as the victim has extensive defense wounds on her arms and hands." Wolfe held up each hand to show them. "This is a frenzied attack."

"Do you have any proof that Rio was on scene prior to the murder?" Jenna peered at the body and then back to him.

Wolfe shook his head. "There is no evidence to prove she was alive when Deputy Zac Rio arrived on scene."

"We figured he must have been there before the murder because the killer would have been covered with blood. It's obvious that the victim's blood loss was extensive." Kane straightened. "We found no blood evidence anywhere outside the house. You've already established Rio was stabbed with a syringe from behind and there is a handprint on the front door-frame. We assumed he stopped on the stoop and was attacked there prior to the murder. He's a competent officer. If he'd walked inside and seen the blood, he'd have pulled his weapon. Rio has a fast draw and wouldn't have allowed himself to be taken down so easily." He sighed. "What did we miss?"

Wolfe pulled up more images of the scene. "More detailed processing of the scene with luminol revealed a droplet of fresh blood beside the bathtub. On inspection of the bathroom, we discovered the pipes below the tub contained a large quantity of bleach. Outside, there's evidence of a fire in the firepit. The embers gave me enough to determine a variety of fabrics. I'd say clothes and towels. From the evidence, the killer struck and used the bathroom to clean up. They showered, used bleach to remove all DNA traces, and burned their clothes."

"No way." Carter shook his head slowly. "There were foot-prints and they matched Rio's boots. You've already established the killer dragged him through the blood wearing his boots. If he wasn't there, how was that possible?"

Wolfe went to the screen array and pulled up image files of the footprints. He changed them through a series of infrared and ultraviolet filters to show them what he'd discovered. "See here under Rio's footprints. Can you make out another boot mark? Maybe rubber boots? I found traces of burned rubber in the incinerator out back. The killer put on Rio's boots after the fact and walked in the blood then went about covering their own footprints. It's ingenious, and without the science we have today to analyze crime scenes, it would have created almost the perfect crime."

"But not perfect." Jenna lifted her chin. "The idea to blame Rio didn't work. They made crucial errors and this is good for us. It means they weren't close enough to him to know he was left-handed, for a start."

"Maybe not, but look at the murders as a whole series of events, not individually. They are incredulous." Carter examined the images. "Someone went to a darn lot of trouble to commit them. Killing, cleaning up, getting a patsy on scene to use as a coverup is remarkable. These crimes are an investigator's worse nightmare." He shook his head. "I'm having trouble absorbing all the information."

Wolfe nodded. "All the details of my findings: the depth and extent of the damage by the sharp forced trauma, are in the detailed notes. The cause of death is heart failure due to loss of blood from sharp forced trauma. The carotid artery was severed and she bled out." He glanced around at the interested faces. "The facial wounds were inflicted post-mortem and I'd say as an afterthought. The wounds aren't so deep as the others and almost calculated in their spacing. You've seen this before in a previous case, so use what you discovered from that one."

"They thought she was watching them—or more likely the killer was afraid the victim could see what they'd done?" Jo moved closer to the body. "Do we know how far back these women were friends? What if all of them were involved with the child abuse? These people seem to be able to find each other. We're seeing more and more of these groups since the internet. If this is so, this quilting circle's members could be the reason behind these murders. Perhaps they knew about Mrs. Jefferson's cruelty and stood by and did nothing... or maybe they participated. The killer hated Mrs. Carson so much they couldn't bear her looking at them."

Wolfe nodded. "I'll write up my findings and get them to you ASAP. I'm sorry I didn't have something more to give you."

"You've given a very clear picture of what happened." Jenna's eyes filled with concern. "We'll concentrate on the list of kids Mrs. Jefferson fostered. This seems like the best motive we have. If any match our suspects or live in Black Rock Falls, we'll at least have more to go on than we do now." She turned to look at her team. "Let's get at it."

# FORTY-FIVE

Deputy Zac Rio listened with interest as Jenna brought him and Rowley up to date. They spent the rest of the afternoon trying to hunt down people all over the state. Bobby Kalo was sending a constant supply of information but it was sketchy at best. Last-known locations offered nothing and phone numbers were nonexistent. He sighed with relief when Jenna told him to head off home to check up on Cade and Piper. His ears still rang from the conversation with Cade. In an attempt to show him Kara Judd was just after his money, he'd informed him about the change in his inheritance. He'd made the only move possible to protect his brother and perhaps show him how people can manipulate others. If Kara dropped Cade, he might be mad for a time, but he'd soon see the way of things.

It was close to six when he arrived home and noticed the white GMC owned by Kara Judd parked opposite. He let out a long sigh, knowing it was going to get ugly. Kara and her sister Amber had Cade twisted around their little fingers. The thought of banning them from visiting had run through his mind, but as he'd taken Cade's truck away and now delayed his inheritance, he'd sit by and wait for the situation to play out. He made his way to the front door, not missing the movement of the drapes over one of the windows. The kids expected him around this time, so someone was watching out for him. He hoped Piper would take his side. She didn't like Amber and Kara. They apparently went through her things, which for a seventeen-year-old is an unforgivable crime.

He stepped into the hallway, removed his hat, and hung it on the peg. A clang filled his ears and pain shot through his skull. Vision blurred, he fell forward into a line of coats hanging on pegs, the cold smell of winter still lingering in the material. He pushed himself up and turned as the heavy copper-bottomed frying pan came down again. His weapon was ripped from its holster but Rio shook his head and turned to face his attacker. Dizzy but ready to fight, he moved to defend himself. "What the hell do you think you're doing?"

"Beatin' the crap out of you." Kara dropped the pan and it crashed to the wooden floor. "Get your hands up." She held the M18 pistol in two hands, aiming straight at his heart. "Walk into the family room and join the others. We need to have a little talk."

Swallowing the metallic taste of blood in his mouth, Rio met her gaze. It was cool and calculated. Her hands didn't shake. He sucked in a breath. The switch the team had made from their Glocks to M18 pistols had come about in the last few weeks. Watching Kane strip it blind in seconds and go through the pros and cons of carrying a military-issued weapon had been impressive, but he'd never imagined having one pointed at him by an irate woman. "Okay, but lower the weapon. You have no idea how to use it."

"Really? This is an M18 pistol military issue, not to be confused with the M18 rifle. This was the beauty they replaced the M11 with, right? I know my weapons and I can shoot this just fine." Kara smiled and nodded toward the door. "Move! Everyone is waiting."

Head throbbing so bad he thought his eyeballs might fall out, Rio kept his hands up and walked into the family room and stopped dead. His sister Piper and their housekeeper, Mrs. Jacobs, sat tied to kitchen chairs with gaffer tape. The tape wound over their mouths and Piper flashed him a terrified look. Behind them holding a sharp kitchen knife, stood Kara's sister Amber. He met the girl's eyes and she stared at him defiantly. His gaze moved over Piper and Mrs. Jacobs. "Are you hurt?"

Piper lifted her shoulders and Mrs. Jacobs just stared into space. "Put down the knife, Amber. Don't make things worse than they are right now. How about we all calm down and one of you tells me what's going on here?" He turned to look at Kara over one shoulder. "It's not too late to turn things around." He peered around the room. "Where's Cade?"

"He's waiting for me up in the mountains." Kara poked him in the back with the pistol. "I promised him I'd make you see reason. Taking his inheritance away was mean. He's not coming home until you change things back the way they were before." She nudged him toward another kitchen chair. "Sit down."

Rio dropped into the chair. "I can't do that. It's signed and sealed. Cade isn't acting responsible right now and it's in his best interest to wait until he's twenty-one to inherit. You see, as his guardian and executor of my parents' will, I get to make all the decisions."

"Then you can change them around again." As Kara dug the pistol into his ribs, she didn't take her eyes off him. "Amber, tie him up good and tight." She gave him a slow smile. "We ain't goin' nowhere until you agree to give Cade his money."

Hostage situations had been commonplace in LA, and Rio had handled a few but never as one of the hostages. "I could agree but that wouldn't get him his money. We're talking about a legal document. I need to see a lawyer and an accountant before anything can be changed. It's not that easy to do." He shrugged, making it difficult for Amber to secure his hands.

"Not until the morning at least." He sighed. "I'd have to make an appointment and then go see them. Nothing can be done tonight, so untie us and go home."

"That is so not goin' to happen." Kara glared at him. She checked his bindings and then padded up and down with the M18 pistol hanging from her fingers. "We'll stay here until morning and then you'll go and see the lawyer."

Rio didn't want to mention the lawyers would be closed until Monday and nodded. He needed all his powers of persuasion to bring this situation to a close without anyone being hurt. "Okay fine, but I can smell my supper on the stove. We all need to eat and use the bathroom. You can keep us all here in the family room, but that's the deal. I'll make the calls first thing in the morning if you cooperate." He shrugged. "You have my weapon and Amber has a knife. No one is going to do anything stupid."

"Okay but I'm going with you to the lawyer's office and I'll be carrying." Kara raised the pistol to Piper's head. "One wrong move and two things will happen: you'll never see Cade again and Piper's face will be scarred for life. Amber will remain here with my rifle, and I'll have your phones. The landline is already cut."

Trying to push down the anger, Rio lifted his head and looked at her. "If you hurt Piper, you know darn well I'll hunt you down."

"You'll never find us." Kara giggled. "You couldn't find us before, could you?" She aimed the pistol at him. "It's a wilderness out there. We could be living anywhere. Maybe in a cave, or in a cabin, or just sleeping rough and moving every night. We could leave the state. You'll never find us but if you do what I want, we won't hurt anything but your pride."

As Kara wasn't threatening to kill anyone, Rio would play her game. He'd make a phony call first up in the morning and hope like hell Kane would understand. He nodded. "That's fine by me. Now untie Mrs. Jacobs. We're not going anywhere." He looked at his housekeeper who blinked back at him. "Just go along with what they say, Mrs. Jacobs. Don't do anything foolish. Make the supper and we'll come into the kitchen one at a time to eat." He looked at Piper. "Same with you, sis. Don't be a hero. I'll give them what they want and they'll go." He glared at Kara. He needed to up the ante and make it a sweeter deal. He recognized her for the money-grubbing woman she was. "If you give me your word not to hurt Piper, I'll have the money released immediately into Cade's account. I won't hunt you down, but I want you to give him a message from me."

"Sure." Kara was almost bouncing with excitement. "What's the message?"

Rio gave her a disgusted expression. "You're dead to me."

# FORTY-SIX

## SATURDAY

Kane rubbed his eyes and leaned back in his chair. "Duffy hasn't left his house overnight. He goes home and stays there and leaves the same time in the morning. Unless he's lying low because he's spotted the camera, he sure isn't acting like a psychopath."

"We'll leave it there for a few days and see what happens." Jenna looked at him. "If he is our man, I can't see him slowing the killing spree now. He'll do something soon and right now he's the best we've got." She reached for her phone. "Hi, Maggie. Is Rio a no-show again?" She paused a beat listening. "No word from him, huh? Okay, if you hear anything, let me know." She disconnected.

Kane looked up from his laptop and frowned. "It's a little after nine. He should have called in by now." He leaned back in his chair. "More problems with Cade maybe?"

"Does this often happen with kids who've lost their parents?" Jenna twirled a pen in her fingers. "Apparently, he was a good kid before his parents died."

Thinking over the time he'd spent with Cade fixing up his truck, Kane smiled. "He's a good kid now, just a little mixed up.

Hormones will do that for a time and dating an older woman is a big deal to him right now."

"If he's sleeping with her, in some states we'd be able to arrest Kara for statutory rape." Jenna shook her head. "That's difficult when the age of sexual consent here is sixteen."

Kane nodded. "Yeah, and he's eighteen in two weeks." He sighed. "Zac is doing his best but he'll always be his brother. The kid needs a father figure in his life to guide him. Someone like Wolfe would be perfect but he's always so busy."

His phone chimed and from the caller ID, Kane could see it was Rio. He glanced at Jenna. "The man himself. I'll put it on speaker." He swiped his phone and Rio's voice came through the speakers immediately, before he could speak.

*"Mr. Bruin? This is Zac Rio. I'm sorry to bother you so early, but I have an urgent situation to discuss. I'd like to see you at your earliest convenience. I know you're tied up for most of the day. Same here, we all are at this time of the year, but this can't wait."*

Knowing at once the call was fake and Rio was trying to get an urgent message across, Kane frowned at Jenna and played along. "Can you elaborate?"

*"It's the private matter we discussed concerning the inheritance for my brother, Cade. I'll need to make some changes."*

Checking his watch, Kane cleared his throat. He needed time to get the team organized. "I can squeeze you in at eleven. Will you be coming with Cade or alone?"

*"No, not alone. There's two of us, Kara Judd, Cade's fiancée will be carrying... I mean, handling his estate from this time forward. She's over twenty-one."* Rio was getting his message over just fine. *"I'll see you at eleven."* He disconnected.

"I'll go and tell Carter and Jo." Jenna hurried from the room.

Kane walked to the door and whistled to Rowley. "Up here, now."

With everyone in Jenna's office, Kane explained the call. "Okay, we're assuming the Judd sisters are holding Rio and his family against their will. Kara is armed and they want Rio to change back the inheritance for Cade."

"Thank goodness." Jo pushed both hands through her hair. "I figured it was another murder. A hostage situation is a nice change of pace."

"Maybe, but I don't have the time to deal with this in the middle of multi-homicide cases." Jenna's mouth turned down. "Honestly, I can't believe Cade got himself involved with those two. He was asking for trouble and now it's happened. I need to nip this in the bud right now. We'll head out and surround the place." Jenna pulled her weapon out of the desk drawer, checked the load, and holstered it before looking at her team. "Unless you have a better idea?"

"We need eyes inside before we endanger anyone." Carter folded his arms across his chest. "I'll go in and see what's happening."

"They'll never believe you went to check on Rio's health." Rowley held his hat in one hand and flapped it against his thigh. "It would have to be me."

Jenna nodded. "Okay but if these girls are smart, they'll check you out for a communication device."

Kane smiled. "They're trying to extort money from a kid and are holding a deputy and his family hostage." He shook his head. "That's not smart." He pointed to Jenna's tracker ring. "Will Jenna's ring fit on your pinky finger? If it does, activate the ring before you go inside and we'll be able to hear everything. If they do check you for a listening device, which is doubtful, they won't know about the ring."

"Try it." Jenna handed it over. "If you're doing this, Jake, don't take any risks. Remember what we discussed about hostage situations. Most are desperate people and will make stupid decisions. The Judd sisters want money. Make it all about making sure they get what they want and leave."

Kane nodded. "I have cash, so offer them an incentive to leave. Tell them, they can take the money and you'll forget it ever happened." He frowned. "Lying isn't a concern right now. It's getting the hostages out safe by any means."

"Got it." Rowley smile ruefully. "Don't tell Sandy I volunteered for this, she'll be as mad as a bee-stung hog."

When the ring slipped on Rowley's pinky finger, Kane looked at the others. "We can go in via Olive and cut through the yards. If they see our vehicles, it might spook them." He looked at Rowley. "Have you got any civvies in the locker room?"

"Yeah, and I'll take Maggie's sedan so I don't spook them. I'll go and change." Rowley headed for the door.

"Okay." Jenna gave a rundown of what she knew about Kara and Amber Judd. "Rio believes Kara is manipulating Cade. He's been falling off the rails since he met her. She's in her twenties and has been around the block more than a few times. I'd say Cade is mesmerized by her. When I spoke to them up the mountain, the only positive thing I'd gotten from Kara was that she was taking her sister to school. There must be some semblance of responsibility there, so doing something like this, which could mean jail time and leaving her sister to fend for herself, seems unusual. They must have some plan that involves Cade."

Kane nodded slowly. "We'll use our coms and go in silent. Rowley will feed us information and we'll decide how to play it in the field." He shrugged. "It's two women and there's four of us. How much trouble could they possibly be?"

"Kara is angry about missing out on the money." Jo checked her ammunition and looked at Jenna. "She only had a couple of days to wait, so the news that Rio had added an extra three years must have ticked her off. In that state, and armed, she shouldn't be taken too lightly. She's been living off the grid, hunting for survival. She'll be one tough cookie."

"We'll head out and get into position." Jenna headed toward the door. "Kane, go and update Rowley. I'll get Duke in the truck."

Kane headed to the locker room as Rowley was heading out. He'd changed his shirt and carried his duty belt over one arm. He looked just like many of the guys in town. "Okay, go up to the door casual-like, ring the bell, and stand way back. If one of the girls answers the door, just say you're there to speak to Rio. You'll have to play it by ear from then on, but press the ring before you go to the door. It takes a few seconds to connect and anything can happen in a few seconds."

"Gotcha." Rowley smiled at him. "I'll lock my weapon in my desk and I'll head out. Is it okay with Maggie about using her sedan?"

Kane shrugged. "I'll go ask her, but I figure after all the years you've known her, she'll trust you with her vehicle." He walked to the front counter and smiled at Maggie. "Mind if Rowley takes your car just down the road to Rio's place? We're checking that he's okay and don't want to tip off anyone if there's a problem."

"You sure can." Maggie pulled the keys from her purse and handed them over. "Just make sure you check in and keep me updated on your status."

Kane took the keys and tossed them to Rowley. "Yes, ma'am."

Jo and Carter had sped off into the distance by the time Kane reached the Beast. He climbed in behind the wheel and headed toward Olive, the road running behind Rio's house on Main. It took no time at all before they met up with Jo and Carter. Both were wearing their FBI jackets. He turned to Jenna. "How do you want to do this?"

"I figure me and Jo take the alleyway four doors down and

go round the front. You hightail it through the backyard behind Rio's house." Jenna indicated to the curious old man peering at them in his front garden. "Maybe speak to him first?" She headed off toward the alleyway with Jo at her side.

Kane explained the situation to the old man and was waved in without any problems. They dashed through vegetable patches and came to a sturdy wooden fence. He gave Carter a nod and they both gripped the top and hauled themselves up just enough to peer over the top. Everything in Rio's house appeared normal. The back door was shut and no one was looking out of the windows. "Let's go."

Kane followed Carter over the fence and they dropped to the ground in silence. Indicating to Carter to go left, he went right and, keeping low, peeked into the lower windows. He had a good view of the kitchen. Dirty plates sat on the table and evidence of both supper and breakfast littered the counters. This concerned him as Mrs. Jacobs was a fastidious housekeeper. There was no way she'd leave as much as a dirty spoon on the table. He turned as Carter came to his side. "There are dirty dishes everywhere. Something's up."

"The blinds are drawn on all the windows. I couldn't see anything." Carter frowned. "No sound from inside. Have you checked the back door?"

Kane pulled out his vibrating phone. "No. It looks like Rowley is heading for the front door now."

"Good time to try that door." Carter moved toward the door. He paused with one hand poised over the handle. "Ready?"

Holding up one finger, Kane listened to Rowley calling out Rio's name.

*"No one is answering the door. It's all quiet. I'll keep trying."*

"The door is locked." Carter turned back to him. "I can try and pick the lock."

"No time. Stand back." Kane lifted his size-fourteen boot

and slammed it into the door just beside the lock. The door splintered and crashed open, hitting the wall and bouncing back. He pressed his com. "We're in."

Pulling his weapon, Kane moved inside. He went right and Carter left. They eased along the wall and checked each room. They found Piper tied to a chair in the family room and Rio in the office opposite, face down in a pool of blood.

# FORTY-SEVEN

"Call the paramedics." Kane's voice came through Jenna's earpiece. "Rio has a headwound but he's breathing. Piper is here but that's all. Carter is heading for the front door to let Rowley in."

Jenna made the call as she ran toward the house with Jo at her side. She pushed past Carter and checked on Rio. He was in bad shape, bleeding heavily from a deep gash on the back of his head. She looked up as Jo fell to her knees beside him. "Stay with him. Rowley, grab some towels and try and stop the bleeding." She looked at Carter. "Where's Kane?"

"Across the hall in the family room untying Piper. She might know what's happened." Carter crouched beside Rio. "Go! I have field medical training and we'll stay with him until the paramedics arrive."

Jenna found Kane cutting Piper from a chair and trying to calm her without any luck. The girl was hysterical and tears streamed down her face. Jenna took her hands and looked her in the eyes as Kane tried to remove the gaffer tape from her hair. "Take some deep breaths. You're safe now." She waved a hand to the open door. "See, Carter and Jo are caring for Zac. He's alive but has had a nasty bump on the head. The paramedics are on their way." She glanced at Kane and then back at Piper. "Come on now, deep breaths, that's right. What happened. Who did this?"

"K-Kara Judd and her sister Amber." Piper shuddered. "Cade went to their cabin with them at Bear Peak after school and didn't come home. They showed up last night and tied up me and Mrs. Jacobs. They waited for Zac to come home and then hit him with the frying pan and took his gun. They wanted Zac to change the inheritance back so they could get Cade's money. Zac said he'd do it but couldn't call the lawyer until this morning. We sat up all night, but Zac insisted we eat and have bathroom breaks. After breakfast, when he made the call to the lawyer, Kara suddenly went crazy. She said she didn't trust him and pressed the gun to his head and made Zac go into the office. Amber searched for money and found none. She kept telling Kara to stop being stupid, but that only made her madder. Kara ordered Amber to dig the knife into Mrs. Jacobs back and take her out to the truck. Then Kara said if Zac didn't come up with ten grand by two this afternoon, they'd throw Mrs. Jacobs and Cade over the ravine." She let out a wail. "Then she told Zac to turn around and she hit him real hard. I could see them from here. He fell on the floor and didn't move. I thought he was dead."

"Has Kara got a phone with her?" Kane tugged off the last strip of tape and looked at Piper. "If so, do you have her number?"

"Yeah." Piper pointed to the mantel over the fire. "Our phones are up there. Mine is the pink one. Her number is in my contacts. It's not locked."

"Thanks." Kane made a call. "Hi, Bobby. Can you find this phone and feed the coordinates into the GPS on my phone. Yeah, it's owned by Kara Judd. She's kidnapped Rio's housekeeper." He waited for a few minutes and looked at Jenna. "Got it."

Jenna looked at Piper. "Jo and Carter will wait with you until the paramedics arrive. We'll go and find Cade and Mrs. Jacobs."

"Kara has Zac's new pistol, the one you gave him." Piper looked at Kane. "He told her to be careful with it but she said she knew all about guns. She tried to force him to open the gun locker but he refused and she stuck the gun to my head." She started to sob again. "He said she might as well kill me because he knew darn well, she wouldn't leave any of us alive and he wouldn't be arming her to kill anyone else." She buried her face in her hands. "She kept hitting him and he didn't even lift up his hands to stop her. He just kept saying, 'Is that all you got?'" She looked up at Jenna, cheeks wet with tears. "He was trying to stop her hurting us, wasn't he?"

Stomach in knots, Jenna nodded. "Yeah, he was keeping the attention away from you, and by saying she should kill you, was taking away her power. It was a very courageous thing to do. He must love you very much."

"We've gotta go." Kane squeezed her arm. "If the signal drops out, we're toast."

"Don't worry, we'll take care of her." Carter walked into the room. "Jo will go with them to the hospital. If you send Rowley back to the office to pick up his weapons, we'll follow as back-up." He looked at Kane. "Where are you heading?"

"Bear Peak." Kane glanced at his phone. "She's gotten a good start on us but we only need to know where she's heading. I'm not planning on risking Mrs. Jacobs life at a showdown on a mountain road." He met his gaze. "We'll be going in nice and quiet to get the jump on her."

Heart already picking up pace, Jenna nodded. "We'll use our com packs for communication. Don't use the radio. Sound carries up there and she's likely got a scanner."

"Okay." Carter moved a toothpick across his lips. "This Kara woman and her sister seem mighty aggressive. She's threatening to kill Mrs. Jacobs if she doesn't get her own way. Why drag an old lady into it when she already has Cade to use as a bargaining chip? Seems a crazy thing to do when Zac has no family attachment to his housekeeper. I mean, she's an employee not family. However well respected, that makes a difference in emotional blackmail." He shrugged. "Want me to ask Kalo to look into her background? There may be more to Kara Judd than we figured."

"I think they're just two money-hungry women but, hey, go for it." Jenna shrugged. "In this town anything is possible."

She followed Kane out of the door and they ran for the Beast. The truck had taken off, spraying the blacktop with dust before she'd clicked in her seat belt. Lights flashing and sirens wailing, Kane maneuvered the truck through traffic and then headed down Main and onto Stanton. The fresh green forest, still patchy with the dead winter bushes, flashed past as the Beast roared into action. Other vehicles became a blur as they increased speed, passing everything, including eighteen-wheelers as if they were standing still.

Mind filling with possible outcomes, Jenna gripped the edge of her seat. She trusted Kane's driving implicitly but the need to hang on for dear life never left her. The Beast had become a part of him and he drove it with complete confidence. In fact, she could see the comparison between the Beast and his sniper rifle. He never missed his target and right now he was aiming his truck between two speeding vehicles. Before she could take a breath, they'd zoomed past and the highway ahead was clear again, although her pulse had increased dramatically. As they headed for the mountain turnoff, Kane silenced the sirens and turned off the lights. They would go in quiet and hope to take control before things had gotten any more out of hand. She had no idea what Kara was thinking or how far she could push her.

The woman had seemed normal enough when she'd last spoken to her, but an attack on a law enforcement officer and kidnapping seemed a little extreme even for her. Was she that desperate for money? She glanced at Kane. "What could have happened to make Kara go off the rails like this? As far as I know, and that's not much, she has been living off the grid for some time, but Amber has been at the same school since Cade and Piper arrived. I recall Rio mentioning that Piper introduced him to a girl who lives in the mountains. I'm sure that's who he was referring to. He was happy she'd made friends."

"I bet he's ecstatic now." Kane shook his head ruefully. "I hope there's no permanent damage. He'd been out cold for a time. That's not good and the blood loss was substantial."

Ahead Jenna made out the flashing lights of the ambulance heading for Rio's house, the siren getting louder as it passed by, and then the sound disappeared as if it had been switched off. The too familiar noise stirred so many unpleasant memories. A shiver went through her as they took the off-ramp and then headed along Rocky Road. The Beast accelerated again, eating up the rough road with ease. Unease gripped Jenna as she clung on tight. In town she had a serial killer running wild and the townsfolk needed her to protect them, but Kara Judd was armed, dangerous, and obviously unstable. Right now, Jenna had no control over what might happen next. The realization made her stomach tighten. The immediate future was unknown. Who would die if she made a mistake? She bit her lip until she tasted blood. Her mind raced so fast with probabilities, it was as if she'd fallen into a raging torrent, and was being swept away into the unknown.

# FORTY-EIGHT

As they moved higher and higher up the winding road, the blacktop turned to dirt and narrowed. Jenna stared at the GPS. They were heading in the right direction but up ahead a turnoff loomed. "Sharp left just ahead."

"The forest is dense here. Her cabin might be disguised." Kane slowed the truck to a crawl and they bumped over the uneven road. "I see tire tracks through the bushes." He maneuvered the Beast forward at a snail's pace and then stopped and pointed at a length of cord caught across the hood. "They have a crude but efficient alarm system." He flicked a glance at Jenna. "They know we're coming." He turned the truck around and backed into a small clearing. "They'll be expecting us to drive into a trap. I'll hide the Beast here and we'll go in on foot. From the GPS, I'd say the cabin, if there is one, is about one hundred and fifty yards up the mountain." He pointed straight ahead. "In that direction. The dirt road will take us right to it."

One thing Jenna appreciated about Kane was his experience in the field. She didn't come close to his expertise in assessing threats and making plans on the run. She nodded. "I think we should split up." She pointed to the right. "The trees closer to the ravine are spaced and I can see an animal track winding in that direction."

"The forest will only go another fifty yards or so." Kane peered into the trees. "If you recall, Bear Peak is surrounded by grassy rocky areas. Most of the recent landslides have been on this side of the mountain. This means we'll be easier to see."

"Okay." She squeezed his arm. "I know Kara had a rifle in her truck, so we have to assume she has that, and the M18 pistol. I want her alive, but if she starts blasting us, you might have to disable her."

"That's a given. In a hostage situation, I'd normally take out the shooter but with two unknown threats in there, it's a whole different ballgame." He slid from the truck and went to release Duke from his harness.

Niggling apprehension wiggled like worms in Jenna's belly as she climbed out of the truck. "Grab my vest out of the back. I'm not taking any chances."

"Let's just hope she doesn't aim for our heads." Kane tossed Jenna her liquid Kevlar vest and pulled on his own. Minutes later he'd assembled his sniper rifle and slung it over one shoulder. "I'll call Carter and update him on the way. He should be on scene soon. Stay safe."

Jenna headed into the bushes. "You too."

She moved swiftly along the narrow trail, keeping to the shadows. Underfoot, the rich pine needle carpet was fast becoming dusty gravel. A recent rockslide had peppered the ground with a variety of unstable debris, and as the incline increased, her feet slipped as if she'd hit a patch of ice. Grabbing hold of the thinning trees, she moved closer to the mountain, her eyes peeled for the women's hideaway. As the trail bent to the left and then hit a straightaway, she could make out a cabin tucked in against the mountain. On one side evidence of the rockslide sat in a mound resting against a small retaining wall, preventing it from spilling into the forest and blocking the road.

Out front was a white GMC, but after using her binoculars to search the surroundings, Jenna found no sign of anyone. She touched her earpiece. "I have eyes on the cabin. I can't see any movement."

*"The sisters are on this side of the pile of rocks."* Kane sucked in a breath. *"They've spotted you, take cover."*

Jenna hit the ground and then rolled behind the closest tree as shots rang out all around her. Bark and wood chips rained down as the bullets whizzed past, clipping the trees. Making herself as small as possible, she kept her back to the tall pine. The smell of freshly cut wood surrounded her as branches fell from the onslaught. The barrage stopped and heart pounding, Jenna scrambled on her belly, searching wildly for a better position. Ahead was a large boulder and she threw herself behind it, coming up on her knees to peek around. The gunshots came again, aiming at the place she'd been before. The bullets cut through the tree, chipping out so many chunks it looked like a piece of a jigsaw puzzle.

Pulling her weapon, all Jenna could do was wait. She couldn't see who was firing at her and hoped Kane had a better view. She caught her breath when Kara Judd came into view, rifle held shoulder high and aiming straight for her, but before she could take aim, a shot rang out and the rifle flew from Kara's hands. The woman let out a blood-curdling scream and spun around. She was yelling, but Jenna couldn't make out a word. One thing was for sure, her attention was now fixed on Kane. Kara's arm hung useless at her side, but she had the M18 in the other hand and was attempting to fire it. Her sister had run for the GMC and spun it around to face the rockslide. Jenna stared in disbelief. What could they possibly hope to achieve? They'd backed themselves into a corner and this was a no-win situation. Her com crackled into life.

*"Get the hell out of there. Run toward the ravine and don't*

*look back. Go now, Jenna. I have you covered."* Kane sounded cool and calm. *"Run."*

Determined to rescue Mrs. Jacobs and Cade, Jenna shook her head. "We have the upper hand. Kara is injured, she'll run out of ammo soon enough and then we go in."

*"Dammit, Jenna, Amber is going to ram the retaining wall and the whole mountain will be coming down on our heads. For God's sake, run. Go now."*

Horrified by his implied intent, Jenna pressed her com. "I'm going. Get yourself out of there now. That's an order."

*"Didn't you hear her confess to the murders? Kara's going to cut up Mrs. Jacobs just like the others. She's our killer and I'm the only one who can stop her."* Kane cleared his throat. *"Run, Jenna, and live for me. I love you."* His com went silent.

Horrified, Jenna gasped as Amber backed up the GMC and then, engine revving, accelerated toward the retaining wall. Heaven help him, Kane was in the direct line of the massive mound of rocks, mud, and trees, and he knew it. Wolfe's words slammed into her. *Don't be his Achilles heel.* She pressed her com. "I'm heading north and I love you too. I'll see you soon."

She turned and ran blindly through the forest, heading into the denser areas and closer to the ravine. Behind her, she could hear the GMC's engine and the squeal of tires as Amber repeatedly crashed into the retaining wall. Rocks pinged off the trees beside her as the mound of dirt trembled and shifted. In her ear she could hear Kane communicating with Carter.

*"Turn back. We'll need a bird in the air. Under fire and the suspects are releasing a rockslide. Jenna is on the ravine side of the mountain. On the right, heading north."*

*"Copy that."* Jenna could hear a squeal of brakes as Carter spun the cruiser around. *"Where are you, man?"*

*"I'm not gonna make it out."* Kane sounded so calm as if he'd resigned himself to dying. *"Duke is hightailing it into the forest, left side toward the river. He knows the forest. Get Atohi to*

*go look for him. I'll disable Kara Judd before she takes me down. Make sure she never gets out of jail."*

*"You got it."* When Carter signed off an eerie silence descended, like a deathly loneliness.

*Oh, my God, Dave.* Jenna ran, jumping over bushes and weaving between trees. If she could make it to the top of the ravine, she'd be past the danger point. In the distance, another single shot rang out. Kane had made the shot, not to kill, but to disable Kara Judd. She wasn't the threat right now. Seconds later, a tremendous roar shook the ground beneath her feet. Bear Peak shuddered with anger. It was as if Amber Judd had woken the mythical giant bear sleeping within the mountain and it was roaring with rage. Lungs bursting with overexertion, she ran, oblivious to the tree branches whipping her cheeks. She reached the top of the ravine and slumped onto a rock gasping for air. The noise sounded like a thunderstorm in a freight train, great clouds of dust rushed toward her, billowing like a wall of water. She rolled into a ball, burying her face in her jacket as the world erupted around her. Sobbing with fear for Kane's safety, Jenna pressed her com. "I'm safe, Dave, but you'd better be running. I don't want to dig your stubborn ass out of the mountain with my bare hands."

# FORTY-NINE

Silence. The sound of the falls below Jenna seemed absurdly normal but the usual sound of the forest had vanished. No birds, not even a rustle in the trees. She blinked, feeling dirt caked on her face, grit filling her mouth. As she reached for her water flask a ton of powder fell from her hair. She washed out her mouth and then drank. It was hard to breathe and she fumbled inside her pocket for a face mask. As she uncurled to sit up, dirt fell from her clothes to join the layer on the ground. Everything around her wore a coating of dust. She touched her com. "Dave, come in. Dave?"

Nothing. She tried again and when her com crackled, she let out a long breath but sadly it wasn't Kane in her ear.

*"Jenna, it's Shane."* Wolfe sounded his usual calm self. *"We'll be heading your way in the FBI chopper. The search and rescue guy is at the stick. I'm coming in with Carter and Rowley. How much of a threat is Amber Judd?"*

Jenna pictured the girl ramming the GMC into the retaining wall and grimaced. "Unknown but treat as hostile, and she's got Rio's M18 pistol. I have no idea if she can shoot or if they're out of ammunition. Kara admitted to being our killer but

I think Kane disabled her. I was too far back to do anything to assist him. I figure from what went down today they're both involved in the murders. I'll head across Bear Peak and back toward the cabin. Kane is there and he might be in trouble. He's not answering his com."

*"I have your coordinates, Jenna. Kane's signal is stationary. Status unknown..."* The sound of the chopper blocked out his words. *"ETA in ten."*

Glancing around to get her bearings in the suddenly unfamiliar terrain, Jenna kept the ravine to her back and headed right. She had to get to Kane but all around her the green forest had been muted to gray as if it were late in the afternoon. The clouds of dust settling had hidden the sun, and the forest was dark and foreboding. Panic for his safety gripped her and she kept pressing her com, constantly calling Kane and moving as fast as possible through the forest. When no reply came, the world seemed to crash down around her. He couldn't be dead, could he? The thought of him buried alive and all alone made her sick to her stomach. She pressed her com. "Dave, hang on for God's sake, we're on our way. Don't you dare give up on me."

Tears streaming down her cheeks, she ran toward his last position. It seemed to take forever before she hit the base of the mountain and, using it for a guide, moved around the perimeter, climbing over anything in her way. Parched and dehydrated, legs aching, she kept going and burst into tears of relief when she found a muddy stream, its clean source coming in a jet of water, ice cold from the top of the snowcapped mountain. After refilling her water bottle, she washed the dust from her eyes and kept running. Above finally came the *whoop, whoop* of the chopper blades and the rush of wind as it passed overhead. Wolfe had found her and it was no surprise when two ropes dropped down close by. A minute or two later, Carter and Wolfe fell from the sky, repelling down with speed. Moments later, Rowley appeared, a little slower but he landed on his feet, and gave her a nod. She ran to them. "Thank God you've arrived. We haven't got much time. The cabin should be about two hundred yards that way." She pointed to the right. "Hurry, Kane isn't answering his com. We need to get to him ASAP."

"Okay." Carter adjusted his backpack and attached a face mask. His expression blank, he'd turned into a Seal in a blink of an eye. "Let's go." He jogged off into the swirling dust.

As Jenna ran beside Wolfe, she glanced at his concerned expression. "Do you know exactly where Dave is?"

"Yeah, from the fly-by, I'm afraid he's under the rubble, Jenna. Even if we'd been on scene, we'd have never gotten to him in time." He glanced at her and shook his head, his eyes filled with sorrow. "We'll secure the prisoners and make sure the hostages are safe and then go and dig him out. You should wait at the cabin."

Gaping at him incredulously, Jenna grabbed his arm. "I'll do no such thing. Have you lost your mind? I refuse to believe he's dead and we're going to dig him out right now. Rowley will secure the prisoners." She glared at him. "That's Dave out there. You're the last person to give up on him. He trusts you to keep him safe, Shane."

"It's not going to make any difference, Jenna." Wolfe pounded along beside her. "I'm so sorry but we're too late. He might be a machine but you know as well as I do no one could survive a landslide of that magnitude."

Anger welled up inside her. "Then you don't know Dave like I do. Get out of my way. I'll go dig him out myself." She bolted after Carter.

They pushed through the forest and Carter came to a standstill as the cabin came into view. He took cover behind a tree and waved at them to do the same. Jenna could hear crying and peered out from behind a thick trunk. Amber Judd was cradling her sister in her arms. From what Jenna could make out, Kara was bleeding from a shoulder wound and had probably passed out. Neither looked a threat. She turned to Wolfe. "They don't look too dangerous. Rowley, go with Wolfe and restrain them. Check the hostages." She turned to Wolfe, pulling out her phone. "Give me Kane's coordinates. I'm going to find him."

"I don't think you'll need them." Wolfe pointed to Duke, digging madly at the edge of a mound of dirt and headed for the cabin.

They all ran across the clearing, Rowley swooping in to handcuff Amber Judd. As Jenna ran past she could see Kara was out cold. "Handcuff her too, hands and feet. She's a psychopath. You really don't want her waking up right now."

"The hostages are alive." Wolfe came out of the front door of the cabin and went to help Rowley. "I'll follow you." He waved Jenna away.

"Let's go." Carter pulled on Jenna's arm. "This way."

Climbing over a mound of dirt, Jenna followed Carter to the other side of the landslide and they ran down through the moonscape toward Duke. Exhaustion gone, she ran leaping over rocks and tree branches. As dirt tumbled down the mountain with each step, Duke looked up at them and barked wildly as he dug, throwing out a wide stream of rocks and dirt behind him. Jenna rounded a boulder and slid to a stop at the sight of a hand holding a sniper rifle high in the air. The fingers moved just slightly but it was enough. "Dave, we're here. Hang on." She fell to her knees and pushed her hands into the dirt. "He's alive. Come on, help me dig him out. Good boy, Duke, dig."

Using her hands, she tore rocks and branches away, scooping away great armfuls of dirt. Beside her Carter was pulling the rifle from Kane's fingers. He'd grasped his hand and was pulling hard.

"Jenna, help me pull him clear." Carter had one of Kane's arms out to the shoulder. "Grab my belt."

Jumping up and taking a firm grip, Jenna dug her feet in

and pulled, using every ounce of strength. A hand pushed through the dirt and she rushed in to grab it. Lifting a two-hundred-fifty-pound man covered with dirt and rocks was like moving a mountain. Seconds later, Wolfe was there, digging out Kane's legs and dragging him clear. The next moment Kane emerged from the mound, coughing and spluttering, but alive. She rushed forward to wipe the dirt from his face.

"Let me care for him, Jenna." Wolfe eased her away and pulled open Kane's mouth and scooped out dirt with his fingers. "Breathe through your nose, good... and now take some water and wash the dirt from your mouth. Don't swallow. Don't panic, your nose is clear, and I have oxygen." Wolfe pressed water to his mouth and Kane made an effort to spit but the muddy water just ran down his chin. "Again. Spit it out." Wolfe gave him more water and this time Kane spat out the dirt two or three times, and then grabbed the bottle, drank, rolled to one side, and spewed.

"Come on man, sit up." Carter dragged Kane into a sitting position. He dusted off Kane's black Stetson and dropped it beside him. "How you saved your rifle and your hat is a story worth hearing." He slapped Kane on the back and got a blank stare in reply.

"Wash your mouth again." Wolfe examined Kane's head. "Where does it hurt?"

When Kane pointed to his eyes, Carter emptied a bottle of water over his head, washing away the dirt. Jenna just sat there and watched, feeling strangely remote. It was like an out-of-body experience as Wolfe methodically checked Kane for injuries.

"He's in shock, but as far as I can tell without X-rays, he's okay. The vest helped and he'd pulled his hat down over his nose and used the boulder for cover. He's a very lucky man." Wolfe's gaze moved over her. "You're not doing so well yourself. You've secured the prisoners and cared for the wellbeing of the hostages. Leave them to us. Carter can handle the extraction. Kane needs you right now. Sit with him, keep up the oxygen, and I'll go check on the others."

Jenna hadn't realized she'd been crying until Duke came up beside her and licked her cheek. She put an arm around him and then noticed his paws were streaked with blood, claws torn from his frantic digging. "You're such a good boy. You saved his life and nearly dug him out alone."

She sat there in the dirt for what seemed like hours, with one arm locked around Kane as he sat staring into nothing, his face covered by an oxygen mask unless he was coughing or spitting. She'd seen Wolfe inject him with something before heading back to the cabin with Carter. She could hear her team via her com, discussing plans with the chopper pilot to send search and rescue out to collect everyone. Carter was hauled up into the chopper by a rope ladder and would return with help to secure the prisoners.

When Kane's hand closed around Jenna's, she turned to look at him. Wet and muddy, his eyes seemed to have lost their faraway look. She smiled at him. "How are you doing?"

"I'm fine." Kane lifted her hand and peered at her shredded fingers and then looked at Duke. "Look at the pair of you. I can't take you anywhere without you getting into trouble." His voice was little more than a croak.

Sighing with relief at hearing him speak, she smiled at him. "You brought down a pair of serial killers by risking your own life. How the heck didn't we have them in the equation?"

"How could we have included them?" Kane rubbed Duke's long dusty ears and brushed the dirt from the deputy's badge hanging from his collar. "There was no link, nothing to make us suspicious of them." He sighed. "I was as surprised as you when Kara just spat out the information. She must have thought we knew she'd been involved. I think her arm is broken and the shoulder was a through and through." He looked at her. "You didn't want her dead, so I had to risk it and bide my time to get a clean shot. She planned to kill both of us."

Jenna nodded. "After doing that, you didn't expect me to walk away and leave you here to die, did you?"

"When the landslide slipped, I rolled beside the boulder. I didn't expect to get out alive and I can't believe my rifle survived. It became my lifeline, stuck against the boulder, it provided me with a little air and marked my position. Although, Duke here, wasn't giving up. I could hear him barking." Mud caked the corners of Kane's smile. "I made all sorts of promises to get back to you, Jenna, and yet again, I've been given another chance." He shook his head in disbelief. "It seems like you're stuck with me."

Spent and an emotional wreck, Jenna leaned into him. "I wouldn't have it any other way."

"Then marry me, Jenna." Kane's expression had turned serious.

Heart bursting, Jenna watched a rivulet of dirty water run down Kane's temple. Dark blue eyes stared at her from a mud-splattered face. He was usually so immaculate and seeing him like this seemed surreal, but in those eyes she could see the real Dave Kane. The kind and gentle person she'd come to love and trust. She dissolved into tears and clung to him, unable to utter a single word, but he just held her, rocking her until the emotion drained away. She sniffed, wiped her eyes on the backs of her hands, and blinked at him. "Yes."

# FIFTY

The cleanup operation happened in a blur. Having an efficient team around her made Jenna's life so much easier. Carter had returned with a chopper and deputies from Louan to escort the prisoners, both would be held for a time at the hospital's secure ward with a deputy on duty around the clock. Watching Kane being strapped to a stretcher and winched into a chopper with Duke had made her feel sick, but she knew he'd be okay. Before he'd left, he'd pressed a set of keys into her hand and asked her to check on the Beast. With Rowley at her side, she'd made her way back down the mountain, her stomach churning at what she might find. As they turned the bend in the road, a shaft of sunlight sparkling gold with dust motes picked out the truck. She grinned at Rowley. "It's dusty but fine."

Feeling a little shaky, she tossed him the keys. "You drive."

"Me?" Rowley gave himself a shake. "Wow!"

Jenna grinned at him and climbed in. "Drop me at the office and take it through the carwash. By the time you get back, I'll have a change of clothes ready for you to take to the morgue for Dave."

"The morgue?" Rowley slipped behind the wheel and ran his hands over it with reverence. "Not the hospital?"

"Nope, Kane hates hospitals. Wolfe will take him to his office, so he can take a shower. He'll look at Duke as well. His feet are cut up pretty bad. The dog trusts Wolfe but hates vets." Jenna leaned back in her seat. "Okay, let's go. I so need to take a shower." She turned back to him. "What did the paramedics say about Rio? Is he going to be okay?"

"He was conscious when they arrived. He'll need sutures in his head and they'll keep him in the hospital overnight for observation." Rowley started the engine and let out a long breath. "Piper is at Wolfe's house. Mrs. Mills is with her. She'll stay there tonight. Wolfe sent Mrs. Jacobs and Cade to the ER. He figured they were both in shock. Cade was incoherent when I untied him."

As they headed down the mountain at a snail's pace, Jenna's phone chimed. "Hi, Bobby, do you have anything for me?"

*"Yeah, those names you gave me, Kara and Amber Judd? They were both fostered, but Kara showed up in Harriette Jefferson's file. She must have been six and went missing around the age of twelve, but showed up halfway across the state at her sister's foster parents. She went back into the system in Helena until she turned eighteen and then took Amber and they just vanished. There were no reports filed around that time to suggest child abuse."* He sighed. *"And I have nothing more on your three suspects. Those guys are squeaky clean."*

Still concerned about how the Judd sisters had escaped scrutiny, she sighed. "Yeah, so it would seem. Kara and Amber Judd are our killers. Kara admitted it to Kane and then tried to kill him in a rockslide. He'll be fine. He shot Kara in the shoulder and likely broke her arm as well, but she'll live."

*"You don't say?"* Kalo sounded astonished. *"Yet the circumstantial evidence was mounting against the suspects. I figured Duffy for sure."*

"Me too but it would never have stood up in court. We were chasing our tails on this one and now we know why." Staring out the window, Jenna frowned. "How many of Mrs. Jefferson's foster kids live in my county?"

*"About seven as far as I can tell, but unless they've caused a problem or made the press, they're like smoke."*

Jenna snorted. "Or time bombs just waiting to be triggered. Keep a file on them. We might need it. I'm pretty sure Kara and her sister's killing spree came from an abusive childhood, and from what I've seen of Mrs. Jefferson's home, it was a petri dish for psychopaths."

*"They could have been killing for years."* Kalo sighed. *"Like I said, they're like smoke. The only reference I found to Amber Judd, and believe it or not there are hundreds of people by that name, was in the Black Rock Falls High School attendance records. She showed up a year ago and before that it said she was homeschooled."*

Staring out the window but seeing nothing, Jenna nodded. "That's her. She was living off the grid in the mountains with her sister." She looked down at her dirty hands and caked nails and shuddered. "I'm looking forward to interviewing both these women to find out what triggered them. Thanks for your help, Bobby."

*"Anytime."* Kalo disconnected.

"I think I know what triggered them, or Kara maybe." Rowley turned onto Stanton but kept the Beast under fifty miles per hour. He hadn't taken his eyes from the road. "When me and Carter dropped Piper at Wolfe's house, Carter was asking her questions and Piper mentioned that Kara went crazy after dropping by one day and seeing the quilting circle. Mrs. Jacobs has them at Rio's house once a month. Piper said Kara was ranting on about not trusting old people and said she needed money to get away."

Trying to fathom how Kara and Amber had slipped under

the radar and brutally murdered four women, she turned to Rowley as the pieces of the puzzle fitted neatly into place. "So, assuming that was the trigger, how did Kara convince Amber to help her?" The image of Amber ramming the GMC into the retaining wall played in her mind and her thoughts went to how poor Mrs. Darvish met her fate. She'd probably seen her sister ramming Mrs. Darvish's truck over the ravine. Oh yeah, Amber would be in it up to her neck. "Strike that question, I've seen Amber in action. They must have planned everything together. Amber is probably the kid on the bike. She's skinny and with her hair covered and wearing a hoodie, she easily passed as a boy. She sure fooled me. I was close by when she came into the office with Mrs. Jefferson's purse and didn't recognize her." She blinked, seeing everything clearly now that she knew two people were involved. "I figure Kara killed and Amber prevented her sister leaving a blood trail by using towels for her to walk on. We found trace evidence of towels on the carpets. Kara showered on scene, changed, and they burned the evidence. This is why we have no viable footprints. They cleaned up the bathroom with bleach. We found evidence of it at all the scenes."

"Yeah, it makes sense." Rowley headed toward the office. "They'd already killed Flora Carson before contacting Rio. Amber drops by his house and gives him the message and then they hightail it back to Carson's house. They'd know he'd write down details and get dressed before heading out. They had at least a five-minute start on him. Plenty of time to hide at Mrs. Carson's house. When he went to the door, one of them delivered the shot in the back. Rio would have staggered inside and they removed his boots. One of them put them on and they dragged him through the pool of blood and set the scene." He looked at her. "But why the mud messages?"

Jenna thought for a beat. "The victims' homes were isolated and I figure Kara was sending a message to the others. She wanted the bodies to be found to instill fear into the quilting circle. That was her goal. She wanted them frightened and living in fear of her, same as Mrs. Jefferson had inflicted on her for however many years."

"Do you think she'll admit to it?" Rowley pulled up outside the sheriff's office. "We have no evidence against them for the murders, only kidnapping and attempted murder of a law enforcement officer."

Jenna pushed open the door. "I hope so. She figures we know everything and some psychopaths love to boast about their kills." She hurried inside.

"Oh, Jenna are you okay?" Jo met her at the door. "Anything I can do?"

Jenna smiled at her. "I'll be fine. I'm just filthy and have a few scratches. You could call the hospital and find out when we can interview the Judd sisters. I want to jump all over them before they change their minds about talking." She walked up the stairs to the locker rooms and stopped to pull a set of clean clothes from her stash. "Kara admitted to Kane she'd cut up the old ladies, so she must have figured we'd found out about her killing spree."

"I'll call the hospital but Carter said Kara had a through and through shoulder wound and a broken arm. The doctors were prepping her for surgery when he left." Jo followed close behind her. "I can't imagine them allowing us to speak to her until the morning and Amber is under heavy sedation. Don't worry, we have them both under heavy guard."

"That's good." Jenna dumped her clothes onto the bench and grabbed towels. She stepped into the bathroom and slid the door shut. After stripping off her dust-covered clothes, she waited a beat before getting into the shower. "Can you stay a minute? I need to tell you something."

"Sure." Jo sounded interested. "What's on your mind?"

Jenna just had to tell someone before she burst. After wrapping a towel around her, she slid the door open a crack and poked her head around it to look at Jo. She wanted to see her reaction. "Can I trust you with a secret?"

"Cross my heart and hope to die." Jo looked at her solemnly. "Although, with exceptions. Please don't tell me you did something illegal. I'm not a priest, I'm an FBI agent."

Laughing Jenna shook her head. "No not illegal. Dave asked me to marry him."

"Uh-huh... I thought something was going on between you two." Jo wiggled her eyebrows. "Kane moving in with you and all last Halloween. Carter said he could see all the signs of a relationship but I wouldn't believe him. You sure kept that quiet."

Jenna shrugged. "We had no choice. I figured it would interfere with our working relationship but it doesn't. Dave's been a little overprotective since he arrived and I don't think that will change. He understands my need to be independent."

"Yeah, he is a really nice guy." Jo leaned against the wall. "I've always known he cared about you. The way he looks at you sometimes is a dead giveaway."

Jenna grabbed shampoo and turned on the shower. "I hope he remembers asking me. He was in shock after we pulled him out of the landslide."

"I don't think much fazes Dave Kane." Jo grinned broadly. "What did you say?"

Jenna poked her head back around the door. "I said yes, of course."

# EPILOGUE

## SUNDAY, WEEK TWO

Jenna woke to the sound of Carter banging on her front door. It had been after midnight when she finally fell into bed. Locating the DA late on a Saturday afternoon had been a nightmare. The ton of paperwork involved due to Kara's injuries sustained during the arrest, her attack on Rio and Kane, and detaining a minor had taken hours to complete. She staggered out of bed and, grabbing her robe, hurried to the front door. She frowned at Carter's raised eyebrow. "What?"

"We've done the chores and Jo would like to start breakfast." Carter grinned around a toothpick. "We thought we'd let you sleep. Have you heard from Kane?"

Jenna turned to look at the clock. "You should have woken me and, no, I haven't heard from Kane at all. Wolfe took him home with him and gave him something to make him rest. Likely he had one of his headaches from hell. He'll contact us when he's ready." She pushed hair from her eyes and stood to one side to allow him and Zorro to enter. "Any news of Rio and Cade? I didn't get any information at all last night apart from they were stable."

"I called before and spoke to Rio. He's okay." Carter

shrugged out of his jacket and hung it in the mudroom. "Cade too. They'll be released once the doctors have checked them over again. I doubt Rio will be back to work for a couple of days. They put fifteen stitches in his head. That woman must pack a punch."

Jenna frowned. "Rio's been through hell and back. I hope he takes a week off. He needs the rest." She glanced up as the clock struck eight. "Oh, look at the time. I'll get ready. I guess we'll be interviewing the Judd sisters?"

"Yeah." Carter smiled. "Rowley called me earlier. He waited for the paperwork last night and dropped by the hospital at seven this morning. He's already charged them both with attempted murder of a law enforcement officer and kidnapping. That will hold them for now."

Hurrying to the bathroom, Jenna waved at Jo coming through the front door. "What would I do without Rowley? I'll be five minutes."

"Take your time." Jo headed for the kitchen. "We won't be able to speak to the doctors at the hospital until they've done their rounds. We have time to go into the office and get all the paperwork finished."

They arrived at the office at nine-thirty and Jenna went through the files to make sure they had everything in order. She made a call to Bobby Kalo. "Thanks for your help with the case. There's just one more thing I need if you don't mind? Will you run another check on Poppy? I still have a niggling feeling about her."

*"I have been checking up on her."* Kalo let out a long yawn. *"She hasn't purchased another phone but used her credit card at Walmart out of Colorado Springs for clothing and personal items. I wouldn't worry too much about her. She has money, I'm sure she's just fine."*

Jenna sighed with relief and drummed her fingers on the desk. She glanced at her watch and frowned. Concerned she hadn't heard from Kane, but not wanting to disturb him if he was sleeping, she picked up her phone again and called Wolfe. "Morning, Shane. How is Dave? Still asleep? And Duke, is he okay?"

*"He left about ten minutes ago."* Wolfe cleared his throat. *"I kind of got the impression he was disappointed you hadn't called him. I told him not to call you as Carter had mentioned letting you sleep, seeing as you worked into the early hours."*

Jenna frowned. "Oh, no. I didn't call in case I disturbed *him*. I figured he had one of his headaches. The steel plate in his head causes him so much pain at times, and I know he likes to sleep when it's real bad. I'll call him now. Where was he heading?"

*"I guess to the office. He's fine. Duke is fine too. He refused to leave his side, even when Dave took a shower. You know how much that dog hates water, yet he climbed in right beside him and just sat there."* He chuckled. *"They both wanted to leave and go home as soon as they'd washed off the mud. Dave is a stubborn man, Jenna. He was hellbent on driving home last night. It was just as well Rowley left the Beast at the office and didn't drop by until this morning to give him the keys."*

Jenna frowned. "He should be here by now. Maybe he headed home?"

*"He didn't say but he did need to pick up meds from the pharmacy, and at this time of the day, the pies are fresh out of the oven at Aunt Betty's."*

"Okay thanks." Jenna sighed. "Catch you later." She disconnected.

"Jenna." Jo walked into the office. "We can go and interview the Judd sisters. Rowley just called. He's been staked out there waiting for the doctors to give us the all clear. When Rowley read them their rights and charged them, Kara asked for a lawyer and Samuel J. Cross has agreed to take the case pro bono."

Standing and staring out the window at Kane's empty parking space, Jenna's stomach twisted. "Just a minute. I need to make a call. I'll meet you downstairs." She called Kane, surprised when he didn't pick up and the call went to voicemail. She left a message. "It seems like we've both avoided calling in case we disturbed each other. A kind of caller's catch-22." She chuckled. "I'm heading to the hospital to interview the Judd sisters with Jo and Carter. Rowley is there already. If you make it into the office, you'll need to file a report on the shooting. I'll catch you later."

She headed downstairs and climbed into the cruiser. As they headed for the hospital, she leaned forward in her seat. "I'd like you both to be involved in the interviews. I need a professional opinion with Kane MIA. I figure Kara is a psychopath, but you will know for sure, Jo, and Amber isn't too far behind. Is it possible for sisters to have the same psychological disorders?"

"Yeah." Jo turned in her seat to look at her. "Psychopathy is genetic. We don't have a specific gene for it yet but that discovery is no doubt just around the corner. You already know a person can be born with a predisposition of developing a psychopathic personality disorder. If that disorder develops or not usually depends on factors in the child's environment. A child brought up with loving, caring parents may never develop into a psychopath or have any of the other psychopathic disorders. However, as it runs in families, it only takes one psychotic parent to trigger the condition. Many kids with the potential find themselves in foster care or on the streets due to a parental breakdown. In this case, both kids being raised in foster care, it would be a toss-up if they survived intact or became a victim of bad parenting or worse." She sighed. "They are victims, you know, and there's very little we can do to help them. Once they start killing, the chance of rehabilitation is practically zero."

Jenna shook her head. "I find it difficult to have compassion for bloodthirsty maniacs. I've seen way too much of their work."

She thought for a beat. "Although I do feel sorry for the kids they once were. I can't imagine the horror of being locked in a closet. It's no wonder Kara is like she is, but it doesn't account for her sister."

"It goes like this." Carter pulled into a reserved parking space outside the hospital. "First you feel compassion for them, then you try and reason with them—and then you die."

After speaking to the doctor in charge of the Judd sisters, Jenna stopped by to check on Rio and his brother. "Hey, so can you remember what happened?"

"Yeah, well most of it." Rio gave a replica of the story Piper had told them.

Jenna looked at Cade. "What about you?"

"I had no idea what Kara was doing. The moment I told her about the change in my inheritance she went ballistic." Cade shrugged. "I went with them to the cabin and she held a rifle on me and then tied me to a chair. Next thing, they showed up with Mrs. Jacobs, then I heard shooting and, well, you know the rest."

Jenna nodded. "Okay, well, take a week or whatever you need, Zac, and get better. Call me if you need anything at all." She headed for the door and took the elevator to the secure floor.

At the front counter, Jo and Carter were speaking to Sam Cross, the attorney. After exchanging pleasantries, they were taken through security and into the ward. Both Kara and her sister had separate rooms. They went to speak to Kara first. Outside the door, Jenna looked at Jo. "You take the lead and we'll jump in when necessary. I don't want to make her any more upset than she is right now."

"Sure." Jo pushed through the door, briefcase in hand, and took a seat beside the bed. "Good morning, Miss Judd. I'm Special Agent Jo Wells and this is Agent Carter. You know Sheriff Alton."

"I'm your attorney, Samuel J. Cross." Cross took a seat on the other side of the bed. "I've agreed to this interview, but you don't have to say anything. However, there is substantial evidence against you for the charges. Do you want to speak to Agent Wells?"

"Why not? I just wanted you here so they didn't railroad me." Kara looked smug. "I don't see Deputy Kane with you? Is he part of the mountain now?" She chuckled.

Keeping her expression neutral, Jenna pulled up a chair and sat down noticing the zip tie securing Kara's ankle to the bed, not that she could do much. One arm was in a cast, the other in a sling. "He's right outside. I figure he'll be interviewing your sister. He has a few words to say to her about her driving skills." She turned on her recording device and waited for Jo to take over.

"Moving right along." Jo exchanged a look with Jenna. "We know about your time with Mrs. Jefferson. We know she locked kids in her closets. What else happened to make you want to go on a killing spree?"

"You don't have to answer. This information isn't pertinent to the case." Cross made notes in his book.

"She does." Jo met his gaze with a frown. "It might explain why Kara felt the need to get revenge on old ladies."

"*Revenge* is a good word." Kara nodded. "Being locked for hours in a dark closet with spiders was one thing, but the beatings she gave us were sadistic. She enjoyed hurting us. She got this look in her eyes, wild like. Then she'd sing like she was saving our souls or something. She was a crazy old woman, but she hid it well. When the quilting circle came to the house, she was like a different person, all sunshine and flowers." She gave a shudder and stared into space. "She'd drag me from the closet and take me downstairs, bend me over a chair, and beat me with a leather strap, all the while singing hymns. She told me she needed to beat the bad out of me." She dropped her gaze to

Jenna. "She was always watching us and I wanted to kill her. I wanted to kill her from the first time she shut me in the dark. Problem is, time distorts memory and everyone seems to look alike. I figured I'd just work my way through the quilting circle. I remember the house had land around it, so I picked the members who lived in isolated houses. It was easy."

"You couldn't have managed that alone." Jo looked up from her notes with a disinterested expression. "The messenger, the messages on the sheriff's office door, none of those were your doing. We know Amber was there for all of them. She helped you by laying down towels so you didn't leave footprints, and from the way she rammed the GMC into the retaining wall, she's probably responsible for pushing Jolene Darvish over the ravine." She smiled. "You prefer to kill hands-on, don't you?"

"I like it bloody. Amber is just a kid but, yeah, she helped me by dressing up like a boy and, yeah, she rammed old lady Darvish over the ravine. I told her she could drive home and we came across the old lady. It was Amber's idea to scare her, but when she saw her that night, she started laughing and, the next thing, the truck went over the ravine. We laughed all the way home. You should have seen her trying to get out. It was classic."

"I think that's enough." Sam Cross cleared his throat. "Maybe we should talk in private before we proceed."

"Nah." Kara flicked him a dismissive glance. "They have me and you know it. I messed up trying to set up Zac Rio. I've done what I came here to do. I'll plead guilty and spend my life in a nice comfy prison for the criminally insane." She shrugged and then winced in pain. "Amber is a kid. They'll go easy on her."

Jenna lifted her chin. "Okay, let's go through the murders one by one."

They spent hours talking and taking statements. The brief time they spent with Amber Judd only confirmed her sister's account. They both seemed resigned to their fate. Black Rock Falls had its own penitentiary. The county being so large, and with so many felons, it had built a prison to rival any state pen. Locally known as County, it housed Black Rock Falls' notorious killers. After writing up the paperwork, Jenna met the DA at his office, which on a Sunday was quite an achievement. He arranged for Kara Judd to be taken to County and her sister to a secure juvenile facility, although he had recommended she be tried as an adult.

It was over. Taking a few deep breaths of fresh mountain air, Jenna walked back to her office. She spotted the Beast outside in its usual space and the familiar tall man in black leaning casually against it, with a bloodhound at his feet. She grinned and hurried across the road. "There you are." She moved her gaze all over him and Duke. "You look in better shape than the last time I saw you. Is Duke okay?"

"Yeah, he's a little clingy, but he's doing just fine." Kane chuckled. "I got your message about our catch-22 phone call situation. We've gotta stop tiptoeing around each other, Jenna. I like you checking up on me. It's nice." He met her gaze. "Are you done here? We need to talk."

*Have you changed your mind about marrying me?* Jenna's stomach tightened into knots. "Yeah, the Granny Killer case is solved and wrapped up neatly. The media has already caught wind of the arrest and Rowley has put out a statement. Now it's in the hands of the courts. At last, we have some downtime. I sure need the rest. Where have you been all day? I tried to call you."

"Oh, I've been kinda busy." Kane smiled down at her. "I needed my hat cleaned and I had to strip down my rifle to get the mud out of it. When I'd finished, I had to pick up a few things and get me some pie." He cupped her cheek. "I figured you needed some space to get things sorted. You didn't need me at the hospital and, as the Judd sisters tried their best to kill me, I figured being there might have caused a conflict of interest."

He stared into her eyes. "Do you remember what we talked about on the mountain?"

Suddenly very vulnerable, Jenna nodded. "Of course, I do, Dave. It wasn't the proposal I'd expected. You know, dinner and flowers, you on one knee. It's every woman's dream, but that ideal flew out of the window the moment you asked me. I'll never forget it or the look in your eyes. It was perfect." She swallowed hard. "Have you changed your mind?"

"My mind was made up a long time ago." Kane pulled her close. "When we went to Helena, I had Wolfe pick up something special for me. It was an opal I purchased from a place called Lightning Ridge in Australia. It reminded me of all the stars in the sky here in Black Rock Falls, and when it moves under the light, it resembles the sun on a green and blue ocean. All these things are part of us, Jenna, and represent what we love. Atohi told me his people believe they are from the Goddess of Rainbows. The ancient Greeks say they are the happy tears of Zeus and bring prosperity and luck." He smiled. "It took some doing, trying to hide the calls back and forth from the designer, but Wolfe collected it for me before all hell broke loose here." He pulled a box out of his pocket and flipped it open. "I don't have flowers or dinner, Jenna. It's just me, Duke, and the Beast, but I want to be with you for the rest of my life." He slipped the ring on her finger.

Breathless, Jenna stared at the incredible stone, surrounded by diamonds, and lifted her gaze to his face. She could see uncertainty in his eyes and smiled, blinking back unshed happy tears. "It's beautiful, Dave. So beautiful."

"When?" Kane's intense gaze flitted over her shoulder. "Dammit. I so want to kiss you. Do we have to keep this a secret?"

Jenna's gaze went to Susie Hartwig and Wendy, who were heading to the office to deliver a pile of takeout. They were standing transfixed on the sidewalk staring at them. "Just one thing: I'll be keeping my professional name as Sheriff Alton to avoid confusion."

"Fine by me. We wouldn't want people being confused now, would we?" Kane grinned broadly.

Laughing, Jenna looked at him. "But—I'll be Mrs. Jenna Kane when we check into hotels. You being so straitlaced and all."

"Well, I do have a reputation to uphold." Kane's mouth twitched up into a smile.

Jenna leaned back and indicated with her chin to Susie and smiled at him. "You sure do. The townsfolk respect you and now you've got them talking."

"Uh-huh." Kane's attention moved back to her. "We're getting an audience."

Jenna stared at the ring and giggled. "After carrying me over one shoulder out of the crime writer's convention ball last winter, I'm not surprised. Is July too soon? Just our close friends... and I'd love to go somewhere hot for our honeymoon."

"I'd prefer tomorrow, but whatever we do, we should have a team on standby in case a serial killer comes to town. We're going on vacation, even if it's only a few days. I'll find a place with no interruptions." Kane's lips curled into a smile as he looked over her shoulder. "Hmm, everyone in the office is watching us through the door. I figure it's time I made my intentions clear." He removed his hat and bent to kiss her.

# A LETTER FROM D.K. HOOD

Dear Readers,

Thank you so much for choosing my novel and coming with me on another thrilling adventure with Kane and Alton in *Pray for Mercy*.

If you'd like to keep up to date with all my latest releases, just sign up at the website link below. Your details will never be shared and you can unsubscribe at any time.

*www.bookouture.com/dk-hood*

It's wonderful to continue writing the stories of Jenna Alton and Dave Kane and having you along. We have so many thrilling new adventures to explore and crimes to solve. I really appreciate all the wonderful comments and messages you have all sent me during this series.

If you enjoyed my story, I would be very grateful if you could leave a review and recommend my book to your friends and family. I really enjoy hearing from readers so feel free to ask me questions at any time. You can get in touch on my Facebook page or Twitter or through my blog.

Thank you so much for your support.

D.K. Hood

# KEEP IN TOUCH WITH D.K. HOOD

http://www.dkhood.com
dkhood-author.blogspot.com.au

# ACKNOWLEDGMENTS

The magnificent Team Bookouture. A wonderful group of very talented people who've made my dreams come true.

My readers, from far and wide. I appreciate each and every one of you for your support and friendship.

1-24
C mw

Made in the USA
Las Vegas, NV
04 May 2023